The
BOYFRIEND
App

Katie Sise

Balzer + Bray
An Imprint of HarperCollins*Publishers*

Balzer + Bray is an imprint of HarperCollins Publishers.

The Boyfriend App
Copyright © 2013 by Katie Sise

Library of Congress Cataloging-in-Publication Data
Sise, Katie.
    The boyfriend app / Katie Sise. — First edition.
        pages   cm
    Summary: Seeking to win a scholarship offered by global computing corporation Public, programming genius Audrey McCarthy writes a matchmaking app but discovers her results may be skewed by a program Public is secretly using to influence teens.
    ISBN 978-0-06-219526-5
    [1. Computer programs—Fiction.   2. Application software—Fiction.   3. Popularity—Fiction.   4. High schools—Fiction.   5. Schools—Fiction.   6. Dating (Social customs)—Fiction.   7. Contests—Fiction.]   I. Title.
PZ7.S62193Boy   2013   2012051821
[Fic]—dc23   CIP
                                                                                         AC

Typography by Alison Klapthor
13 14 15 16 17   LP/RRDH   10 9 8 7 6 5 4 3 2 1

First Edition

To Luke, for everything

Part 1.0

chapter one

It was lunchtime in the social battleground better known as Harrison's upperclassman cafeteria, and I was staring at Aidan Bailey.

Voices chattered around us and I was distracted—too busy wondering if anyone could see the hair on the back of my neck stand up as I looked into his dark-blue-denim eyes. So my guard was down when my ex–best friend, Blake Dawkins, pushed out her chair and straightened to her full five feet nine inches. (Plus two inches of metallic kitten heels = seventy-one inches of physical perfection.) But then Blake caught my glance and took off across the linoleum. I snapped out of my trance when I realized her kitten heels were *click-click-click*ing in the direction of my lunch table.

I was sitting with my three friends, the ones Blake's new BFFs, Joanna and Jolene Martin, named *troglodytes* on account of some of us inhabiting the computer lab like a spiritual home. Being that troglodytes are a race of humanoid monsters from Dungeons & Dragons makes me question the Martin sisters' secret activities. (Takes one to know one, if you catch my drift.)

Nigit Gurung was prattling on about an algorithm he wrote, and then saying he could've played Wolverine in *X-Men*. I sensed we were moments away from a conversation about coding, encryption, or video games—any of which Blake could use as ammunition—so in a last-ditch effort to save us, I changed the topic to Homecoming.

Mistake.

"So who are you guys thinking you'll take?" I asked, my voice raising a notch as Blake stalked closer. "To Homecoming, I mean."

Nigit scratched the skin beneath the collar of his THIS SHIRT IS A MUNITION tee, the black one with lines and lines of code splashed across the back—the one he wore yesterday, too. "Homecoming?" he asked, the way some people might say, *Plantar wart?* "You mean like the dance?" Nigit had smooth brown skin, thick hair, and wide, dark eyes behind Coke-bottle glasses.

I pretended to study my plate. The potatoes au gratin were my mom's newest addition to the Harrison menu. And she'd slipped me an extra slice of meatloaf, which was extra nice, considering she's a vegetarian and Harrison's lunch meat is disgusting.

Did I mention my mom works at Harrison as the cafeteria supervisor? Yeah. Uncomfortable.

Aidan tapped a binder filled with financial-aid printouts. I liked watching the way his long fingers came to rest on the paper. His cuticles were so . . . *messed up*. Like he'd just destroyed them doing some boy thing.

"Are you going, Audrey?" Aidan's low voice rasped in the middle of words and curled up at the edges.

"I'm thinking about it," I said, sipping water and tasting metal. Not technically a lie: I was thinking about *not going*. And right now I just wanted to get going. Out of the cafeteria.

Aidan's dark blue eyes blinked, lingered on mine. He almost made me forget about Blake. Almost.

"Or maybe we can exploit a flaw in the HTTPD software to alter the web page and mess up the candidates for Court," he said. He pushed up the sleeves of his gray wool sweater and exposed his muscular forearms. "I nominate you and Mindy for coqueens."

Melinda "Mindy" Morales, my third friend at the table, smiled in silence. *In silence* is the way Mindy does everything. She has a speech sound disorder, which means she can't make certain language sounds the right way. *Fish* sounds like "Fis," and that's only the tip of the iceberg. Mindy's speech problem wasn't really a big deal in elementary school, but by the time we got to junior high, it was like a ticking time bomb. She just couldn't get rid of it. She does better in Spanish because it's her native language, but hardly anyone speaks Spanish at Harrison, so that's no help. And it doesn't matter that she's super pretty: There are some things most people can't—or won't—get past. She flew under the radar until freshman year, when she caught Blake's attention as my new best friend. Blake termed her *es-st-st-stupida*, and it stuck. (It's a sound disorder, not a stutter, but whatever, Blake.) Now Mindy's making straight Cs because she won't speak in class.

"Over here, Blake!" yelled Annborg Alsvik, the exchange student who got caught having sex with herself in the drama department's costume closet while wearing nothing but the curly red wig from *Annie*. Annborg whipped out her hot-pink buyPhone and snapped a photo of Blake on her linoleum catwalk. Annborg was obsessed with Blake. She started a fan website called OMGluvUBlakeGodBlessBlakeandAmerica.com, where she posted photos. She captioned the photos with things like: *Thirsty Blake drink water from fountain.* Or, *Blake wear shiny shoe with pointy toe.*

Blake stopped to pose for Annborg and my sweat turned ice-cold.

"Don't you need a date to go to Homecoming, Audrey?" Nigit was asking as Blake tucked her chin and pouted at Annborg.

Aidan fidgeted with his binder. A flush crept over the skin near his inky hair.

Blake gave Annborg one more pose (draping her arm over her head and partly shading her eyes—straight out of *America's Next Top Model*) and then told Annborg to get a freaking life before starting toward our table again.

Nine feet. Eight feet. Seven feet away . . .

"I could get a date if I wanted to," I told Nigit. Total

lie. I hadn't had a date since freshman year. I'd kissed a few guys, but not anybody worth talking about, especially not with Blake six feet away. I'd never actually even had a boyfriend. (Maybe I needed new clothes. Or maybe I shouldn't have cut my almost-black hair into a pixie cut, even if the lady at the Clinique counter said it made me look gamine. She also said my green eyes were *to die for!* But then she tried to sell me a fifty-dollar moisturizer, so who knows.)

Blake had enough boyfriend-getting power for both of us. A few tables away, her BF (lacrosse king Xander Knight) was busy being hot and stoic while the rest of her pack laughed and pointed at my lunch table.

"Real-live video, like the YouTube!" Annborg shouted as she ran alongside Blake, catching it all on her phone. Blake's sequined miniskirt went *swish, swish, swish*, like a soundtrack for her strut. I flashed back to the afternoons Blake and I used to spend in my mom's closet, trying on heels and skirts that were too big for us. We used to stage fashion shows in my parents' bedroom, and my mom would pretend to judge the looks, like on *Project Runway.*

Xander turned to watch Blake. Mindy's and my shared Xander Knight Obsession meant we'd memorized the golden flecks that sparkled in his hazel irises. I felt my stomach twist for the split second he caught my glance before looking away. Like I didn't exist.

In junior high, Xander was that kid who wore the same clothes three days in a row, clammed up when a teacher called on him, and played by himself at recess. I was always super nice to him because the other kids weren't, but then he outgrew me (literally) by sprouting seven inches and growing muscles and chiseled features. He still wore the same clothes too often (a variation on broken-in corduroys and a vintage T-shirt), but he wore them so well no one gave a crap.

And now the tables have turned, and I'm the freak.

Xander settled his glance on Annborg, who was yelling, "Every person check out OMGluvUBlake-GodBlessBlakeandAmerica.com for real-time video!" as she jumped over books and bags to get her footage. Within seconds, there were dozens of eyeballs darting between Blake and me from all across the cafeteria.

Someone help me.

The clicking noise from Blake's kitten heels stopped. She flicked a lock of jet-black hair over her shoulder. Then she jutted out her hip and leaned forward with both hands against the table. Every part of Blake was tanned and toned—even her boobs. Like Jennifer Aniston. Or Jessica Rabbit.

The heady, floral scent of her tuberose perfume wafted in the air between us.

We stared at each other.

Nigit was the first to move. He took a swallow of his latte and made a loud gulping noise that ricocheted across the table and somehow spurred Blake into action.

"Hello, Aubrey," she said. I rolled my eyes. Acting like she forgot my name was Blake's numero-uno favorite game.

"Audrey," I corrected her.

Blake smirked, and her beauty mark popped like a punctuation mark. She pointed at my rabbit's foot, nestled in its permanent position on the right-hand corner of my lunch tray.

I've carried my rabbit's foot for exactly three years to the day. Since October 12, freshman year. When it happened.

"So what's *that*, Aubrey?" she asked in a singsong voice that curled across the table. Her shimmery gold fingernail matched the UNIVERSITY OF NOTRE DAME logo key chain attached to the rabbit's navy fur.

She knew what it was. Of all people, Blake *knew*.

I looked up at her and thought about all of our secrets. I thought about how she lost her virginity to Xander Knight's cocaptain, Woody Ames; how she lied and promised Xander he was her first; how she worried her only real feelings were for our Hot Gym Coach, Mr. Marley; and how she could cry only when cartoon characters got hurt, but not real people.

And then I thought about what she knew about *me*. How the only reason she started dating Xander in the first place was because I had a massive crush on him. How I never even told her. How she just *knew* from the moment I spun a bottle and my breath caught when it landed on him. How I crawled on my hands and knees across the Martin sisters' basement floor like I was begging. How I was about to kiss him when she elbowed between us and told everyone Xander was off-limits, that he was hers.

I was frozen, so I just answered, "My lucky rabbit's foot?" My words made a horrible question-mark sound at the end, like we were on a game show and she was asking me the hundred-thousand-dollar question.

"And is it working?" Blake asked slowly, like she was talking to a kindergartner. The cafeteria had quieted and her voice echoed over the tables. "Are you . . . *lucky*?"

There was only one right answer—the one she wanted: *No. I'm not lucky. I'm maybe even* un*lucky*—but I couldn't bring myself to say it. Admitting it meant admitting the person I had loved most was wrong.

"Leave her alone," Aidan growled. He turned to me. "Ignore her, Audrey."

But I couldn't. Adrenaline coursed through my veins. "Maybe I *am* lucky," I said instead.

Nigit took that moment to burp, loudly.

"Classy, Nigit," Blake said, pronouncing *Nigit* so it rhymed with *digit*. Nigit's Indian, so obviously his name is pronounced *Nih-jeet*, which Blake of all people knows because their dads were roommates at Notre Dame back in the day.

Blake's glare returned to me. "How about I get this for you?" she asked, her dark eyes flashing. She yanked my lunch tray from the table and held it high above her head like a cocktail waitress.

Mindy mouthed *No*. And then a hush fell over the lunchroom. There was only the faint hum of the vibrating vending machine.

Blake spun around and took off with my tray.

"No, *wait*." I shoved my chair from the table. "Blake, stop," I said, panicking as I stumbled after her. I saw

10

the rabbit's navy fur puff over the lip of the tray. The Dumpster was five feet high. There was no way I could get my rabbit's foot from the lunch-food slop if she tossed it in there. *"Please,"* I tried again, but Blake was power-walking now, every muscle in her legs glistening beneath her airbrushed tan.

"Audrey!" Aidan must have come after me.

A hundred pairs of blinking eyes bore into me as my skull-and-crossbones Vans squeaked across the floor. Sweat trailed down my spine like a finger.

Blake stood in front of the Dumpster with her arm at a ninety-degree angle. Annborg was trying to get it all on video, but she tripped and dropped her phone. My tray seesawed on Blake's palm. She smiled at me as she threw the contents into the Dumpster.

I lunged.

My fingers caught the gold buckle of her snakeskin belt as I tackled her and we crashed into the side of the Dumpster. We dropped to the floor and Blake let out a shriek. She rolled onto her back, and somehow I ended up on top of her, inches from her face. Her nostrils flared and her lips curled into a snarl. It was the first time I'd ever seen her look ugly.

Students clattered around us in a half moon. Aidan was still calling my name from somewhere in the mix of bodies that swarmed us. Heat rose to my cheeks and tears started, blurring my vision and making me see double. I blinked to see two Joanna Martins elbowing through the crowd (and trust me, one was enough). Joanna knelt beside me and put

11

a warm hand on the side of my face.

"Audrey?" My mother's voice cried out my name as she tried to push through the students. I could just make out the plastic hairnet she wore bobbing up and down between the faces that stared at me.

No, Mom, this is the last thing I need right now.

Joanna's fingers dug into the side of my cheek. *"Loser trog,"* Blake snarled, moments before Joanna knocked my head into the Dumpster and I passed out.

chapter two

This is South Bend, Indiana. Standing out is not the point.

Everything that got messed up is traceable to the day my dad died in an accident at Blake's dad's megamillion-dollar empire, R. Dawkins Tech.

October 12, freshman year. The day everything changed because of a mistake.

But that's how it goes. One glitch in the matrix and I could kiss life as I knew it good-bye.

In math or code, these sorts of anomalies don't happen. Formula + Predictable Outcome = Safe. That's why I spend my days in the computer lab and my Friday nights testing how hard it is to hack into various South Bend institutions' secure websites. Answer: not very.

And things were going so well.

In the summer before freshman year, when we were

all fake-smoking cigarettes and freezing one another's bras at the Martin sisters' sleepover parties, I was a vision of popularity. It wasn't just my impeccable spin-the-bottle aim landing me seven minutes in heaven with hotties like soccer star Briggs Lick (perfect last name for your first French kiss, right?). It was the fact that those boys *wanted* to kiss me.

Because so what if big boobs didn't grace my 115-pound frame, and so what if all my clothes were borrowed from Blake. I had looks. I had attitude. I had smarts.

I was fearless.

But then high school started, and my dad died, and I basically lost it. And even though Blake never took it out on me, angling for social position among kids three years older brought out the worst in her, like high school itself had made her cruel. It started with small stuff, like calling luge-obsessed Nina Carlyle the Fat Slob on a Sled. But it kept escalating, like when she buried Joel Norris's inhaler in the courtyard, or started stealing stuff from the cafeteria while my mom's back was turned. Worse, she'd look at me and smile like I was in on all of it. And I'd just stand there too numb to say anything.

I was barely hanging on back then. I was trying so hard to be okay without my dad, but I wasn't. And then, one day, Blake pushed a girl with scoliosis into a gym locker and soaked her back brace in the sink.

I was only fourteen. But when your dad dies, you get what sad *really* feels like. So when Scoliosis Girl stood there crying with her curvy spine and no back brace, I snapped.

I used my blow-dryer on the back brace and picked the girl first for my softball team. And that afternoon, I changed my Best Friend Status to Single on the Public Party Network.

Nobody defriended Blake Dawkins, not even on Public Party. She was crying in her bedroom when her father barged in. She told him what happened, and he capitalized on our fight and said I'd told him she was "sexually active," and then grounded the living daylights out of her. (He'd probably found the diary she kept on her laptop and didn't want to admit he'd snooped. Because I'd never told *anyone*.)

But Blake believed him.

This is a Catholic town. Most girls aren't having sex in ninth grade. And the ones who are certainly don't want their fathers finding out.

Blake never forgave me.

And, look. After I lost my dad and then Blake, I got kind of weird, too. Take the root of today's Dumpster Debacle: that navy-blue-dyed rabbit's foot with little white toenails hanging from a gold Notre Dame logo key chain. I was way too old to be attached to a stuffed animal—especially the foot of one—but my dad gave it to me before school on the day he died, and said, "Audrey, this will bring you luck." He was superstitious like that, which was fun when I was younger, but old by the time I was fourteen. Instead of thanking him, I rolled my eyes.

After his accident, I couldn't help but think that if he'd just held on to it, he would've been okay. Which meant I couldn't let the rabbit's foot go. Like, ever. Three years later, I get all kinds of freaked out if it's not right next to me or on my person.

Since nothing exciting ever really happens at Harrison High School (besides the odd senior girl sneaking into a Notre Dame football tailgate and making out with a college guy) everyone knew about my dad's accident at R. Dawkins Tech. They knew about my weird rabbit's foot, and why I carried it. And even though this was senior year when we're all supposed to be perfect, my quirks still paled in comparison to scandals like Annborg having solo sex in the costume closet. Or Barron Feldman having diarrhea in the colon section of the *Bodies* exhibit. Or Kevin Jacobsen smoking a joint during the SAT break.

You might even say my dingy rabbit's foot was old news.

Until the Dumpster Incident. Thanks, Blake.

My dad's boss, Robert Dawkins, and his wife, Priscilla, gave my ex–best friend a head start by naming her Blake, the figurative equivalent of stamping her birth certificate: *I'm a Huge Deal.* Blake Andrea Dawkins is the girl who saunters through Harrison's halls with a glossy, pink-lipped smirk on her heart-shaped face, having a way better time than everyone else, sort of like high school is an exclusive party and she's the only one invited. Don't deign to approach her unsolicited, because she'll give you a heavy-lidded blank stare that reminds you of the worst news of your life: You're not her.

Everybody said first semester senior year would suck, and so far everybody was right. But there were only two hundred thirty-nine more days until I could escape Harrison High School. Two hundred thirty-nine days until I could break free from the place where I'd fallen from grace and get away from the group of people who'd witnessed my loss. Two hundred thirty-nine days until I could start over as someone new.

College was where I dreamed all the good stuff could happen. Because even if my mom and I couldn't afford a college that matched my test scores (at least, not without accumulating a quarter-million dollars in debt), I still wouldn't have to be *here*. Harrison High School would only be a place from my past. Nothing more.

By the time I woke up in the nurse's office, the story had spread through Harrison like wildfire. Blake Dawkins and Joanna Martin told everyone I'd gone crazy and attacked Blake after she'd kindly offered to throw away my lunch. Who was going to cross Blake and Joanna?

My mother scheduled a meeting with the principal to detail the version of events she saw, but I begged her to cancel. She reluctantly did.

She reassured me on our walk from the school nurse to the school social worker that she found the rabbit's foot. I guess she pushed a table against the Dumpster, and then used her banana clip to get it, like in that arcade game where you try to pick up a stuffed animal with the metal hook. It was currently being soaked in Palmolive. "Well, I worried they wouldn't have the same model at the Notre Dame bookstore anymore," she said.

We hadn't been back to the Notre Dame bookstore since my dad died. The three of us used to go on weekends and try on T-shirts and Windbreakers, and then we'd browse my dad's favorite books about football legends. Sometimes we'd buy stuff, but usually we'd just look.

I clutched an ice pack against the side of my skull and said, "Thanks, Mom." And in my head I thanked her for not mentioning the real reason she saved the rabbit's foot.

We stopped in front of a dirt-colored wooden door with G103 written in black marker on masking tape.

"I guess this is it," my mother said. A small red line trailed over the side of her face where her hairnet had been on too tight, but her shiny brown curls still looked pretty good. I wanted to tell her so, but it was hard to talk to my mom at school.

"Audrey?" she said. I pulled my ice pack from my head, sure we were about to have a moment. But then she said, "No computer tonight. And no internet. Except for homework."

My mom has never understood why it isn't okay to take away my computer. My dad was the one who taught me all sorts of coding techniques and encryption algorithms, the one who taught me how to script in Python and introduced me to *Smashing the Stack for Fun and Profit* (the unofficial Hacker Bible). And when my mom used to come into my room and tell us to *get outside and enjoy the fresh air*, my dad and I would smile at each other, our own way of saying, *This is so much better than riding bikes.*

When I was little, my dad saw I had the hacking itch, just like he did. It's something that starts in my toes and spreads to my fingertips—an all-consuming desire to see how something works, to reverse-engineer the inner mechanisms of software. My dad knew exactly what to do about the itch. He started me in Linux when I was eleven—an open-source software system popular among the geek set—which meant I could navigate the operating system used by the majority of servers in the world before I got my period. We moved from learning how to pilot the OS to creating simple scripts, and then onto actual programs. He didn't just teach me how to do it—he taught me *why*. We studied hacker philosophy like *The Cathedral and the Bazaar*. My dad believed software, should be open and shouldn't have restrictive licensing—*Free as in speech, not as in beer*, he used to say. We were practically religious in following the open-source philosophy because it produced the most stable software that anyone could have access to. It meant you could take code already in place, patch it for problems, and make it better.

My dad's beliefs became my beliefs. And when he taught me how to find vulnerabilities in software, he imparted the most important wisdom of all: Don't use what you know how to do to hurt people.

Because once you know this stuff, you have responsibility.

Blake's dad never got how capable my dad was with computers. He never even gave him a chance. He kept him working as a mechanic on the machinery, and hired his Notre Dame undergrad friends or his MIT grad friends for the programming stuff. And I think my dad was too nervous to ask for a chance. That part made me hurt all over. The idea of my dad feeling nervous. At home, with us, he was different. At home, he knew everything. He could put my favorite music into my video games. He could add characters so that my games were different from everyone else's who played the same game. And if we couldn't afford a certain game, he could build one that was even better.

And that was just video games. When it came to computers, my dad could do anything.

I still remembered the first time I chose a party over one of his programming sessions. I still wished I hadn't.

The door marked G103 swung open and a petite blond girl appeared.

"Audrey McCarthy?" the girl asked. Her eyes were the color of pool water. I tried to piece together which grade she was in—she was the kind of pretty that doesn't usually go unnoticed at Harrison.

"We're here for Mrs. Condor," my mother said, shifting her weight and smoothing a hand over her wrinkle-free khakis.

The girl's face widened into a smile that exposed tiny white teeth. "I'm Mrs. Condor," she said in a warm southern accent. She turned to face me. A delicate gold necklace caught the light at her collarbone, and twinkled. "And you must be Audrey."

This girl—no, *woman*—was the school shrink?

"You just look so *young*," my mother said in the high-pitched voice she saves for when she's embarrassed.

Mrs. Condor's already-wide smile went bigger, like Anne Hathaway's does. "Why don't you come on in, Audrey, and we can talk," she said. Her voice made *comeonin* one word. And *Audrey* sounded slow, like *Ahhh-drey*, not like the fast way most people say it.

I ducked under her arm with my ice pack pressed to my head. A cuckoo clock on the wall let out a chirping noise, and a yellow bird shot forward and dipped its head. Weird.

I figured Mrs. Condor would want to talk to my mom privately about my rumored aggression problem, but instead she gave my mother a wave and shut the door. "Welcome," she said. It was one of the few times I've heard someone say that word and sound like she really meant it. She gestured at the space around her and said, "Impressive, isn't it?"

I wasn't sure if Mrs. Condor was making a joke, and I didn't want to hurt her feelings and laugh if she wasn't. Room G103 was windowless like the computer lab— which was exactly where I would have been right now if it weren't for Blake—and so tiny it must have been a closet at some point, or a janitor's equipment room or something.

But Mrs. Condor was tiny, too, so at least she fit.

"Care to sit?" she asked, moving behind a wooden desk with a circa 2003 Compaq and a framed photograph of two kids propped on the lap of a buff guy with blond hair, who sat in a canoe. If these people were her family, they looked like an advertisement for L.L.Bean.

I sat in a metal folding chair that squeaked beneath my butt. Mrs. Condor had put a pillow on top, maybe to make it seem less like the waiting area in the DMV. The box of tissues next to the chair leg reminded me that I should probably still be crying.

Mrs. Condor sat behind her desk and tapped her fingertips near a mouse pad with a picture of a mouse on it. I love tech irony. "So do you want to tell me about what happened today, Audrey?" she asked.

Silence hung heavy in the stale air between us.

"Um," I stalled. I didn't really know how to talk to this lady. This was therapy, which I'd only seen in the movies. My mom tried to get me to see a grief counselor after my dad died, but I'd refused. I wasn't sure how another person could fix the hole I'd felt ever since our buzzer rang at midnight and we'd opened the door to see a cop.

"I just stopped by Ms. Bates's classroom," Mrs. Condor said.

"If you can call that geek closet a classroom." I forced a laugh. I wasn't sure why I was so nervous.

Mrs. Condor tapped a peach fingernail on her desk. But she didn't say anything like *How interesting* or *Do you consider yourself a geek, Audrey?* Which is what I thought a shrink in the movies would say.

"Ms. Bates says you're her top female student," she said instead.

"I'm her only female student." Not technically true, but true in the sense that I'm the only female student in her advanced Java programming class. The one where we work on games and building apps and everything's open source. The one where Aidan and Nigit and the other guys don't realize there's a girl in the room.

"Why don't you tell me what it is you like so much about computers," Mrs. Condor said.

My lips pursed and shot to the side. "Everything?" I said. I waited for her to ask me another question, but she didn't. So I kept going. "I love how quiet it is working on my computer," I said. "And how certain I am of what I'm doing, and the outcome. How there's a formula for things that makes sense." I wasn't sure the last time I'd said three sentences in a row about my feelings. I was about to feel more, but then the loudspeaker crackled, followed by the familiar sound of our principal clearing his throat like he'd swallowed a bug.

"Hello, Harrison students," Dr. Dawkins barked. Aloysius A. A. Dawkins is our principal. In the computer lab, he's known as Triple-A or the Battery. He's always wearing brown suits that make him look like a graham cracker, and he also happens to be Blake's uncle, a fact she likes to keep on the DL unless she needs something. (Like, say, getting out of detention for stealing Charlotte Davis's wheelchair—from the restroom, while Charlotte was peeing—and riding around the hall in it, waving like English royalty.) Plus, Blake's bona fide rich-guy father does stuff like sponsor the yearbook and myriad school trips, like the upcoming Stanford Lacrosse Invitational that Blake's boyfriend's starring in. And a bunch of Harrison parents work at his company, R. Dawkins Tech. So everyone pretty much loves him. Except Blake and me. We used to spend all our time at my apartment, because we never knew what kind of nasty mood Blake's parents would be in. In junior high, Blake told me she wished my parents were hers, and that way we could be sisters, and she could live with us.

Blake's Uncle Battery went on, "This is a special

announcement to inform you of a nationwide competition open to all persons aged thirteen to eighteen." He let out a chuckle. He was generally very satisfied with himself. "And with our excellent record in technological studies, I'm feeling highly optimistic that the winner could be someone right here in Harrison, listening to this very announcement right now, given by your devoted principal."

My stomach churned as the Battery mouth-breathed through the intercom. A possible tech competition made my nerves light up like Christmas decorations.

"Public Corporation has launched a nationwide competition for the most innovative mobile application . . ." the Battery droned on.

"Mobile application?" Mrs. Condor repeated.

"App," I explained. My fingertips itched the way they do whenever I get those first pricks of excitement about something.

"Public is a generous company," the Battery said, sounding like a fanboy. And why wouldn't he? His brother, Robert Dawkins, made his millions by investing in Public when they were a little tech company operating out of their now-CEO Alec Pierce's attic. Fast-forward a few decades: Public ruled every teenager's world with the creation of Public Party (a social networking site), buyJams (music-for-purchase website), the buyPlayer (handheld device to play said music), and then, of course, the buyPhone, the Beast (a handheld computer), and the Fiend (a laptop, available in Skinny and Skinnier. Marketing slogan: *Get Skinny with the Fiend!*).

Public's gear was the best, too. Kids went nuts for it. They stumbled around the Public store wide-eyed and amped up, spending all of their money there. I was currently grounded from entering the store because I kind of went bat-crap crazy, too, when my mom said I couldn't get noise-canceling headphones that Public advertised as Drown Your Parents Out.

Anyway. Besides the XXXPhone (for adults only) that tanked in the marketplace, the Public product creators were geniuses (or at least, marketing geniuses) and the Dawkins family was Public royalty.

The Battery bug-cleared his throat again and went on, "The winner will secure a trip to Public's worldwide headquarters in Ecru Point, California; spend a day with the Public tech team; and receive two hundred thousand dollars in college scholarship money."

Little black dots swirled in my vision.

Two hundred thousand dollars? Any college I could get into paid for?

"Details of the competition will be posted on HarrisonHS.edu, along with all rules and regulations. I'd like to take this moment to introduce all of you to our technology teacher, Ms. Bates. If you choose to participate, you can visit Ms. Bates in room M107 with any computer-related questions."

Ms. Bates came over the loudspeaker and invited everyone to participate. She said a few other things, too, but I couldn't focus. My heart was pounding as my mind scrolled through existing mobile applications. The really successful apps: Foursquare. Angry Birds. Words with Friends. That one everybody used to get where your phone turns into a beer glass.

Two hundred thousand dollars.

Problems. Solved.

Mrs. Condor was doing the Anne Hathaway smile as the Battery came back on and wished us luck. Then the announcement was over.

I sat there with my back ramrod straight, like if I moved, this might all go away. I tried to slow my heartbeat, but I couldn't. How was I going to think up—and build—an app that Public Corporation would give me two hundred thousand dollars for?

A wave of nausea hit—the kind you get when you want something the instant it's dangled in front of you: You want it so badly you almost wish you never knew it existed in the first place, because that way it wouldn't hurt so hard when you couldn't have it.

It wasn't just that two hundred thousand dollars could pay for MIT, or Harvard, or Stanford. It wasn't just that if college were paid for, my mom and I could make our rent each month *and* have enough left over for my music and video games and her romance novels and fancy-French-food cooking habit.

It was the fact that I suddenly understood—with completely clarity—that building the world's most innovative mobile application and winning this competition could change—and *save*—my life.

chapter three

I stared at the raised bronze numbers marking 313 and stuck my key in the lock. Our heavy black door caught against the frame. I had to bang my shoulder against the wood to set it free, eventually catapulting myself into the apartment. "Roger needs to fix this," I said to my mom's back. Roger is our apartment complex's good-for-nothing super who wears cutoff jean shorts and Tevas year-round. "Or it's gonna stick more until we can't open it, like last time," I went on, dropping my black backpack next to our Leaning-Tower-of-Pisa coatrack.

I was trying to be casual.

My mom stood at the counter, chopping onions faster than people with their own cooking shows. (She'd learned all kinds of fancy ooh-la-la cooking because she trained with Chef Antoine in the basement of Villa Madri. She'd traded lessons with him for late-night weekend dishwashing.)

I smelled garlic, and I was pretty sure she was making my dad's favorite dinner: pissaladière, saucisson en croute, and salad Nicoise with seared tuna. She'd made his favorite dish on the anniversary of his death sophomore and junior year, too.

"We're eating at six," she said. She bobby-pinned a dark strand of hair behind her ear. "And I meant what I said about the computer."

"No!" I accidentally screamed. "Mom, *please*," I tried again, softer. "There's this contest. And I just need to research some things about building apps."

"I taught you better than to react to nastiness like you did today," she said. She picked up a mason jar and started shaking it way harder than she needed to, like it was the vinaigrette that pushed Blake.

Fear clenched in my chest. I *needed* my computer tonight. "If I won the contest, I could . . ." I stopped myself. I didn't want to mention money stuff today of all days, when we were both already on edge. Even with a hefty financial-aid package, college was going to be a reach, and I'd still have to work, like, twenty hours a week. My babysitting jobs weren't going to cut it—I needed to learn how to waitress in the next two hundred thirty-nine days.

The TV was on, and fifteen-year-old pop star and Public spokesperson Danny Beaton was staring at me and the rest of America, saying, *"Don't you want it, girl? The Public buyPhone 17.5 can be yours for only seven hundred ninety-five dollars. Complete with YouandDanny, the new app where I show you how it will be, girl, when the lights are off and it's just you and me."*

I took a breath and tried a different tactic. "But the app contest is sort of like homework, when you consider—"

"*N-O* spells *no*, Audrey." My mom has a tiny nose like mine, and smooth, fair skin that blushes from her cheeks to her ears when she's upset. I backed away as a splotch of vinaigrette flew through the air. It landed next to the framed *Home Is Where the Heart Is* cross-stitch my aunt Linda bought us at the St. Therese Little Flower Catholic Church's Kris Kringle Craft Show.

A lump burned my throat and I tried to swallow it like gum.

Whenever I used to cry, Blake would sing the theme song from the *Friends* reruns we watched together at the top of her lungs until I stopped crying and started laughing.

The way I missed her sometimes was so pointless.

I crossed the living room to my bedroom. Our apartment has a kitchen in one corner of our living room and two bedrooms right off another, so you can't really make a dramatic exit by stomping off somewhere. I shut my door too hard to make a point, and then collapsed onto my bed.

The kitten falling off a shelf on my HANG IN THERE poster stared at me. So did Thom Yorke from Radiohead, looking slightly cooler than the kitten.

Two hundred thousand dollars . . .

A dark spike of hair fell in front of my eyes, and I tried to finger-comb it back into place.

No computer. No computer. No computer. (Thom Yorke

nudging me: *OK Computer.*)

I could brainstorm. Just my brain and me. Storming up ideas.

College. College. College. Ivy League. Other smart kids. Communal bathrooms. Shower shoes. Shower caddies. With shampoo from Bath and Body Works that smelled like raspberries.

I was really fixed on the shared bathroom thing, for some reason.

Bathrooms. Showers. Bathrooms. Toilets. An app that found a clean public bathroom within a quarter-mile radius of your location? No. Logistics too impossible . . . I'd have to create a system for judging the cleanliness factor of every public bathroom in the United States. Plus, bathrooms are gross. I didn't want to be known as the Public Bathroom App Girl.

I inspected the chips in my black-and-silver nail polish. *It's a statement,* I'd told my mom when she commented on the alternating polish colors. *A statement of what, exactly?* she'd asked.

Maybe a nail-polish app that told you what color to wear depending on your outfit? No, stupid. An app that taught you how to use SAT words in sentences? Probably already existed. An app that predicted the future? Might be kinda hard.

Here's the thing about apps. It's easy to come up with a simple app (like, say, SmellyPet, the app that reminds you to give your dog a bath every three weeks, which I just came up with in three seconds). But it's hard—*really* hard—to do a good one. Not that the programming is such a problem, or the code, but the original idea. The simple, sweet original idea . . .

I rolled over and stared at the current love of my life: Hector, my custom-rig desktop I built myself. Hector was like the best kind of boyfriend: smart, trustworthy, and always there when I needed him. I watched his green light blink and listened to the purr of his fans as though he were trying to signal he felt the same way about me.

I kicked off my Vans. Not being allowed to troll around Public Party made me want to more than ever. Some virtual Xander Knight stalking might be the only thing that could take away the sting of today—his lacrosse pics are *that* legendary.

Sometimes I looked at Xander's pictures and remembered how it was when he watched me crawl across the basement floor before Blake stopped me. How he glanced down at the bottle, and then up at me. How a tiny smile crooked his lips when our eyes met.

PING! went my buyPhone. I sat up straighter when I saw the text was from Aidan. My mom never said anything about texting.

Aidan: hey whats up

Me: nothn

Aidan: u going 2 win the contest? 200k?

Me: yeah right

Aidan: today when you weren't in lab bates said nigit and me should work 2gether. so we started our app.

31

That stung a little. I didn't know what to write back.

Aidan: I should of texted u tho to see if u wanted to work with us. But hey the good news is now u don't have to split the money when u win like we do. ha

Aidan and Nigit were amazing programmers. They were sure to come up with something good.

Me: I get it.

And I did. But I still wished they'd thought of asking me.

Aidan: hey auds

Aidan was the only person who called me *Auds*. I liked it. I liked practically everything he did. But I couldn't let on that I liked him *like that*.

I have three real friends. If I messed things up, I'd have zero. I remembered what it was like after my falling-out with Blake, before Mindy, Aidan, and Nigit adopted me. There was no one who I could look at who would look back at me.

I didn't want to go there again.

There were two hundred thirty-nine days left. I needed to play it safe. So I obsessed over Xander, who I could never have.

Aidan: did you see info bates cut and pasted onto MOOG bout how to build an app?

Me: not allowed to use my computer tonight

Aidan: ???

Me: long story

Aidan: hey auds you ok?

I imagined his dark blue eyes holding mine, and the

shiver I felt when he looked at me—like the day only *really* started when we saw each other.

Me: yup. c u tmorw

When Aidan first transferred to Harrison freshman year, all the girls freaked out and tried to make him their boyfriend. But Aidan was so shy he clammed up every time someone approached him, and pretty soon, all the girls gave up. But then last year for a few weeks, Aidan dated some girl at a private school in the next town over. She was beautiful and funny, and she wore pink tank tops and long, flowy skirts. I was nothing like her.

Anyway. I knew he was talking about what happened with Blake today, but I didn't want to get into it. And I didn't feel like texting anymore. I felt like having someone real here with me in my room, telling me that I actually might have a chance to win the contest. Telling me my ideas were genius. Telling me I was pretty even if my hair never did the right thing.

What I wanted was a boyfriend.

Aidan texted again. **now that I know ur into homecoming . . . dance fundraiser tmrw. u bakin cookies?**

Not unless I could build an app that would find me a homecoming date. Now *that* would be worth four years at MIT. AppDate, maybe. Or GuyApp. AppLove?

Aidan: or u secretly inventing the greatest app ever?

And then I had it. I knew what the simple, sweet idea was. I knew what my MIT-winning app would be. Everyone in the world would want it. It would make my mom and me millionaires. I'd be on talk shows with Mark Zuckerberg. I'd have the universe in the palm of my hand.

Everything that went wrong would be right again.

Introducing: the Boyfriend App.

Get the app. Get the guy. It would work—even for me. It had to.

chapter four

Lindsay Fanning honked four times—four more times than my mom and my aunt Linda told her she was supposed to—just as I pushed through the door and spilled into the parking lot. Lindsay was technically my cousin, but she was way more like my sister.

The sky pegged water pellets at the windshield of her 1995 Acura Legend. I swung open the car door and tried to close my umbrella, but it wouldn't budge. Rain soaked my hair. I finally got the thing to shut, and climbed inside. I could smell my strawberry shampoo as I sank onto the leather seats.

Lindsay's platinum-blond bob was pin-straight and rain-resistant, thanks to some chemical treatment that had been banned by the FDA. "You look like a drowned skater boy," she said, adjusting the neon-yellow rope that framed a lucite cameo at her throat. "Though the whole androgynous thing is pretty on trend right now." Lindsay wants to be the *Deputy Fashion Director at a Major Fashion Magazine by Age Thirty or Die Trying*, as she puts it on the home page of her blog.

Lindsay's eight-year-old sister, Claire, waved a leather crop from the backseat. She pointed to the black velvet riding helmet dwarfing her head. "Look what Lindsay and me found on eBay," she said.

Claire refused to go to third grade in anything other than equestrian-style clothes. She practiced riding her bike around the neighborhood, pretending it was a horse and whipping the back wheel with her crop.

"You look great," I told her. Then I handed her an article I'd printed out about the horse who played Mr. Ed on TV.

Lindsay cranked up the windshield wipers and sped through the road behind our apartment complex. She had the AC blasting because she suffers from what she terms *hot flashes caused by an overactive metabolism*. The hair on my arms shot up like a forest of icicles.

"I heard about yesterday," Lindsay said in a hushed voice. She'd missed the Dumpster incident because she was chairing the Homecoming planning committee (theme: Paris Fashion Week, Lindsay's suggestion) and they met during lunch. "And I IM'd you like a million times last night to see if you were okay."

"I wasn't allowed to use my computer," I said.

Lindsay nodded sagely. "My mom took away *Vogue* last week when I went over my spending limit on buyJams, so

I know how you feel." She leaned too close to the steering wheel, like she used to when our dads took us to drive bumper cars. "I can't stop myself from downloading music once I start," she said. "Do you think there's some kind of twelve-step program for that?"

I looked at her and saw she was totally serious.

Lindsay clapped her leopard-print flat on the accelerator and fishtailed onto Route 31. Route 31 led from our apartment complex by the highway past the University of Notre Dame, past crappy hotels like Ho Jo and Motel 6, past the deliciousness of American Pancake House, to Harrison High School.

My cousin wasn't winning any awards for her driving. And I was already nauseous when I thought about surviving school today. The only thing making it better was obsessing over how I was going to take the Boyfriend App from fantasy to reality. Since I wasn't allowed to use my computer last night, I'd found one of my dad's leather journals and brainstormed the old-fashioned way, sketching out the design architecture of the application with a pencil and eraser in pseudocode. Pseudocode just means nailing down the functionality in broad terms. Like say: *When the user hits X button, Y will happen.* Later I would go back and write the code in an editing program in a much more specific way that my computer would understand.

I yanked the journal from my backpack. Lindsay swerved around college kids who were wearing Notre Dame gear jogging along the side of the road, blissfully unaware of what a bad idea it was to run in the rain near Lindsay's car-weapon. Notre Dame college girls always looked golden and bouncy and happy. Whenever I saw them, I tried to pick out whic students studied in the engineering program, or did research at the department for nanoscience and tech. I tried to pick out which college girls I was like.

The first half of the journal was filled with my dad's pseudocode for scripts to automatically restart computer systems should they be stopped. It was the kind of thing that had entered the market recently, but my dad was already working on a functional prototype years prior. He was way ahead of the curve.

I wondered if he'd ever gotten his courage up enough to show Blake's dad.

I flipped through his code to my dog-eared page. My notes were scraggly and crooked. When we built apps, Ms. Bates taught us to beware of building while ideas were too nebulous, while limits were undefined. You had to set up parameters of what you wanted to create.

1) An app that finds the perfect boyfriend
If I want to win the contest, I need a universal app that can work for anyone and everyone—even me.

2) Perfect Boyfriend = Perfect Match
People will need to download the Boyfriend App (the BFA) and register by completing a highly detailed questionnaire. In order for the BFA to work, a registry with superpersonal information is a must. The BFA needs to know everything about you. If you're claustrophobic and scared of big dogs,

the BFA can't match you with a boyfriend who loves packed movie theaters and has a Rottweiler with a spiky collar named Kill Boy.

3) This is NOT a dating app.
The BFA takes any preconceived notions about digital matchmaking and injects them with steroids to create a virtual Boyfriend Finder. An alert sounds on your cell phone when your Top Love Match is within 100 yards. Say you're walking by the theater and the alert rings out: It turns out your perfect boyfriend—the guy who is totally made for you—is on stage running lines for King Lear. There's no more missed opportunities, no more mistakes, no more chance happenings thrown away because you weren't paying attention.

WHO NEEDS FATE WHEN YOU HAVE THE BOYFRIEND APP?

I jerked forward as Lindsay slammed to a stop twenty feet in front of a red light. "Someone needs to teach Blake and the Martin sisters a lesson," she said.

Claire took a break from drawing horse heads in the steam on her window. "You can say that again."

Lindsay said it again, but Claire didn't laugh. Neither did I.

I snapped the journal shut and slunk farther down against the leather. Lindsay didn't know the feeling of being not liked, and I was grateful for that. I don't know what I'd do if anyone was mean to her. Everyone's loved Lindsay since she entered the world via cesarean section, nine days before I did. She had a group of friends, but she usually just hung out with anyone she found interesting in the moment. (Though she avoided Blake & Co. out of loyalty to me.) To top off Lindsay's lovability, in the summer between our sophomore and junior year, she did the coolest thing anyone at Harrison has ever done, which was to spend three months in New York City at FIT on a grant awarded by Kate Spade. She came back all worldly and everything, and everyone noticed. Between FIT and her fashion blog, she was sort of untouchable.

And just like Xander with his probable lacrosse scholarship to Stanford, and Blake with her guaranteed acceptance to Notre Dame (now that her father had donated millions for a workout facility to be called the Blake Andrea), Lindsay was practically guaranteed a spot at FIT next fall. So she had zero idea what it was like to have to go to college somewhere you weren't excited about. Which meant she often said things like, *Where are you applying, Audrey?* Or, simply, *Where're you gonna go next fall?* Which just made me feel worse. If I ended up at Holy Cross Community College to avoid debt, I wouldn't really be *going* anywhere. It was embarrassing.

Lindsay's crystal doorknocker earrings slapped the side of her face as she turned to look in my lap. "That journal's kind of retro Audrey McCarthy circa fourth grade," she said. She slammed on the gas while her head was still turned. "Are you sure you're okay?"

She rested a hand on mine. I wanted her to put it back on the wheel.

"I'm fine."

"You're lying."

"Maybe. But I don't want to get into it right now."

Lindsay attempted to angle the car into the elementary school's parking lot still holding my hand. She gave up when we rolled over a soda can on the lawn, and then made tire marks on the grass as she gunned back on the road. We pulled up to the school's front entrance, but Claire wouldn't leave the car until Joelle Martin was out of sight. (Joelle was the third Martin sister, and in Claire's third-grade class. In addition to being bullies, the three Martin sisters all have Jo names. How not cute is that?)

Joelle and her Hello Kitty book bag finally disappeared behind a bus, and Claire got out. She shut the door and waved a shaky good-bye with her crop.

"I wish Joelle Martin would get lice," I said through an overly wide smile, waving encouragingly at Claire through the windshield.

"I wish Joelle Martin would get rabies," Lindsay said, waving and smiling, too.

On our way to Harrison, we passed Lindsay's mom power-walking beneath a golf umbrella. My aunt Linda's main concern in life was traffic, which was why she walked a mile every day to her job as a receptionist at South Bend Dental. She wouldn't take a ride—even when it was raining. Lindsay shook her head and said, "Oh, Linda," as we passed. Linda gave us a thumbs-up.

At Harrison, Lindsay shot me sideways glances as we inched through the parking lot. The downpour washed the grime from Xander Knight's artfully decrepit motorcycle. Lindsay was about to pull into an open spot when she realized Blake's white Jeep Grand Cherokee occupied the space to the right. It was an unspoken rule at Harrison that you didn't park on Blake's left because she didn't like having to squeeze between cars or have restricted room to open her door.

Lindsay's wipers swiped the glass, barely able to fend off the rain. She jerked the wheel and pulled next to the sand-colored Prius I knew was Nigit's by the bumper sticker that read: NO, I WILL NOT FIX YOUR COMPUTER. I wondered if he and Aidan had spent the night brainstorming app ideas.

Lindsay turned off the car. "Balenciaga's new handbag is so gorgeous I want to take it behind school and have sex with it," she said, rummaging through a metallic makeup bag. "Is that wrong?" She fished out a magenta-colored gloss and ran the wand over her lips. "I'm spotlighting the collection on *FBM* today."

Lindsay has more than forty thousand uniques (a.k.a.: readers) on her blog, *Fashion Becomes Me*, and tweets to another twenty thousand. *FBM* got sponsored with an AOL ad this summer and that's how she bought her used Acura for eleven hundred bucks. Nearly every girl at school reads *FBM*—even Blake, though she'd never admit it to Lindsay. (I know, because Lindsay once charmed me into getting Blake's IP address, which I did by emailing her a web page that logged her IP as soon as she connected. Then I matched her IP to comments left on Lindsay's blog nearly every day. Like: *OMG Lindsay luv ur blog! Totes buying Vena Cava LBD for Homecoming!*)

If you're wondering: *Yes*, it *is* tempting to hack into Blake's computer and mess with her life. Except I'd be breaking my dad's rule: Never use what you know to hurt people.

Still, I'd fantasized about what I could do to make her stop coming after me. Like setting up a backdoor on her system and installing a keylogger for unfettered access to everything she ever typed—including passwords for pictures, documents, emails, bank accounts, *everything*— and then emailing secret romantic Blake/Woody pictures to Xander. Or, I dunno, connecting via said backdoor and launching a Denial of Service attack on the FBI. (That meant I could get Blake's computer to launch its own attack by flooding the FBI's server with connections. And then I could hide in the bushes and watch as federal agents showed up on her doorstep and hauled her away.)

I wished I could be meaner. Because there were so many more options.

Lindsay and I got out of the car and squished together under my umbrella. Rain soaked the bottom half of our legs as Lindsay went on about how drop-crotch pants can be flattering if you pair them with the right heel. I nodded along and reminded myself it was already Thursday—all

I needed to do was get through today and tomorrow and maybe everything would be forgotten by next week. I ignored the little voice that whispered *Yeah, right,* as we made our way into Harrison.

chapter five

I swung open the door to the computer lab. It wasn't even eight a.m. and the air was already five degrees warmer than the rest of school. Plus, there's something about the way black T-shirts and black socks produce BO in epic proportions—that, plus some trogs don't shower as often as the rest of the planet—and our tiny, airless space was less than 400 square feet.

My gaze landed on Aidan hunched over his notebook. His lashes were so long they appeared to brush his high cheekbones as he jotted notes. His hair was dark and wavy, like Lake Michigan at night, and his broad shoulders angled to a slim waist. One hunter-green Converse was balanced on the opposite knee. He tapped the rubber sole with his mechanical pencil. I looked away before someone could catch me staring.

White paint flaked on our four windowless walls. The

bulletin boards that framed the room overflowed with computer-related newspaper clippings—the most recent about Infinitum CEO Jane Callaghan's relaunch of the InfiniPhone Universe due out next month. (Infinitum was Public's biggest competition. The crowd of Infinitum users was smaller, but more devout.) And then there was the latest Public campaign: *The buyPhone 17.5: a Sexier SmartPhone: Just Because You're Smart Doesn't Mean You Can't Be Sexy.*

No one even looked up as I took a seat at computer #15 in the back left corner of the lab. The trogs didn't care about what happened yesterday, maybe because they were so steeped in building scholarship-winning code that my social faux pas was already old news, or maybe because they'd done way worse themselves. Like when Joel Norris dropped his tuba onto the big toe of head cheerleader and first violinist Carrie Sommers one week before the Circle of Stars National Cheerleading Competition in Indianapolis. The Harrison High pyramid was never quite the same. Neither was Joel's social status. Harrison was unforgiving like that, especially if you messed with a popular girl.

Someone had written MOBILE APPLICATION DAY on the board in yellow chalk, and drawn a stick figure holding a cell phone with a thought bubble that read: TWO HUNDRED THOUSAND BIG ONES. I was about to take out my journal when I saw Mindy's mane of caramel hair obscure the pane of plastic on the computer lab's door.

Her dark eyes caught mine. She shoved a piece of paper with block letters scrawled in green marker onto the plastic partition: U OK 2DAY?

46

Maybe it's only me, but whenever anyone asks if I'm okay, I just feel upset again. I gave her a nod and faked a smile. She considered me through the plastic for another moment before disappearing down the hall.

Three thin rows of wood with five computers each lined the lab. Aidan and Nigit sat directly in front of me. Aidan turned as I took my journal from my backpack. He was a few inches over six feet, and even while we were both sitting, I had to look up to meet his navy eyes.

"You want some help, Auds?" he asked. His deep voice was quiet, like it was just for me to hear.

Aidan had grown up in a tiny town in Maine, which made sense, because something about him reminded me of a fisherman. Not just the well-worn cable knit sweaters, perfectly broken-in Levis, or the permanently mussed hair that made him look like he'd just climbed off a fishing boat: It was a quality I couldn't put my finger on, like patience, or fortitude or something. He was both kind and tough. Most people don't have that combination.

Aidan, his mom, and his little sister moved to South Bend during the winter of freshman year, so he never knew me as Popular Audrey. He never knew me as a girl with a dad. He never knew me as anyone other than a hoodie-wearing freak who carried a rabbit's foot and who other guys stayed away from. Somehow him not knowing what I'd lost took the pressure off.

"I think I'm okay," I started. "I actually brainstormed last night and I—"

"Aidan, we need to *focus*," Nigit said, adjusting his glasses. "Sorry, Audrey," he said under his breath.

Aidan gave me a long look before turning back to his computer. A text alert pinged my buyPhone.

Aidan: talk later

Ms. Bates looked up. Her dove-white hair was cut just beneath her jaw. She always wore red lipstick, and she always looked like an old-fashioned movie star. Bates was in her sixties, but you could tell she was drop-dead in her day. She was by far the most glamorous teacher at Harrison—even Lindsay said so—and she was definitely the smartest. We trogs got her all to ourselves.

"No phones, Audrey," Ms. Bates said. "Only code."

Bates went to grad school at MIT alongside Robert Dawkins, Public CEO Alec Pierce, and Infinitum CEO Jane Callaghan. It was weird to think of them all being grad students together. She never told us stories about them—no matter how hard we pressed. Only Google talked, telling me a Hannah Marie Bates worked with Jane Callaghan in New York City in the seventies before Jane Callaghan was *Jane Callaghan* and Infinitum was *Infinitum*. Sometime in the early eighties, Bates returned to her hometown and started teaching technology.

"Sorry, Ms. Bates," I mumbled. I swiped a layer of vanilla-flavored gloss onto my lips and logged on to Public Party, where an ad popped up: *Danny Beaton Wants You to Party Your Face Off with the Newest Public buyPhone!*

Confetti sprinkled across the screen. *Hello, Audrey McCarthy. Ready to start the party? Enter Your Password.*

I logged in and clicked on my home page. I'd made my wallpaper dark gray and swirly, kind of emo, like in a Victorian house. It used to be pink, but now my Party

Guest Connections had dwindled, so I figured my page should match my social standing.

An icon popped up. *Lindsay Fanning sent you flowers.* I clicked on it and a virtual bouquet bloomed above a note that read *Chin up, Cuz.* The flowers faded like a mirage, and that's when I saw it. Front and center on my wallpaper.

BLAKE ANDREA DAWKINS: *Now your little Dumpster toy is just like you: TRASH!*

A bunch of Harrison kids "loved" it. I scanned the list of loves—the Martin sisters, Annborg Alsvik, Carrie Sommers the cheerleading violinist, another girl I tutored last year for the SATs. I took the slightest bit of comfort that Xander wasn't on the love list. Sweat warmed my palms as I deleted the post.

The murmurs and keyboard-clicks around me softened. I heard my dad's voice.

You know who you are, Audrey. Nobody can make you feel bad unless you let them.

Just because we didn't have a lot of money didn't mean we were trash. I knew who we were, even if no one else did.

I logged off and took a breath. Nobody—not even Blake—was getting in the way of my Big Idea.

I SSH'd into my home computer. (It's an encrypted connection, so school can't see what I'm doing. Call me paranoid, but I didn't want to leave a trace of my app in the lab.)

The blank screen gave me the familiar feeling of hope— like I could create something from scratch with meaning.

A problem is solved one step at a time.

It was what my dad used to say whenever we worked on homework or computer code.

So what's the first step, sweetheart?

The survey. It was the key to creating the match-up algorithms.

Variables, arrays, loops, and sanity checks splashed through my mind. Something electric shot through the air as my fingertips touched down and started to create.

SURVEY PART I.

What do girls really want in a guy, anyway?

I tapped my finger on the mouse.

> Kindness.
> Honesty.
> Hotness.
> Nice to your parents but not too nice.
> Smart.
> Faithful.
> Probably good at sports. (But if he's a drummer, then okay if he's not good at sports.)
> Good dresser.

I wasn't really sure what made one guy a good dresser and another guy a sucky one. Maybe I could build the survey like a multiple-choice question test.

How does your ideal boyfriend dress?
Like a rap star/Like a business mogul/Like a jock/Like a

prep/Like a douche bag (Oakley sunglasses, pink collared shirt with the collar up)

What does your ideal boyfriend look like?

Clean-Cut/Stubble/Mustache/Goatee/

Brad Pitt from *Seven Days in Tibet*

FatBoy/Soft-Around-the-Edges/Toned/

Brad Pitt from *Fight Club*

NBA-star Tall/Regular Tall/Medium/Short/Seriously Short

Black Hair/Brown Hair/Red Hair/Blond Hair/Dyed-a-Funky-Color Hair

What kind of shoes does your ideal boyfriend wear?

Converse/Nikes/Penny Loafers/Doc Martens/Flip-Flops/

Dirty Bare Feet/Brad Pitt's dress shoes from *Ocean's Eleven*

I found most things in life could be illustrated with a Brad Pitt reference from the pre–Angelina Jolie years. Maybe he was old now, but someone with proven, lasting sex appeal was more my speed than a flash in the pan like Pop Boy Danny Beaton, whose concert Lindsay, Claire, and I were going to in a few weeks in Indianapolis at the Lucas Oil Stadium. Claire had won front row seats from a Public Party Preteen contest. Obviously I preferred Vampire Weekend and Radiohead to Danny Beaton, but I was secretly excited.

And that was a good survey question.

What kind of music does your ideal boyfriend listen to?

Danny Beaton/Vampire Weekend/Radiohead/Phish/

Miles Davis/Metallica/Mozart

I did a few more questions about favorite songs, movies, forms of exercise, and hobbies, and then moved on to dating stuff.

What is your ideal first-date cuisine?
Italian/French/Japanese/Chinese/Pizza/Hot Dog/Vegan/
Something that won't blow my Weight Watchers Points tally.
What are your favorite topics of conversation?
Sports/Pop Culture/Celebrities/Technology/Fashion/
Politics/I don't wanna talk, let's just make out.
How do you want your boyfriend to vote when he turns eighteen?
Democrat/Republican/Independent/Socialist/
Don't care as long as he's hot.
How does your ideal boyfriend keep his bedroom?
Cleaner than an operating room/Pretty neat/Some clutter/The floor's covered in his boxers and cartons of half-eaten Chinese takeout.

Then I made a section called Boyfriend in Action with questions like:

How do you want your boyfriend to greet you?
Yo!/Oh. Hi./Wassup Girl/Howdy Partner/Hello, Lover/Hail Princess
What kind of presents do you want him to bring you?
Flowers/Candy/Stuffed Animals/Jewelry/Video Games/
No Presents. I'm so not materialistic.

What's your ideal date?
Riding his motorcycle/Strolling on the beach/
Expensive dinner at the hottest restaurant/Dinner at a
dive/Go out to a movie/French-kissing on the couch/Wii
bowling/Picketing at an animal rights protest.
How often do you want to hang out?
Practically never: My girlfriends are cooler/A date every
few days/Daily hangout/Like we're handcuffed.

It turned out that not ever having had a boyfriend
primed me for writing the survey. I'd spent endless hours
fantasizing about what I wanted and what I didn't.

On page six of the survey, I did moral dilemmas. Like:

**Say your boyfriend was caught in Target stealing a
pack of Jujyfruits. Would you:**
Call the cops/Break up with him on the spot/Give him a
lecture outside the store but keep dating him/Roll your
eyes but secretly be glad he did it while you chow down
on Jujyfruits/Join in the fun and steal two Butterfingers.

I felt a twinge as I read over the questions. Blake and
I had spent practically every afternoon in seventh grade
reading quizzes like these in *Seventeen* magazine. Blake
bought the magazines for us, even though my mom said:
Not till you're seventeen, to which Blake said, *That's missing
the point. We need to know all this stuff* before *we're seventeen.*
We had to hide the magazines in an art-supply box under
my bed.

I was searching *What do girls look for in a boyfriend?* on Google to make sure I'd covered everything when the bell rang. My back was stiff from arching forward. My butt was asleep with sharp, stabbing pricks where blood used to flow. But as I scrolled over the pages in front of me, there it was: the survey that would form the bones of the app. Tonight, I'd start hacking away at a code.

"You're all going to have to dig deep," Ms. Bates said as the bell quieted. "Program as your most innovative creative self." As we gathered our stuff, she went on about pushing ourselves to do something that had never been done before (which was mildly impossible). Then she reminded us to log on to Public's website as soon as we finished building our apps.

Here's how it was supposed to go: We submitted our apps to Public; they went live and were available for download. During the weeks the contest ran, download was free. The Battery had missed a few key details. Public was granting *two* grand prizes: one for the Most Innovative Mobile App (decided by Public) and one for the Most Popular Mobile App (the app with the most downloads worldwide). Both grand prizewinners would secure the college scholarship. And—bonus—every student in the Most Popular App winners' high school would get the newest edition of the Public Beast twenty-four hours before its official debut. (Beast 5.0, valued at $995.00.) And every student in the Most Innovative Mobile App winners' high school would get a buyPlayer and speakers.

I ran a hand across my eyes and tried to blink away the

screen's glare, but it felt like my brain was glazed with a neon white glow.

"Auds?"

I turned to see Aidan. He had a habit of tugging his inky black hair between his knuckles and now it shot out on one side like porcupine quills. "I'll walk you to gym?" he asked.

I nodded so hard I hurt my neck. Then I tried to be more casual, and said, "Time to get my dodgeball on." *Time to get my dodgeball on?* "Thanks for walking me," I tried again, making my voice sound ladylike instead of like an androgynous skater boy. It was another Top Ten Reason I didn't have a boyfriend—I said weird stuff.

"I figured, especially after what happened yesterday," Aidan said.

I looked up as he moved closer. I took in the smooth skin stretched tight over his strong, angular jaw. "I wasn't sure if you were okay," he said.

I wanted to tell him I wasn't really okay. But Nigit was staring at us. "Your diary?" Nigit asked, pointing at my journal.

"Not exactly," I said, suddenly embarrassed. I fumbled to fit the journal into my backpack's front pocket without crushing my rabbit's foot.

"So what're you guys working on?" I asked Aidan once we were in the hallway and out of Nigit's earshot.

Aidan's dark blue eyes glinted as he glanced around us. "It's a philanthropy app," he said. I liked how he didn't need to tell me to keep it a secret. He already knew I would. "You enter how much time you have to spare—on a certain date, or right then in the moment, and then the app tells you how you can help people based on your location and the time you're willing to commit."

I chewed on my bottom lip. It wasn't just a good idea; it was meaningful. The Public contest people were sure to love it. "That's really good," was all I managed to sputter out.

Charlotte Davis cruised down the hall in her wheelchair. Two soccer players wearing dark red Umbros and Harrison jerseys nearly toppled us as they jumped out of her way. (Sometimes she purposely steered it at people, especially Blake.) Aidan put an arm protectively around my shoulders. "What about yours?" he asked, guiding me toward a bank of lockers. He was stronger than I would have thought, and I felt little sparks of heat where his hand touched.

My idea suddenly felt stupid. Here Aidan was saving the world one charitable app user at a time and I was trying to get myself a boyfriend.

"It's sort of an app that finds a girl a boyfriend," I said.

"Really?" Aidan asked, arching an eyebrow. His mouth hinted at a smile. "Are you looking for one?"

Heat streaked through me. I was trying to figure out what to say when Jolene Martin rounded the corner with Xander.

"Audrey!" Jolene shouted, loud enough that everyone in the hallway turned to stare. The mole on her chin was like a clue that telegraphed: *This Girl Is Actually a Witch*. She made her fingers into an *L* on the top of her forehead.

Aidan stopped.

Xander was big, but Aidan was bigger. His large frame stood completely still, forcing Jolene and Xander to move awkwardly out of our way. "Oh, I get it," Aidan said sarcastically to Jolene. "*Loser.* Your sign language is groundbreaking and original." His hand on my arm felt protective, like a shield. But then Jolene made a fist and shook it in my direction.

It gave me shivers.

The Martin girls had made fun of me for years—ever since their Glory Day arrived and they took over my position as Blake's BFFs. But Joanna actually hurting me yesterday was a first.

Xander's hazel eyes caught mine. I swore sometimes he looked at me the way he did that one time in Joanna's basement.

Jolene was still laughing.

Aidan told them to get lost, and then held me closer until I felt dizzy. "Auds," he said, low enough so only I could hear him. "They're mean because it makes them feel better about their sucky lives. What a crap way to exist, right?"

"I should go," I said. I ducked away, worried he was going to see how I wanted nothing more than to stay with him, safe beneath his embrace.

chapter six

Two dozen bottles of Mountain Dew and seven thousand lines of code later, the app was built.

Here's basically how I did it, and it's easier than you think.

Building an app means writing lines and lines of code. Think of code like instructions. As the programmer, the code you write tells the app what to do.

I wrote the code in an editing program called Textmate. (Think Microsoft Word for app builders: Like how Word has fonts and formatting, my editing program has ways to help me write code.)

So, if you took a picture of app building, it would look like this: me wearing pajamas sitting in front of Hector the Computer typing code into an open window.

The code I typed might look like this:

```
Distance = user.location()—target.
```

```
location();
If (distance < 100) then
Target.isMatch = yes;
Else
Target.isMatch = no;
```

That code will determine the distance between the user and a potential match and, if the match is less than one hundred yards away, mark the target as a potential match.

I don't need an actual phone to test my code because a simulator runs a version of the phone on my screen. So once I've written some code, I run it on my computer, click around to see if it's doing what I want it to, and then go back and edit.

Programmers usually talk about code in terms of quantity of lines written. So say I have a monster session: I could write a few hundred lines of code in one night. But if I spend hours debugging problems, I might end up with only a couple new lines after a full night of work.

But there are *always* bugs—lots of them—so you have to be prepared. As a programmer, your job is to figure out where they are and squash them.

Like any app, the BFA had its own unique components, like the survey. Once I perfected the survey, I created filters for the multiple-choice questions. The app had to have a brain of its own to decipher how certain answers matched up with others. The filter made it so that if you preferred a short, bald, kleptomaniac fatboy, the app matched you with one. I built an external database to code the data so the answers could be pinged to that. Then, I got the app to use GPS to sort through all survey answers within a five-mile radius. Geo location triangulated each user's position in relation to other users. The results were sorted. Matches were created. Then the external server returned back the match results to every user's buyPhone.

Once I'd built the core functionality of the app, I had to skin it. Skinning an app means dressing it up. You take your clunky bits that work together (but don't yet look like anything) and make them look pretty. Programmers call how the app looks the user interface. The better your app looks, the more likely users will want it, and I needed to get the design exactly right. So I pored over dozens of fashion magazines I borrowed from Lindsay. I tore out a bunch of pages—everything from a cartoon of Cupid to a photo of a couple snuggling over chocolate pots de creme, to an ad for bright white designer sunglasses. I wanted the Boyfriend App to look super romantic and chic, but glam, too, like a valentine combined with the shiny engagement ring the girl contestant gets on *The Bachelor* when the guy proposes. After making a bunch of stuff that wasn't quite right, I came up with a sleek, bright white icon with a pink diamond-studded heart set inside. I stared at it for hours until I *knew* it was right. I could feel it.

I mocked everything up in Photoshop before slicing the screens and skinning the app. Once the user was within a hundred yards of her match, I designed the UI so that the app sent an alert to her phone with his name and position written in a cursive script with a swirly border. Like this:

Boyfriend Alert:
BRAD PITT. 24 YARDS SOUTHEAST.

I created a flashing arrow graphic that worked like a compass to guide the girl in the direction of her perfect match. The boys had to wait for their match to be revealed to them. Which happened only if the girl chose to reveal the evidence on her phone that they'd been matched.

And *boyfriend* was really just a word. I made the app to work for girls wanting girlfriends, girls wanting boyfriends, boys wanting boyfriends, and boys wanting girlfriends.

Each night, I took a break from coding around ten to download new music from buyJams. Downloading music on buyJams was like being in a trance. There were so many Radiohead songs waiting for me to purchase. And then all icons popped up: *If You Like Radiohead, Public Suggests . . .*

I usually snapped out of it somewhere around midnight, and went back to building, debugging, and chugging soda.

On Wednesday, I sat next to Aidan in lab. I was closer to him than my usual seat one row back, and his nearness was making me dizzy. His eyes widened just a little when he saw me sitting there. His glance passed over the bare skin of my collarbone and I suddenly felt naked.

Sunday confession, here I come.

I cleared my throat. "I need your help with something," I said.

Aidan turned his chair so he was facing me. He leaned back and crossed his arms over his broad chest. There was trouble in his smile and my pulse went erratic. Each second put me more on edge.

"Whatever you need," he finally said. Then he reached forward and yanked my chair closer. Our knees were touching and my head felt full of cotton.

I swallowed.

"So for my app," I started, trying not to focus on how close we were, how it felt to have him touching me. "I need guys to download it and take the survey and be potential boyfriends for the girl I get to test it out."

"Are you the girl?" he asked evenly.

"What? No, *no*. Of course not." I let out a nervous laugh as Nigit and Joel Norris sat down. Aidan convinced them to download the BFA, too, and then Bates came in and started a discussion on cross-site scripting.

That night, I texted Mindy and explained the gist of the app.

Sounds so cool, she texted back.

So . . . I texted. **Any chance you would try it for me? Be the first girl user?**

She radio-silenced me for a few minutes. Then she texted: **I want to help you. But I'd be too chicken to ask out the guy I got matched with. I'm sorry, Audrey! Lemme know if I can do something else!**

I was already worried the app wasn't going to work. Now I was freaking out. I needed someone I trusted to test it.

The next afternoon, I was still drinking Mountain Dew and jittering about the app when Lindsay pushed open the door to Farrah's Finds. "Chin up, Audrey. Shoulders back," she said as a bell celebrated our arrival with a muted *ding*. "Your posture sucks."

Farrah's Finds was a vintage store located in a strip mall on Edison sandwiched between Her Story (my mom's favorite romance bookstore) and a World of Video (which smelled like cigarettes and lemon air freshener).

Lindsay sighed as we slipped through a curtain of purple plastic beads. "Heaven," she said.

If this was heaven, I was going to take up sinning. Rows of musty-looking furs, stretched-out vintage T-shirts, and high-waisted jeans that would make even me look fat lined the walls. Glassy-eyed mannequins were posed around the store wearing 1960s fashions with dingy handbags slung over their shoulders. I envied the fact that they couldn't smell the mothballs.

Farrah herself sat behind the register swathed in a paisley scarf and a snug silk blouse. "Lindsay!" she trilled. She bounced a little and her droopy water-balloon boobs got a second wind. "How's my favorite fashionista?" Farrah had a fake accent, the kind that makes you think of rich people drinking tea and playing cricket. I was pretty sure she told Lindsay fake stories, too.

Farrah *blah blah blah*ed about wearing white after Labor Day and some other equally boring stuff, and then excused herself to retrieve a shipment of estate jewelry she called *exquisite*.

Lindsay turned to me. She tapped a hot-pink fingernail on the glass counter. "Did I ever tell you Farrah met editrix Diana Vreeland on a catamaran in Monaco and inspired

Diana's stacked-bangle look?"

There were so many words in that sentence I didn't understand. "Diana who?"

"Diana *Vreeland*," Lindsay said, like I'd asked who George Washington was. "Only the twentieth century's greatest arbiter of style and elegance."

"Listen, Lindsay," I said, running my fingers over a golf-ball-sized cocktail ring displayed on a plastic hand. "I need to ask you something."

Lindsay unfolded spectacles the size of Oreos and put them on. "I can barely see Loulou de la Falaise in these," she said, squinting at her phone's screen. Loulou de la Falaise was what she called her buyPhone.

I'd rehearsed my speech in my head all afternoon during classes. "You know that app contest Principal Dawkins announced?" I started.

Lindsay nodded. Her green eyes shrank behind the prescription lenses.

Nerves shot through me, but I forced myself to go on. "I have this idea called the Boyfriend App."

Lindsay's fingers froze on the buckle of a Kelly green snakeskin wallet. She glanced at me with an expression I couldn't read, partly because her eyes looked so weird in the spectacles.

I clammed up as she cocked a well-shaped eyebrow.

"That's a really catchy title, Audrey," she said, running her hand over a rhinestone tiara.

"Oh. Um, thanks," I said, emboldened. "So I built it, and I just need someone to try it out. There's this survey

64

you'd have to take, and a bunch of guys I know already downloaded it onto their phones." I left out the part that the only guys I knew well enough to convince to do it were the six computer-lab guys. "You'll download the app to Loulou de la Falaise, and once you take the survey, the Boyfriend App sends you an alert when your top love match is within one hundred yards, and—"

"I haven't had a boyfriend since Jonas," Lindsay interrupted, referring to the college guy she met at FIT who made dresses out of pizza boxes. "Do you really think I'm ready to move on? To find happiness again?" Her eyes got all glazed. "Do you think I'm ready to resubmerge myself in the waters of love?"

Considering she hadn't talked about Jonas in, like, a year, the answer was probably yes. But I put my hand over hers solemnly anyway. "I think it's time," I said gently, like we were in a Lifetime movie.

Lindsay's lashes started blinking rapid-fire like they always did when she got excited. I knew I had her.

My cousin put the sparkling tiara on her head. "I'll do it," she said.

chapter seven

Contestant Number 13079: Audrey McCarthy. Harrison High School. South Bend, Indiana. THE BOYFRIEND APP. Available for Download. Users: 7. Click Here for More Information.

"How exciting, Audrey!" Ms. Bates said the next afternoon in the computer lab. Her tall, thin frame was wrapped in a knee-length cashmere cardigan. She'd pinned her smooth white hair into a tortoiseshell clip.

It was Friday at the start of lunch period, and the lab was packed with Harrison students wanting Bates's help building their apps. Students I had no idea cared about programming filled the seats and the regulars waited outside the door, acting pissed. Joel Norris peered through the glass, looking like he was going to drop his tuba. Again.

"You're the first Harrison student to submit," Ms. Bates said, smiling.

I sucked in a breath. I hoped I hadn't rushed anything.

"The Boyfriend App," Bates read aloud.

I felt more nervous by the second. Ms. Bates knew *everything*. It was one of the first times I hadn't asked for her advice on a computer project. "It finds boyfriends," I blurted.

Bates pursed her crimson lips. She looked unsure, so I tried to explain it more like the computer nerd she knew me as instead of a teenager with a boy-crazy streak. "The app user fills out a survey," I said. "And the Boyfriend App sorts the results of anyone in a five-mile radius who's also completed the survey. It sends the user an alert when her top love match is within a hundred yards, so she can approach her possible love target if she wants to."

Bates gave me another smile. But this one was smaller. "It's sort of like a dating website?" she asked slowly, like I'd just described the Boring App.

"I—I think people will like it," I said. But now I was freaking out again. Bates had cut my giant innovative idea down to its knees.

"I think perhaps you should dig deeper, Audrey," Bates said, eyes narrowing. "You're capable of much more, and if you just—"

PING!

I'd never been so relieved to get a text from Mindy.

Let's eat in the Books. K?

Mindy was referring to the library. I mumbled good-bye to Ms. Bates and promised I'd try harder. I loved Bates, but she'd never even gotten married. She probably forgot how important it was to have a boyfriend.

I made my way to the library and silently thanked Mindy a hundred times for not having to be the one to suggest eating as far away from the cafeteria as possible this week. I was hurrying past the girls' bathroom when I heard crying noises. Not like I'm trying to win a Teen Compassion award, but I really think—as a rule—you should stop for crying. I pushed through swinging doors into the bathroom.

Blake stood hunched over the sink. Her hair was like a black curtain covering her face and arms. The silver charm bracelet she got for her thirteenth birthday dangled on her slim wrist. Her head jerked up, and her dark eyes went wide when she saw me standing there. She took a quick step back. She looked panicked, like an animal who'd been cornered.

Maybe I should've run out of the bathroom right then, but I stupidly couldn't help myself when it came to her.

I swallowed. "Are you okay?"

Mascara smeared beneath Blake's thick lower lashes. She didn't say anything for a few beats. She just stared at me. When she finally said, "You don't get to care anymore. Remember?" her voice was practically soft, like even though she was trying to say something mean, she couldn't make her tone match.

It still stung. "Whatever." I turned to go, but she grabbed my arm. Her brown eyes looked crazed. I couldn't decipher if she was about to tell me what was wrong, or punch me.

"Audrey," she said, her voice catching. Her grip tightened. She was freaking me out.

"You're right," I said as her nails dug into my skin. "I don't care anymore." It was a lie, but she let go of my arm and backed away like she believed me.

I couldn't get away from her fast enough. I shoved through the door and hurried down the hall. I could still feel the cold grip of her hand on my arm. What was *wrong* with her?

In the library, I followed the scent of peanut butter to a circular table sandwiched between rows of leather-bound books. Aidan and Nigit sat next to each other with their heads bent over Nigit's *World of Warcraft* notebook. Mindy wore a honey-brown sweater that matched her hair, and she was dipping her knife into a jar labeled PEANUT BUTTER. EXTRA CHUNKY! Her eyes crinkled when she saw me. I smiled back and tried to forget about Blake.

Aidan's dark hair was sticking out on the side like he'd slept on it funny, which made me think of him in bed. And that brought on a sudden fantasy of us rolling around in bed, with him in the tissue-thin vintage Metallica T-shirt he'd worn last summer that made me crazy.

I was giving myself a fever just imagining it. I tried to think of something neutral as I made my way toward my friends.

Puppies running in a field.

Nigit drummed his knuckles on the wooden table where students had carved dates as far back as 3/25/86 and wrote things like C.S.+T.H.= LUV 4 EVA. I wondered if C.S.

and T.H. were still together, planning their retirement. Or maybe one of them was in jail.

I dropped my paper bag onto the table and sat between Nigit and Mindy.

Aidan glanced up at me and smiled. He put on a navy-blue baseball hat that matched his eyes.

Nigit slapped a hand over his notebook page and gave me a dirty look.

"Chill, dude," Aidan said. Dark curls stuck out like wings beneath the hat. The collar of his gray knit fisherman's sweater nearly touched the curls. "I told her about the app," he said, pinching a mechanical pencil between two fingers. Then he smiled at me. I couldn't breathe until he broke our stare and returned his gaze to the notebook.

"PhilanthrApp," Nigit announced, straightening. If he had feathers, they would've fluffed.

I fidgeted with the zipper on my green hoodie. Mindy said it made my eyes look like emeralds, so I was trying to wear it more often. "Sounds awesome," I said.

The hair on Nigit's skinny brown forearms grew from the pinky side of the arm toward the thumb—the opposite of everyone else's—but it didn't seem to bother him. "It's unbeatable," he said, a grin quirking his lips. "Not that it isn't also altruistic of you to find people boyfriends," he added.

I ignored him.

My phone pinged with a text from Mindy. **Looking at Xander makes me suspect Leonardo DiCaprio had sex with a girl angel eighteen years ago and they made him**

I was about to text something back about Xander's hotness when Lindsay's voice echoed across the library: *"What the freak?"* A rhythmic *DING DING DONG DING* punctuated her words. I turned to see her platinum-blond bob shimmering beneath the library's fluorescent lighting as she stared at her buyPhone. Her black jeans were slashed down the sides like a bear had mauled her. "Audrey? Can I talk to you for a sec?" she asked in a sky-high-pitched voice. She yanked me behind the cover of a bookshelf where our eighty-year-old librarian's aide, Glenda, pushed a waist-high cart.

Glenda was legally deaf, so no one ever got in trouble for talking in the library. "Good morning!" she yelled, even though it was the afternoon.

Lindsay shoved her phone in my direction. "This *has* to be a mistake." Her screen flashed with the Boyfriend App's graphics: the swirly blue border framing the words *Boyfriend Alert!* in romantic cursive script. The blinking green arrow pointed in the direction of our lunch table. Beneath the arrow flashed: *NIGIT GURUNG. 7 YARDS NORTHWEST.*

"It worked," I breathed.

"It's obviously malfunctioning," Lindsay said, shifting her weight from one motorcycle boot to the other. Her wide green eyes mirrored mine. "Nigit? Me?"

"Lindsay, please," I whispered. I couldn't lose her—not now. "The app matched you. Maybe it sees something we don't."

Lindsay glanced through a space in the bookshelf at my

friends. Nigit arched forward. The puffy-paint Link from THE LEGEND OF ZELDA crinkled on his T-shirt as he gesticulated about a quest he'd recently started in *WOW*. Even Aidan's eyes were glazed.

Lindsay pursed her fuchsia-colored lips. "You owe me." She spun on her heel and bolted toward our table. "Is this seat taken?" she asked, pointing to the one next to Nigit.

Nigit stared through his Coke-bottle glasses. I worried he'd forgotten how to carry on a colloquial conversation.

"It's open," I squeaked.

Lindsay shot me a death look.

I sat next to Aidan and took out my stainless steel canteen. "Eco-friendly," I remarked, fumbling to make conversation.

"Hi, Lindsay," Aidan said to the back of his hands. I always forgot how shy he could be in front of other people. Which made me even more grateful for the way he'd stood up to Jolene in the hall.

Nigit stared at Lindsay's forehead like she was a Cyclops from one of his video games come to life. Were my friends and I this glaringly antisocial all the time?

Without speaking, Mindy managed to be the most welcoming. She smiled as Lindsay sat, and proffered a ginger candy.

"I loved the short story you wrote for English," Lindsay said to Mindy, unwrapping the candy. Mindy was a killer writer. "Was Anna's bouquet a metaphor for her lady parts?"

"Um, Lindsay," I started.

Mindy's face reddened as she mouthed *No*.

"Is that Ganesh?" Nigit asked, his voice accusing. He shoved his head into Lindsay's personal space and examined a gold charm on her necklace.

Lindsay nodded. Nigit let out a cackling laugh. "And you know who Ganesh is?" he asked. "Or, lemme guess, is your necklace just a faux-spiritual fashion thing?"

Lindsay glared.

"Speaking of fashion," I said. "I'm sure you all know my cousin Lindsay has a fashion blog with more than forty thousand readers." But I'd lost my audience, and no one seemed to care. Nigit and Lindsay locked eyes like they were in a staring contest to decide who hated the other one more.

"Duh," Lindsay said. She went to flick her hair over her shoulder and missed. (She only recently had it chopped into a bob, and sometimes she forgot it wasn't long anymore.) She recovered quickly, fishing inside her ostrich-embossed purse and retrieving a granola bar. She took another glance at Nigit, who obviously didn't believe her. "You mean Ganesh, Remover of Obstacles?" she quipped. "Sometimes called Ganapati, Vinayaka, or Pillaiyar? *Yeah*. I think I know who he is."

Nigit's dark eyes widened. "How do you know about Ganesh?"

Lindsay patted Nigit's hand like he was a small child. "The worship of Ganesh isn't restricted to India and Hindus, Nigit. I'm a Buddhist. As Ganesh is the Patron of Letters, I often invoke his name at the start of my blogging sessions."

I swallowed a bite of baked potato and wondered what my very Catholic aunt Linda thought about her daughter's eastern spiritual leanings.

Aidan's eyebrows arched into mini lightning bolts. Nigit stared at Lindsay like she was the Public prize money. He reached into his backpack and retrieved a figurine the size of a thumbnail. It was the same Ganesh-elephant thing Lindsay had around her neck. He sat it on the table between them. I thought about displaying my rabbit's foot, but I thought it might kill the mood.

"May I?" Lindsay asked.

Mindy held her peanut-butter sandwich in midair and glanced between Nigit and Lindsay.

Nigit nodded. Lindsay gently picked up the tiny green statue. "Jade?" she asked as she examined it.

"Jade," Nigit confirmed. "It was a gift from my mom for Diwali. I keep it on my puja table when I'm not here."

You know when you look at somebody—*really* look at them—and no matter how long you've known them, what you see surprises you? Something about the way Lindsay stared at Nigit made me want to see what she did. I peered through Nigit's thick glasses to see dark, intelligent eyes. His brown skin was clear and smooth, and his lips faded from dark pink on the outside to the pale pink of rose petals.

"I wish I had a puja table," Lindsay said softly. "But my parents would freak. They already think my mala beads are weird."

Aidan caught my glance as Lindsay and Nigit went on

about their meditation practices. I gave him a small shrug and tried to look nonchalant, but I was breathless. The pool of guys with the app was so small I knew it was a fluke—but I still couldn't help but freak out a little that the Boyfriend App was *working*.

"Last night while I was meditating, I couldn't get Prada's extra-mini miniskirt out of my head," Lindsay was saying as she cracked open the top to her Dr Pepper.

Nigit nodded sagely. "My family went to India last year and got Sanskrit mantras during a ceremony." His index finger touched the shiny jade trunk of Ganesh. "Those help during meditation when your mind wanders." He gripped the base of his statue, and glanced away. "I could teach you some," he finally blurted.

"Really?" Lindsay said, her voice fluttery.

Nigit nodded. He grabbed Mindy's bright red apple and took a massive bite, like that was somehow normal dining behavior.

Mindy and Aidan exchanged a glance.

"There's a religious shop downtown," Lindsay said, adjusting the hot-pink sleeve of her sweater. "No one knows about it. No one at Harrison, anyway. They have all kinds of statues and crystals. Wanna go?"

Nigit's pale pink lips opened and closed like a goldfish.

"Yeah," he said. "I do."

"Think of a limit as the value that a function approaches as the input or index approaches a value," I told Rachel Levey that afternoon.

I tutor on Fridays after school. Don't go getting the idea that I'm one of those Key Club or student government kiss-ups who live for volunteer work, because I'm not. This isn't going on my college application. But my dad was big on *using what you're blessed with to help others,* and it's not like I can offer makeup-application tips or social-etiquette lessons.

Freshman year, I set up a corner table in the cafeteria after school with a sign that said AUDREY MCCARTHY, ROGUE TUTORER in red Sharpie. Kids came.

Before my dad died, Blake would sometimes come, too, and do her homework next to me if she didn't feel like going home. Three years later, tutoring reminds me what it was like to be the old me. It was the one place where everybody still showed up to hang out.

I'd angled my table next to the water fountain in front of a Public poster that read PUBLIC WANTS *YOU* TO GO TO COLLEGE. The poster showed a blond girl with ripped jeans and bare feet sitting in front of a run-down house. A thought bubble over her head read: *No student debt?* And then Danny Beaton (who, apparently, could read thought bubbles) was superimposed onto the picture, saying, "That's right! Just build the most innovative mobile application the world has ever seen!"

When I finished teaching Rachel Levey about limits, she started telling me about her mom cheating on her dad. I'm not good at that many things, but I'm *really* good at secret-keeping. You learn a lot about other kids from tutoring, especially if they come once a week, like therapy.

I kept secrets like how Charlotte Davis had panic attacks; how Xander's teammate Barron Feldman had medical-grade IBS—which was becoming less of a secret due to his frequent bathroom emergencies; how Zack Marks hunted deer like a psycho killer but also took ballet lessons two towns over; and how Jolene Martin's mind mixed up the order of the letters in a word. (Not that she came for tutoring anymore since my falling-out with Blake.)

I told Rachel I was sorry to hear that. She shrugged. Then she switched gears and asked, "With whom are you going to Homecoming?" Rachel's grammar was better than her math. I was about to say I wasn't planning on going, when I saw him.

Xander.

His khaki-colored corduroys hung loose at his hips. He took his earbuds out, then stuffed his buyPlayer in his pocket.

What was he doing? Was he looking at me?

A janitor named Rosie pushed a yellow bucket along the cafeteria's floor. Gray water sloshed over the sides and onto the linoleum. Rachel Levey was asking me something, but I couldn't focus. "Audrey," she finally said, loud enough to pull me from cognitive paralysis. "Are you all right?"

I cleared my throat. "Low blood sugar. See you next week."

Rachel did a double take when she passed Xander, but he didn't seem to register her. Because it was official.

Xander Knight was staring at me.

I was too nervous to stare back, so I focused on his tan,

muscular forearms. When he stepped closer, I saw the hair on those was blond and spiky, too. His hazel eyes were the color of almonds covered in gold dust. They sparkled even more than in his Public Party pics, even more than I remembered in Joanna's basement.

I slipped my rabbit's foot into my bag from its spot by my canteen. I didn't need to remind Xander of the Dumpster Incident.

Our Hot Gym Coach Mr. Marley strode through my line of sight whistling the Harrison Victory March. The high-pitched melody zinged across the cafeteria as Xander Knight did the unthinkable. He spoke. To me.

"I need help with something," he said.

It was the first thing he'd said to me since that night at Joanna's when we stood together on the porch, minutes before the game of spin the bottle. *I like your sweater,* he'd said back then. And it made me happier than I'd ever been, even if the sweater was Blake's. And then he'd taken a step closer. He'd put his hand on the porch railing, close to mine. Closer. Closer. Until our fingertips were touching.

But then Jolene Martin had burst onto the porch and called us inside for the game. Xander pointed to a dark cloud swollen with rain. *A storm is coming,* he'd said. And then the storm came. And those were the last words he said to me.

Until now.

"Can I sit?" he asked, gesturing to the empty chair beside me. He didn't wait for an answer. He sat and arranged his notebooks in a mini tower. The vending machines where Nigit got his lattes buzzed like a hive of bees. A pungent whiff of Xander's cologne made me feel woozy, but it'd been so long since I'd been close enough to sniff him that I kept doing it. He was a spicy mix of sweat and man-cologne: like if you combined how Brad Pitt would smell in *Babel* and *Meet Joe Black*. I tried to get my breathing under control as he unloaded a chemistry textbook. His bicep flexed as he opened the book and I tried not to watch.

"I don't understand ionic bonds," he said, his voice gruff. He wouldn't look at me. He just stared at the textbook.

Please, God, let my voice work.

"Well," I started. One word went okay. Now I needed to string together a few at a time. "Ionic bonds are formed between two chemicals with oppositely charged ions." *Success.* "So, like, take table salt."

"Sodium and chloride," Xander said.

"Exactly. Sodium and chloride are all the way at opposite sides of the periodic table. But opposites attract." I couldn't help myself. It had to be said. "In chemistry. And sometimes in real life."

Two hundred thirty-two more days. Why not?

Xander looked up. I got lost in those almond-colored eyes. Shades of green came to life now that the sun was streaming into the cafeteria. A little like almonds covered in mold, but not in a bad way.

I dropped my glance back to the periodic table. "An ionic bond is considered a bond where the ionic character is greater than the covalent character."

"I get it," Xander said quickly.

He did?

Xander ran a hand through his buzzed blond hair. "Audrey, listen. About the other day, with Blake. I should have—" But right then his lacrosse cocaptain, Woody Ames, rounded the corner drenched in sweat. He slammed another guy with his lacrosse stick, making me glad to be a girl. "Like I said, I think I got it," Xander said suddenly. "The opposites attract thing." He stuffed his textbook into a black EMS backpack. I didn't want him to leave. I wanted to know what he was going to say.

chapter eight

"If this date goes well, you're going to need it," Lindsay said an hour later when she took @TheBoyfriendApp live on Twitter. We were in my bedroom, eating Twizzlers. "And are you ever going to take down that kitten poster?"

We'd already dissected Xander's weird half sentence, which Lindsay couldn't interpret either. Mindy and Lindsay thought Xander was hotter than hot. Still, I never told them what happened freshman year with him. I didn't know how to put it into words. Nothing had even *happened*. It just felt like it had—to me, at least.

Besides, not telling them meant we were all on the same Xander-level. Easier to obsess over him that way. Easier to distract Mindy and Lindsay from my other feelings, which was crucial to my survival.

Two hundred thirty-two more days.

Lindsay and I argued over the wording of my Twitter

bio (I wanted: *Audrey McCarthy's Public Mobile Application Contest Entry.* Lindsay wanted: *Make Love on your buyPhone*) until we finally compromised on: *Find Love with Audrey McCarthy's Debut Mobile Application: The Boyfriend App!* We entered a URL linking my entry on Public's website for download.

Lindsay wouldn't talk about what happened at lunch between her and Nigit. "Only time will tell if your app is legit," she said instead, dismissing me with a wave.

She took off to get ready at her house and I stared at Hector the Computer. Something felt off during Xander's tutoring session. It was like he didn't really need tutoring.

My fingers itched to hack and figure it out. There's a known flaw in Harrison's website code involving the login authentication, which I could exploit, thereby able to dump the database and search Xander's first-semester chemistry scores to find out what was really going on. Whether he was faking it.

I know how bad that sounds. But I didn't buy that Xander didn't get ionic bonds. When I'd said *table salt,* he'd jumped right in with *sodium and chloride.*

And I remembered him being smart freshman year, when we still used to talk. It could be a prank. Something Blake roped Xander into. I knew what it was like to be Blake's number one. Like you were special. Like she chose you.

When she asked you to do something, you did it.

If it *was* a prank, then maybe today was the first stage. It could be something elaborate, some way to embarrass me in front of everyone. And I needed to be prepared before I got my head slammed into another Dumpster.

I stared at Hector for five minutes straight before I gave up. No matter how much I wanted—no, needed—to break in, I couldn't spy on him like that. Sweat pricked my palms as I pulled up Twitter instead. At least I knew Xander had other motives, ones that probably involved his crew. At least I could be ready.

I cracked open my bedroom window. It was a home football weekend and the sounds of the Notre Dame marching band filtered through the window with bleating trumpets and the *rat-tat-tat* of a snare drum. I logged in to Twitter. Nigit was picking Lindsay up at six, and I prayed he'd gotten rid of the life-sized cardboard cutout of Sephiroth he sometimes drove around with in the backseat.

At 6:14, Lindsay tweeted.

@FashionBcomesMe: with Nigit at Spirit Trade, South Bend's Premier Religious Memorabilia Shop #FirstDate

Lindsay posted Twitpics of Oriental rugs covering the walls in swirly gold, maroon, and navy. A small Indian man stood behind a long counter. He stared into Lindsay's camera with a bewildered look on his lined face. Nigit stood next to him, pointing to a glass case of jagged quartz stones and miniature statues.

@FashionBcomesMe: Nigit taught me in Hindu sacred texts Lakshmi has the object of uplifting mankind. Luv her even more.

Nigit held a statue of a female figure with dark hair and flowing red robes. Lindsay captioned the photo: *Lakshmi: Goddess of Abundance. Bringing back the layered look of 2005. Who wears it better? Lakshmi or Kate Hudson? Vote here www.fashionbecomesme.com*

I clicked on to Lindsay's blog, where she'd uploaded side-by-side photos of Lakshmi and Kate Hudson wearing a flowing maroon skirt with a gold bandeau top. Within minutes, hundreds of Lindsay's followers cast their vote. I wasn't sure whether to be more surprised about the Hindu deity's fashion coup or the fact that nearly a thousand of Lindsay's readers were following her date with Nigit.

@FashionBcomesMe: So cute! Pic.twitter.com/ ldwOwTOz

Nigit held a stone Buddha in his arms with a whopping grin on his face. I'd never seen him smile like that. I switched over to *FBM*, where Lindsay posted a photo of her and Nigit making peace signs in front of a small waterfall (the kind you see in a dentist's office that's supposed to make you relax, but doesn't, because *you're at the dentist*). The camera's flash made Lindsay's shimmery gold V-neck glow like she'd caught fire. Nigit's forest-green button-down was too big for him in the shoulders, but he looked nice, like he was trying.

Beneath the photo, comments loaded onto the page faster than I could keep up with.

Jenny96: You two look so cute together!

StyleGuru: Zen waterfall is a spring/summer must-have accessory, right, Lindsay?

GiaGirl: Nigit's hot. Need more pics.

@FashionBcomesMe: Have no idea where we're off to now. Nigit's surprising me!

If Nigit was planning the rest of the date, things could turn. The last time he planned a night out for Mindy, Aidan, and me, we ended up at a low-rent version of Comic-Con, South Bend–style. We had to go home early because Mindy got trampled by a herd of boys dressed in *Dissidia Final Fantasy* costumes and sprained her wrist.

"Audrey?"

I nearly fell off my chair.

"Are you all right?" my mom asked. Tiny crow's-feet were scattered on the skin around her light eyes, like whiskers. My dad's XXL Notre Dame football sweatshirt bunched over her arms.

"I'm fine," I said. I hadn't told her about the Boyfriend App yet, and I didn't want to explain why I was following real-time updates of my cousin on a date. That would look even worse than not being on a date myself.

"I thought we could watch *The Bachelorette*," my mom said. She tucked a brown curl behind her ear.

So, my mom and I tape every season of *The Bachelor* and *The Bachelorette* and watch it religiously. I don't usually admit this to most people. But I can't help myself when it comes to reality matchmaking. I love watching the sparks fly between potential boyfriends and girlfriends. I love the passionate kissing. I love how they talk about being vulnerable and taking their relationship to the next level even when they've only known each other for three days.

And I love the dramatic fights because it usually means they'll make up with more passionate kissing.

"Um, I'm sort of busy," I said, cracking my knuckles even though I knew she hated it.

Sometimes the way my mom looked at me made me feel like the only thing she wanted in the world was for me to be okay, which made me feel guilty when I wasn't okay. "'Bye, Mom," I said, sounding ruder than I meant. I opened my mouth to tell her we could watch our show tomorrow, but she'd already closed the door.

@FashionBcomesMe: Spoiler alert: we're headed in the direction of the Golden Dome!

@FashionBcomesMe: On the Notre Dame campus. Exact destination TBA

@FashionBcomesMe: Side note: ND students—are you out there? Y'all need a lesson in Making Fleece Fashionable. Will blog about it this week

Lindsay posted a photo of a beautiful gray brick building I recognized as Dillon Hall: a dorm on Notre Dame's south quad, where my grandfather—my dad's dad—worked as a janitor. Cool Daddy Pop-Pop is what Lindsay and I called him until he passed away when we were twelve. I hadn't been back there since my dad died, but I knew that campus like the insides of Hector the Computer. My dad was smart, like me, but he and his family could barely scrape together the money for Holy Cross, the South Bend community college my dad went to. That didn't stop him and my grandfather from roaming Notre Dame's campus for hours on end.

I used to think it was stupid, how he cared so much about something he couldn't afford to be a part of. Something out of his grasp. Now I was starting to understand.

Nigit's brother Suraj was a sophomore at Notre Dame. Maybe Nigit was taking Lindsay to a dorm party?

@FashionBcomesMe: Coolest. Date. Ever. With Nigit's brother Suraj and his girlfriend Kavya. Suraj cooked!

Lindsay posted a picture of a makeshift table in Suraj's dorm room covered with food.

On and on it went. And the more Lindsay blogged and tweeted, the more her followers linked her blog, retweeted, and hashtagged *LindsayAndNigit*.

A little before ten, she tweeted from one of the lakes on campus: **Will he kiss me?**

Her readers were hooked. *I* was hooked.

@FashionBcomesMe: he kissed me! the most amazing #firstdate ever, and it's all thanks to @TheBoyfriendApp!

My Twitter account caught fire as hundreds of users followed me. My fingers zinged over the keys doing follow-backs like Lindsay instructed. Breathless, I checked my profile on Public's site.

Contestant Number 13079: Audrey McCarthy. Harrison High School. South Bend, Indiana. THE BOYFRIEND APP. Available for Download. Users: 111. Click Here for More Information.

Every time I refreshed the page, more people had downloaded the app!

Users: 144

Users: 209

Users: 298

Next to a scrolling bar on their home page, Public listed the contest entries with the most users. There was an app called Doggie Did that found your dog's poop in the dark using a heat sensor, which led the way with 2,783 users. App number two on the list was called Dress Hot (you submitted a photo of your outfit and the app taught you how to Make It Hotter) with 2,105 users, and so on.

My user numbers were climbing, but not as nearly fast as the apps on the home page. It was a self-fulfilling prophecy: Obviously the top ten apps displayed front and center on the site were the ones Public buyPhone owners would think were the best, resulting in way more exposure and potential users. It was like high school: Somebody decides you're popular, or not, and his or her opinion gains momentum, suddenly becoming the truth about you. If I could just break into the Top Ten list, I'd have all the free publicity in the world and a chance at winning the prize for the Most Popular App.

Users: 307

Users: 339

If only I'd submitted it sooner! My fingers flew over the keys, following high-school and college students on Twitter who seemed like maybe they'd be my *target market*, as Lindsay called it. But there was virtually no way to compete with the most popular apps.

I texted Lindsay: **We need to get the BFA into the top ten.**

I'm roping bloggers in now, she texted back. *Lots of them wanna do a post on u.*

I watched as the numbers skyrocketed for the Top Ten apps. *Thnx, L. But we need a miracle . . .*

chapter nine

"Strike!"
          Ten bowling pins ricocheted with a riotous clatter.
My shoes squeaked on the shiny wood floor as I victory-
danced my way across the lane.

It was 2-FOR-1 SUNDAYS at South Bend Bowl &
Arcade, and a strobe light glittered from the ceiling when
someone bowled a strike. Aidan and Mindy were covered
in sparkling checks of brightness as they clapped.

"You're a weirdly good bowler, Auds," Aidan said,
grinning. His long body leaned back against the booth.
His ivory sweater made his curls appear even darker.

"Thanks," I said, mentally filing the details of the
parent/child bowling league my mom and I played during
sophomore year in a folder marked *THINGS YOU
DON'T EVEN TELL YOUR THERAPIST.*

Today was Mindy's idea. I'd been holed up in my room

for the seventeen hours since Lindsay and Nigit's date doing Twitter stuff for the app like Lindsay taught me (minus the one hour I babysat our neighbor's toddler) when Mindy texted: lets see the luvbirds in action . . . South Bend B & A at 4?

Raspberry-colored barrettes clipped Mindy's caramel waves away from her face. She caught my eye as she tapped a pearly green bowling ball the size of her head. "Too heavy," I said, nodding when she picked up a smaller brown one.

"Are you *sure* you're not secretly pro?" Aidan asked. The bowling alley was dimly lit and his blue eyes were dark like lake water. The corners crinkled as he teased me. "Between bowling and the Boyfriend App, you seem to have plenty of options for college scholarships."

Mindy laughed and I felt myself blush. It was good to hear him say that, whether or not it was really true. It was better-than-good to be here with him.

In the arcade behind us, twangy electronic noises sounded and an elderly couple with matching gray bowl cuts blew up an ATM machine in a video game called *Bank Robbery*. In the lane next to us, four Notre Dame kids—three girls and one boy—sat clustered together, laughing. Textbooks stuck out from their bags, like maybe they were taking a study break. I watched the way they moved, how sometimes they touched one another's arms when somebody said something. I liked how they seemed so sure of themselves. I imagined how, after today was over, they'd return to their beautiful campus and tiny bedrooms in Gothic dormitories. Or maybe meet with a professor. Or study with their roommates at the brown brick library covered with a shining mosaic. How could we live in the same town and occupy entirely different universes?

"You're number fifty-nine on the Most Popular App list," Aidan said. I stopped staring at the ND kids and turned to Aidan. A white glow illuminated his jaw as he studied his buyPhone. "No one else from Harrison has even broken the ten-thousand mark," he said.

I took a breath, letting myself get my hopes up again. Maybe there was a chance. "You never know," I said. It was all I could manage.

"You need to download it, Auds," Aidan said, still holding my glance. "The creator of the app has to be one of its users. That's like the number one rule of tech." He looped his thumb into a hole in his Levis. "And you never know who it might match you with."

He smiled. My toes curled. Was there any way he meant that it could match us? Had he thought about that?

Mindy was absorbed in her turn bowling and she wasn't paying attention. So I just said it. "Hopefully someone tall, dark, and handsome."

Like you.

"Or just tall and dark," Aidan said. The low rumble of his laugh made my body turn on like a light switch. It was definitely the first time we'd ever officially flirted. Or was it? Was I overreacting? Maybe he wasn't referring to himself. Maybe he was just messing with me. I felt totally nervous trying to figure it out. And then Mindy threw a gutter ball and Aidan went to clap, but his chunky black techno-watch caught the bottom of his sweater. It pulled at the hem and exposed the way his stomach muscles formed a *V* above his jeans. It put me over the edge. I had no idea where I was until his clothes lowered and I could breathe again.

"You, on the other hand, need to stick with creative writing," Aidan said to Mindy, making her laugh. I faked a laugh, too, and tried to act normal. But now I had visual confirmation of the beautifulness of his stomach muscles. Jesus. There was no going back.

Bowling shoes squeaked behind us.

"What's up, earthlings?"

My mouth dropped, and the synapses in my brain were too confused to close it. Nothing—not even Lindsay's rabid texting and blogging about their trip to U.P. Mall yesterday—could've prepared me for Nigit's outfit. Tight-fitting black jeans hugged his scrawny legs and cut off at the ankles. His hair was slicked to the side. A white leather belt with a shiny silver buckle cinched his waist. A skinny tie draped over a slim-fitting white shirt beneath a black sateen dinner jacket. He looked like the cool guy in an electronica band who stands off to the side and plays a cymbal. Or a Bollywood movie star walking the red carpet. He looked amazing.

I glanced at Lindsay. It was the first time since kindergarten that I didn't notice her outfit first, but not even her peacock-feather hairpiece and gold-framed cat-eye glasses could distract me. She was gazing, googly-eyed, at Nigit.

The smooth skin on Aidan's forehead creased. Mindy stared.

Somebody had to say *something*.

"Nigit?" I finally sputtered, trying to keep the gasp out of my voice.

"'S'up, Audrey?"

"Um, nothing. Want to bowl on my team?"

Nigit peeled his eyes from Lindsay. "Totes."

What kind of alternate love universe had the Boyfriend App uncovered?

"Cool," Aidan said, recovering. "I'll take Lindsay and Mindy. We'll need best out of three to beat Audrey anyway."

A cocktail waitress strode by with a tray full of margaritas, ignoring us. The scent of lime and tequila mixed with the bowling alley's sweaty-sock smell as Lindsay and Nigit picked bowling balls. It turned out both of their favorite colors were orange. "You should see the way mandarin lipstick brings out my eyes," Lindsay told Nigit. They then proceeded to go straight to first base right there by the ball return.

I fake-cleared my throat. "Aren't you a lefty, Nigit?" I asked, gesturing to the white leather glove on his right hand, the one currently in my cousin's back pocket.

Nigit depocketed. "This isn't a bowling glove," he said, fanning his fingers. "It's part of my weekend look."

Lindsay set her ball down with a *thud*. "Nigit took my Men's Fashion Quiz on *FBM*," she said, smoothing a platinum lock into her hairpiece. A pear-shaped

94

faux-diamond stud took up nearly all of her earlobe. "One of his style icons is Michael Jackson."

"Rest in peace, Michael," Nigit said, pointing his gloved index finger toward the ceiling. His body contorted into a surprisingly impressive three-step moonwalk. "And you should always wear a signature piece." He nuzzled Lindsay's cheek before turning to me. "You rock for building the Boyfriend App, Audrey." He clasped his hands together in a prayer position and bowed his head. "It's a life-changer."

I was so distracted by Nigit's personality transplant that I didn't see the nightmare that had descended on our bowling lane.

"Looks like there's garbage in the alley today."

My body registered Joanna Martin's voice before my mind, and a sick feeling slivered through me. I turned to see Blake, Jolene, and Joanna wearing matching black leggings and witchy expressions.

"Perfect," Aidan said under his breath.

The Martin sisters' highlighted blond streaks were pulled back to expose Angelina Jolie–esque cheekbones and icy-blue eyes. They framed Blake like evil bookends. Xander stood off to the side. He did a double take when he saw me, but then he looked away and fiddled with his buyPlayer. He took out his earbuds and stuffed them into a pocket of his corduroys. "Come on, Blake," he said, gesturing to an open lane farther down the alley.

But Blake didn't move. She pointed at Nigit. "What's up with Nidgiot?"

Nigit blinked.

"Leave him alone," I said, my nerve endings on fire.

Jolene let out a barking laugh. Xander averted his glance, but the three girls stared at me until my legs felt wobbly.

A high-pitched singing voice rang crystal clear through the bowling alley.

"Thrillerrrrr."

It took me a minute to realize the sound was coming from Nigit.

"Thriller night!"

Nigit's gloved hand flew high toward the ceiling. His other hand grabbed his shiny silver belt buckle, and his limbs started moving at different speeds, exactly like Michael Jackson does in the video.

"And no one's gonna save you from the beast about to strike!"

Nigit's voice was a little off key, but his dance moves were killer, like his body was part rubber and part Paula Abdul. Pins clattered in the next lane over and the strobe light came to life again. It bathed Nigit in pulsing white light and made him look even more awesome.

Nigit dance-jumped toward Blake and her cronies like he was doing a special performance just for them. He ran a hand through his slicked-back hair and then slammed it back to his side.

"So let me hold you tight and share a killer, thriller."

He kicked his legs, twirled in a circle, and ended the move by grabbing his crotch, thrusting it forward, and scream-singing, *"Ow!"*

A little girl in a neighboring lane started clapping.

Aidan, Mindy, and I stood gaping. Lindsay joined the little girl with maniacal clapping. Aidan whistled and Mindy let out a squeal. "Go, Nigit!" I yelled.

Nigit turned to face us and bowed with a hand flourish like a court jester in the seventeenth century.

Blake looked even more nauseous than the time we had bad yellowtail at South Bend Sushi-Saurus. Joanna shook her head. Jolene stood there with both layers of teeth exposed and a glazed expression on her face. Xander glanced between them and us.

"You're lame," Joanna said.

"And you're mean girls," Nigit shot back. "Way past the time when the movie was cool."

"I'd rather be mean than lame," Jolene said. But the insult fell flat and Jolene averted her eyes like she knew it.

Aidan linked his arm through mine. "You *would*," he said in his low voice, laughing. And then Mindy laughed, too. A giddy feeling came over me. I watched in disbelief as Nigit spiked forward onto his toes again and did another crotch grab. Lindsay giggled and clapped her hands again, like it was awesome to be a part of us.

Blake stared at me in a way she hadn't for a very long time. She stared as if it was just us, the way it was every afternoon after school, and again on the weekend mornings when we left the Martin sisters' sleepovers and went to hang by ourselves in my apartment. And then her lips curved, and she smiled at me like she always used to, like nothing could come between us. And then she laughed, and said, "Your father was lame. And now he's just dead. One less

McCarthy to fit in your tiny apartment." She shifted her weight. "Your family's a joke."

I felt nothing for one full breath. There was only blood swirling in my ears and the steady thud of bowling balls against the wood.

But then something inside of me splintered.

No one spoke. Another bored-looking cocktail waitress passed with an empty tray and a cigarette behind her ear. A mom cheered in the neighboring lane when her little boy bowled a strike and set off the strobe lights.

My bottom lip shook. I clamped my top teeth over it hard, tasting blood.

Aidan pulled me to him. He held me like he'd done it before a thousand times, like he already knew the curves of my body. I felt his breath against my ear. His voice was like steel. "I'm getting you out of here."

I tried to focus on the contours of his face, the strong cut of his jaw, the flushed skin over his cheeks. His cherry-red lips were slightly parted, and up close I could see the ghost of a scar just above them. I let my hand fall over his and felt how solid he was.

But then bowling pins shattered, snapping me back to reality.

Joanna and Jolene were laughing. Their shoulders shook and the strobe light made their movements jerky and robotic. Xander was looking at the floor, his shoes, the back of his hands—anywhere but me. Blake still looked like she was about to be sick, and suddenly I felt sure I was going to be sick, and I didn't want to embarrass myself in front of Aidan. So I pushed him off and started to sprint. Fake explosion noises blasted from a *Buck Hunter* video game. I dodged the cocktail waitress and nearly knocked over the elderly couple with bowl cuts. I heard Aidan and Lindsay call after me as I passed the skinny guy collecting tickets, the bartender pouring blue liquid into a martini glass, and the dad holding his little girl's hand. I ran harder, as though I could push through everything that hurt.

I shoved the glass doors. The bright sunlight blinded me, and my body folded like a paper doll. I crawled over to a yellow parking-lot bumper and dropped my head into my hands. My cheeks were wet and I had the strange feeling I was bleeding, but when I looked down, there were only tears on my fingers.

I closed my eyes and didn't open them until I smelled Mindy's vanilla perfume. She dropped to her knees right there on the gravel. "Audrey," she whispered, low enough that no one else could hear that it sounded like "Oh-drey."

"Are you okay?" Lindsay asked, squatting next to Mindy. Nigit stood close to Lindsay, fidgeting like he was nervous.

Aidan knelt beside me. His face had darkened and he looked furious. And then his hands were on me again, lifting me to my feet. I didn't want him to let me go.

They were all saying stuff as we walked to Lindsay's car, but it was hard to focus. I wanted to tell my friends I was okay, but I couldn't. I couldn't say anything at all.

Aidan, Mindy, and Nigit watched from the parking lot

as Lindsay nearly crashed into the letter-board sign advertising 2-FOR-1 FUN!

I swore I saw Blake glancing through the bowling alley's door. But the sun was glinting against the glass, and I probably just imagined her.

chapter ten

Lindsay tried to talk to me about what'd happened as
we sped along Route 31, but there was nothing to say.
Navy flags with slogans like HERE COME THE IRISH! waved
on manicured lawns, left over from yesterday's game. The
car smelled like the glue Lindsay used to cover her hair
clip in feathers.

I counted the seconds until I could be alone with Hector.

We pulled up to the courtyard in front of our building.
Claire played with her toy Breyer horses in the grass with
my mom.

I checked my reflection in the rearview mirror. (I didn't
want my mom to know I'd been crying. I didn't need the
questions.) My skin looked paler than ever, and my hair
was messy, but my green eyes were bright. I didn't wear
makeup—no matter how many times Lindsay advocated
for mascara—so nothing was smeared.

Clank. Clank. Clank. Roger, the super, tossed cans and plastic bottles one by one into a green-painted trash can.

"New *man*dals?" Lindsay asked, gesturing to Roger's leather footwear, which looked like something one of the disciples would wear. "Where are the Tevas?"

Roger's cutoff jean shorts were shorter than usual, and even from the car I could tell he'd shaved his legs. His Chihuahua, Nicorette, nosed a crumpled can of Diet Coke near his feet. Lindsay rolled down her window. "Roger!" she shouted, her eyes narrowing on his shiny legs. "How do you keep your skin so moisturized in cold weather?"

I put a hand to my forehead.

Roger moved to the car with Nicorette darting circles around him. He considered Lindsay, and then glanced around like someone might be listening. "Two parts Lubriderm to one part Vaseline," he finally said, taking a sip of grass-green liquid from a plastic cup. Nicorette barked. "Apply after the shower."

Lindsay put the car into park. She looked at Roger as if he'd solved a complex algorithm. "I am *so* blogging about that," she said as I got out.

Claire kissed my mom's cheek and raced toward us, her dirty-blond hair streaming behind her. "What's Ubiderm?" she asked, climbing into the front seat.

Lindsay's hand covered Claire's, making me wish I had a sister. "You going to be okay, Audrey?" she asked.

I pushed up the emerald sleeves of my hoodie and nodded. I hated the way she was looking at me. And the last thing I wanted was to make conversation with my mom, who was already staring from the courtyard with her hands on her hips like she knew something was wrong.

Lindsay opened her mouth like she was going to say more, but then an engine growled in the parking lot and a rusted Toyota Camry pulled into the spot next to hers. A HARRISON HIGH REJECT sticker was pasted beneath one that read MUSCLES ARE FOR HIGH SCHOOL. BRAINS ARE FOR LIFE.

The car coughed and sputtered. Aidan opened the door and stepped onto the gravel.

My pulse quickened. A flush crept over Aidan's pale skin as he stared at me, and I felt unsteady on my feet again. What was he doing here?

Lindsay was talking, but I couldn't pay attention. Claire told Aidan he looked like her imaginary stable hand, George, and then Lindsay and Claire were off.

"George shovels horse manure," I told Aidan, not quite meeting his gaze. My fingers went to my rabbit's foot in the front pocket of Lindsay's hand-me-down skinny jeans. I felt on the verge of a freak-out. I was still embarrassed about what happened at the bowling alley. And Aidan had never been to my apartment before. And then there was my mother, staring at us from twenty-five yards away.

"He's probably very attractive, though, right?" Aidan asked. His broad shoulders scrunched and he looked unsure about his joke.

I smiled despite my nerves. "He's an extremely hot stable hand," I said, relaxing the tiniest bit.

At least we were far away from South Bend Bowl & Arcade.

"You kids want to come upstairs?" my mom called to us, as if we were twelve. She lifted her skinny arm and gestured to our window like she was Vanna White and our apartment was a vowel.

I didn't want Aidan seeing my kitten poster. And I didn't want my mom eavesdropping on us. So I gestured to the dirt path that led behind our apartment. "I was thinking Aidan and I could walk," I told my mom as we crossed the gravel into the courtyard. I made my voice sound upbeat, like I was craving fresh air.

Aidan's hunter-green Converse were untied and he stumbled. His cheeks flushed even brighter as he caught himself. "Hi, Mrs. McCarthy," he said. He knew my mom from the lunch line.

My mother smiled like Aidan was a Publishers Clearing House representative holding an oversized check. I had a feeling she was going to say something embarrassing, and she didn't let me down.

"The tater-tot boy," she said. "Extra tots."

"That's me," Aidan said.

"Mom. Really?"

"Call me Marian," she told Aidan, winking.

I pulled my hair into a short, spiky ponytail. Dark pieces started falling out before I even finished tying the rubber band. "I'll be back before dinner, Marian," I told her, like I made the rules and she didn't have a standing decree about always eating together. I kept my head down as we rounded the path behind the apartment complex. I wasn't used to being with Aidan by myself outside of school. I wasn't really sure what to say.

Aidan's hands were shoved deep into his pockets. His long, lanky gait was more relaxed when it was just us, like he was perfectly okay with his place in the world. Like he was way less nervous than I was.

The tangerine-colored sun framed the leaves like a golden halo. Aidan pushed aside spindly branches and held them for me to pass. The trees thickened, leaving just enough sunlight for us to avoid rocks and divots. The birch trees were my favorite. As we walked, I traced my fingers over the silvery-gray scrapes that covered their white trunks. "We're almost there," I said softly.

Aidan didn't ask where *there* was. I liked that he trusted me. And I liked how it felt to be with him by myself and without my friends. The way it would be if he were my boyfriend.

But he's not your boyfriend. Not by a long shot.

Little brown birds filled the silence with tiny squeaks. The path widened and Aidan slowed until we were side by side. I was hyperaware of his movements and how each one either separated us or made us closer.

I prayed for the ones that made us closer. I inched my hand farther from my side until it brushed his. My skin felt electric. I wanted to take his hand, to lace my fingers through his.

If he liked me, I would know.

Cold air snapped through me as we emerged from the mouth of the trail onto a small clearing. Large rocks surrounded a pool of dark-blue water that spilled over a fallen log into another smaller pool. The birch trees surrounded it in a perfect circle, like gatekeepers. On the far side of the pool, my dad and I had arranged the smaller rocks into a cave, where we used to store things like sticks and loose change. Things my dad called treasure. I couldn't bring myself to disassemble the cave. Even after he was gone and I stopped hiding things there.

The air smelled clean and wet. The tightness in my chest loosened as I took in the water, and the birch trees. It was my secret spot. Only Blake and Lindsay knew about it from when we were little. And my dad, of course. And now, Aidan.

Aidan's eyes passed over the water. He nodded like he appreciated we were somewhere beautiful.

"Do you want to sit?" I asked, gesturing to the smooth, flat rock that jutted over the water's edge.

Aidan nodded. I realized how much taller he was than my dad—he had to crouch so his head wouldn't hit the low branches.

I hurried to sit first. I didn't want to be the one to decide how much space should be between us.

Aidan took his time. He picked up a twig and rolled it between his hands, like he did in the lab with his mechanical pencils. I imagined those hands on me. My body felt like a sparkler just thinking about it.

I held my breath as he sat cross-legged, facing me. His knee touched my calf and my nerves pulsed.

"You're still wearing your bowling shoes," he said.

"Crap."

He laughed but it didn't last. His dark lashes lowered as he studied the twig. When he lifted them, his gaze was far away, like he was remembering something.

"My dad left us," he finally said. He traced the twig over the hole in his jeans. His breathing was jagged and it made his words come out in tiny portions. "I don't know what we did . . . my mom and my sister and me . . . to make him leave." He snapped the twig and let the pieces fall. "But he left."

A pit formed in my stomach. It was how he said the words. Not just sad, but unbelieving, like he couldn't understand how something so terrible had happened to him and his mom and sister. I knew exactly how that felt.

Aidan's hand rested on the rock. Without thinking, I reached forward and touched my fingertips to his. Warmth rushed through me. He didn't move his hand away. He looked up. Leaned a tiny bit closer. Then he said, "I'm glad what you had with your dad was good."

When somebody gets taken away from you, people try to say all kinds of things to make you feel better. Like how time heals (it doesn't) or how sorry they are (who cares?) or how God has a plan (if He does, why is it crappy so far?). This was the first time someone said something that helped a little bit. I was grateful for it.

Wind gusted and rippled the water's glassy surface. Aidan set his twig in the water and we watched it drift away. His Army-green jacket was a few shades darker than his Converse, and my eyes settled on a tiny tear near the elbow. I took in how big he was, sitting there in a place where I was usually alone. The jacket's corduroy collar was unbuttoned, and I saw twine resting against the smooth, pale skin of his neck. It was the kind of thing you would hang a key from, or something you didn't want to forget.

I hugged my knees to my chest. "He wasn't even supposed to be at work that night," I finally said. My heart clenched like a fist. I didn't want to feel the pain that came with talking about my dad. But I wanted to tell him.

Aidan sat very still, watching me.

"My dad did mechanical work for Blake's dad's company—making new engine parts usually, or fixing stuff. One night, Robert Dawkins called my dad in to work on some special project. Something he said only my dad would know how to do. My dad was working late when he had an accident with the machinery."

My joints felt like seams unraveling when I said the words. It was the worst part. Imagining my dad getting hurt. My mind couldn't always do it. Because when I did, I fell into something so painful I didn't think I would make it out. "I sometimes think about whether or not he had time to be scared," I said.

Aidan took my hand and held it while I cried. Silence settled. The wind curled through the trees and rippled over the water. In the quiet I felt the day ending and darkness falling.

"It was just a mistake," I finally said, to myself as much as to Aidan. "He'd worked with those machines for so many years. And it was so unlike him to make a mistake with something mechanical." Then came the part I couldn't reconcile, the part that kept me up at night. "If one thing had gone differently—if I'd begged him to stay home, instead of taking on Robert's stupid important project—then he'd still be here." I couldn't help but think about all the reasons he should still be alive, and how there had to be some way to fix the mistake. "You know how the South Bend newspapers love R. Dawkins Tech," I said. "Whether or not Robert Dawkins knew they were going to print what he said, they did. *It's a tragic accident. But my company has a zero-tolerance policy for negligence in the workplace. Francis McCarthy was careless.*"

I'd memorized those words. My dad had worked for Blake's dad for fifteen years, and that's what he got. His name dragged through the mud.

Aidan's grip on my hand tightened.

"Blake assured me her dad didn't mean it. That he was out at a bar and said something stupid that got overheard by a reporter. But the damage was already done. My mom was so hurt."

Aidan didn't look unsure anymore, like he had when we'd stood outside my apartment. He looked like he understood me. "And you were hurt, too," he said.

I nodded. The sky had darkened so quickly. When I looked up from the water, I could barely distinguish the leaves from the shadowy heaven above them. A low rumble of thunder sounded. I kept going anyway.

"The weird thing is, after the accident and everything Blake's father did, Blake held on to me tighter than ever. She stood closer to me in school, like she was protecting me, or trying to protect *us*." A blood-red leaf fell onto the water. "But too much had changed."

We were quiet for a few moments, and I wondered what Aidan was thinking about. The water was black now. "We should go," I finally said. My voice didn't sound like my own. The high-pitched nervousness was gone, and I just sounded exhausted.

Aidan stood first. He pulled me to my feet for the second time that day. Then he leaned forward until there was only a breath between us. There was an intensity in his dark blue eyes that I hadn't seen before. His hands went to the small of my back. My heart raced. I couldn't figure out if he was trying to—

I panicked. "We should go," I said again. I turned and Aidan's lips brushed my cheek. I felt his mouth, soft and warm against my skin. My body went wild, and then my thoughts did, too. It took everything I had not to freak out as we walked back along the trail, and the conversation that had just been so natural between us suddenly felt strained. I tried to joke around with him, but Aidan all at once seemed unsure again. What had happened back there?

Was my cheek where he'd meant to kiss? Was it just a friend thing?

Or had he been about to *really* kiss me?

chapter eleven

*B*rrrrinnnnngggg!
    I fumbled for my ringing phone. "Lindsay?"

"Wake up! I can tell you're slouching just by your tone of voice."

"It's three in the morning," I said, pressing my wrist against my eyes. I'd fallen asleep at my computer.

Lindsay puffed an exhale. "Stop stating the obvious and get onto Public's site."

My fingers shook as the page loaded—my mind already going to places it wanted to be. The PUBLIC logo flashed bright orange against a metallic silver background. My eyes found the Most Popular App list on the right of the screen.

It was there. *It was there!* The Boyfriend App was number seven on the Top Ten list!

I screamed. Lindsay went nuts on the other end of the

line. "It's happening!" she said. "You're going to win this thing; I know it."

I could barely breathe. "But *how?*"

"Two words: *Danny. Beaton.*" Lindsay squealed. "He's always been one of my personal heroes. And now he's the Boyfriend App's!"

Danny Beaton. Public spokesperson. Teen heartthrob. Rock star. I remembered the exact moment he followed Lindsay on Twitter. She hadn't shut up about it for weeks. I clicked on Danny Beaton's Twitter page and what I saw sent my heart ricocheting in my chest:

@DannyBeaton retweeted Lindsay's tweet about the Boyfriend App to his 18,239,087 followers.

Lindsay's Twitter following had jumped by thousands and so had mine.

My fingertips blazed as I clicked on @mentions. Danny Beaton had started a fire: Thousands of Twitter users retweeted Danny's tweet about the BFA or started their own conversation, hashtagging TheBoyfriendApp and commenting about it with all kinds of stuff ranging from normal—@CutieCT: look out, potential BFs. here I come—to a little odd, like @AlaskaGirlBrrr, who tweeted: hey @TheBoyfriendApp! Just downloaded you. Am I gonna find me my made for 4ever Eskimo. Kiss kiss! And then there was the downright creepy: @BruceBlogs: Genius girl Audrey McCarthy @TheBoyfriendApp what do I have to do to make you my Girlfriend App? Invite me to South Bend! Go Irish!

Lindsay had never entered my location, which meant

people like @BruceBlogs were Googling me to find out where I lived. I didn't think I'd ever done anything Googleable before.

I scrolled through TheBoyfriendApp hashtags. A bunch of guys who downloaded the app bemoaned how they had to sit around and wait for a girl to approach them with her match results. This ignited a Twitter conversation about whether or not I was a feminist.

"This is balls-out!" Lindsay was saying when a knock sounded.

My door flung open. "Sweetie?" My mother's dark frame was silhouetted against the hallway's bright light. "Are you okay? Did you have a dream?"

I said good-bye to Lindsay, promising I'd do even more Twitter PR stuff, and turned to my mom. It *did* feel like a dream. "I'm okay," I said. "I'm maybe more than okay." I patted the space next to me. The ergonomic chair was big enough for us to squeeze next to each other. It was how my dad and I used to sit.

"I want to show you something," I said.

My mom sat next to me as I logged on to my Public entry. I took a breath, and clicked.

chapter twelve

"*We both know you got what it takes, girl! Oh-oh-oh!*"
It was Monday morning and I hadn't slept since Lindsay's three a.m. phone call. Neither had Lindsay. She was wired on Starbucks and singing along with Danny Beaton on the radio while banging her hand on the steering wheel.

"Do you want me to recite my Top Ten Things I Love About Nigit Gurung list backward?" she asked, curving into Harrison's parking lot. Her eyeliner curled into what she called a Sophia Loren cat eye. I was about to protest when I spotted a crowd of students waiting on the lawn in front of school. A half dozen sat on the granite ledge of the *Eros Sleeping* statue. The rest stood in a cluster staring at their buyPhones. Blake, Joanna, and Jolene were trying to push through the students, who were too absorbed in their screens to jump out of Blake's path as usual.

"What the—?" I said under my breath. My heart sped up as Lindsay and I climbed from the Acura and started across the lot. My mind played movies of kids waiting by the flagpole to watch a fight—if Blake had spread the news about a confrontation, maybe a bunch of kids were waiting to watch?

"Audrey!"

I didn't recognize the redhead calling my name from the outskirts of the crowd.

"That's her," a Goth girl with a rose tattoo on her neck said to her friend. Goth Girl wore a black lace veil that trailed to the floor, like a wedding-funeral mix.

"Go, Audrey!" cried Francis Noonan, my freshman-year softball pick with scoliosis.

If I was about to weather another Blake fight, at least a few kids seemed to be on my side.

Carrie Sommers stepped from the crowd in her cheerleading uniform and hollered, "You might be good at basketball, you might be good at track, but when it comes to building apps, you might as well step back!" She raised her maroon-and-yellow pom-poms and shook them crazily.

With the exception of Blake, Joanna, and Jolene, everyone broke into applause. I heard my name echoed and the clatter of gossip. *Holy. Crap.* My nerves spiked as we crossed the pavement. I couldn't help it—I started to slow my steps, afraid of the crowd.

"Keep going, Audrey," Lindsay said through the bright white smile she'd plastered on her face. She linked her arm

through mine. *"And stand up straight."*

The crowd swarmed us and swallowed me. I scanned for Aidan, but I didn't see him. An Asian girl with blunt-cut bangs patted me on the shoulder. A guy named Marcus I knew from AP Chem said, "Genius app, Audrey."

A tall, gangly basketball player raised her hand to high-five me. I stood on my tiptoes to connect our palms. "Congrats on the top ten," she said. Her teammate stood next to her with a forehead full of butterfly Band-Aids covering Frankensteinesque stitches. "You gonna win us all Beasts?" Stitches asked, staring at me like I was going to be in trouble if I didn't.

A girl with red-rimmed glasses I knew from a tutoring session on particle physics tapped my arm. "So how long will it take us to get matched?" she asked, adjusting her plastic headband.

I glanced over the dozens of eyeballs fixed on me. Had all of them downloaded the Boyfriend App? "Um, well," I started. "It can be different for everyone. The app will match you to the best guy for you based on the current applicants within a five-mile radius. But you have to be within one hundred yards of your match for the alert to go off on your phone. So that you can, like, go to him and tell him."

Public speaking wasn't exactly my forte. And Blake was only a few feet away with glassy black locks hanging over her shoulders like Cher, freaking me out. Joanna stood to Blake's left, her lips pulled back to expose dull, white, rectangular teeth that curved at the bottoms, like an upside-down row of tombstones. I swore Jolene's mole was twitching.

"So do you know Danny Beaton personally or something?" asked Carrie Sommers, her pom-poms fluttering in the wind.

Lindsay jumped in before I could say anything. "I'm working on PR for the Boyfriend App," she said, raising her hand as if to silence everybody. "So if anyone has any further questions, you all know where to find me. Public Party. Twitter. *Fashion Becomes Me.* If you haven't already, please sign up for my RSS feed for updates." Lindsay pulled me from the crowd and onto the sidewalk leading to school. "We have to keep them wanting more," she hissed.

I glanced over my shoulder to see everyone watching us walk away. None of them had looked at me like that in years.

DING DING DONG DING.

My shoulders tensed as the Boyfriend App's alert rang out. A squeal sounded over the crowd's murmurs. "I've been matched!" It was Goth Girl. The metal spikes on her dog collar caught the sunlight. She held her phone high in the air and girls clamored around her to see the flashing graphic. She was nearly knocked to the pavement when the stitched-up basketball player grabbed her phone. "Ty Bennet?" Stitches said, studying the screen. Goth Girl yanked her phone back. She glanced over the heads of the crowd. "Who's *Ty Bennet?*"

A sophomore wearing a tan bomber jacket with US Navy wings pinned to the shoulder strode across the parking

117

lot. His blond crew cut and aviator sunglasses made him look like he'd just stepped away from fighter-pilot training camp. "I'm Ty Bennet," he said in a silky-smooth, talk-show-host voice. He lowered his sunglasses and took in the crowd. Goth Girl glanced between Ty and her phone, where my programming meant an arrow was pointing in Ty's direction, and his approximate distance was flashing across the screen. *Five yards. Four yards. Three yards.*

I couldn't help but notice Blake, staring wide-eyed between Ty and Goth Girl, just as enraptured as the rest of Harrison.

Wrinkles creased the caked-on white powder on Goth Girl's forehead. "We've been matched," she said, holding up her phone.

I had to give it to this girl. She didn't seem to care about the potential of public rejection. Maybe she got all that fear out of her system when she started wearing black lipstick in eighth grade. It had to be freeing, not giving a crap what anyone thought.

"Seriously?" Ty asked, a blond eyebrow cocking dubiously. He studied Goth Girl's phone and for a second I was sure he was going to laugh. But then he took in the crowd's stare and puffed his chest. "Awesome," he said.

Lindsay saw her opening. "And the Boyfriend App finds love again," she announced. She shook her head wistfully like nothing warmed her more than two kids in love. "Audrey and I will be participating in a Q-and-A session on Twitter this afternoon at three."

I was about to mention I already had a session at three—

with Mrs. Condor. But I figured reminding everyone about my mandatory school social worker visits wasn't on Lindsay's PR agenda. I'd have to beg Mrs. Condor to reschedule.

"Remember," Lindsay went on, "the more you convince your friends to download, the bigger our pool of potential love matches."

"So go get 'em, Harrison!" Carrie Sommers cheered. The bell rang, and like some sort of Pavlov's dog situation, Carrie Sommers did a split jump. "Go! Fight! Win!"

I'd never been so fired up by team spirit. Was this really happening? Was I going to win this thing?

Cafeteria today? Mindy texted a few hours later.

I was ready and Mindy knew it.

The lunchroom smelled like new tires mixed with spaghetti. And it was louder than usual—maybe because I was trying to pay attention to conversations instead of ignore them. Echoes of *did you download Audrey's app?* mixed with *have you been matched?* and *can you believe she was matched with* him*?* Everyone was staring in my direction like I'd just gotten a boob job.

"Hey, sport," said Nina Carlyle as I passed. Her friend Anna said, "She's an Olympic hopeful. She calls *everyone* sport," and laughed, like the three of us were in on some great joke. A table of six girls wearing homemade T-shirts with Danny Beaton's face on them that read INDIANAPOLIS OR BUST! looked up from their phones with a fawning chorus of, "Hi, Audrey!" "Hey!" "What's up, Audrey?"

Even when I got tongue-tied, Lindsay made me promise I'd at least smile and wave. "Together. At the same time. Do we need to practice?" she'd asked.

Marcus from AP Chem sat with a handsome sophomore named Tim who played the saxophone. Tim winked at me. "Killer app," he said, linking his arm through Marcus's. I smiled. (And waved.)

Aidan sat alone at our lunch table. I flashed back to yesterday in the secret spot behind my apartment, like I'd done so many times since he'd gotten in his car and pulled away. I felt feverish just thinking about being alone with him, the way he'd leaned in close, his lips against my cheek. A faint smell of woodsy cologne lingered in my memory of what had happened. Things had been sort of weird in lab that morning, but I couldn't tell if it was because he'd meant to really kiss me before I messed it up, or if it was because Nigit was sitting between us and being snotty about my app. And once all three of us had gotten into our normal trog-programming routine, Aidan had warmed back up. So I still wasn't sure what to make of everything. And I couldn't ask Lindsay's or Mindy's opinion, because what if it was nothing and I blew my cover?

But what if it was *something*? What if it wasn't all in my imagination?

Aidan broke into a grin when he saw me walking toward our table. He held up his buyPhone with Public's home page flashing. "You're number four on the Top Ten list, Auds," he said as I sat across from him. "This is *unreal*." He held up his hand and I high-fived him. His fingers slipped through mine and held them for a second that felt like an eternity.

I couldn't contain my smile. And I couldn't stop imagining what it could be like to go to a private university and walk out of it with no debt. Maybe somewhere covered in ivy? It was impossible not to get my hopes up when everything was shifting. And I'd downloaded the app that morning, so I couldn't fight the nervousness I felt when I thought about who I'd be matched with. What if it was Aidan? I'd imagined it a hundred times since I'd downloaded: the alert ringing out and *AIDAN BAILEY* flashing across the screen. I'd show him my phone, and then what would he do? What would *we* do?

"I'm sitting with my boyfriend today, ladies," Lindsay singsonged as she passed her group of friends, holding Nigit's hand up like a shiny trophy. Lindsay's friend Diana, who wore weird headpieces and liked to be called Princess Di, called, "We love you, Linds!"

Lindsay's friends all smiled like we lived in some weird utopia where girls didn't get pissed when they got ditched for a guy. Then they resumed staring hopefully at their buyPhones. I'd never seen more phones displayed across the cafeteria. Hot-pink and purple cases mingled with black, navy, and metallic ones.

Lindsay squeezed my shoulder before she and Nigit sat. Mindy joined us, unloading a Thai wrap that smelled like lemons and peanuts. Nigit crossed his ankle over his knee, looking relaxed in his skinny black pants and sateen dinner jacket as he talked to Aidan about the China and Japan localizations for PhilanthrApp. He pulled his white glove from his fingertips and rested it next to his latte. Any other day he would've gotten made fun of. Any other day people would've pointed and sneered. Any other day he would've endured *trog, nerd, loser.*

Not today.

"Check out the Vampire Girl and Aviation Boy Hotness," Lindsay said, scooching her chair closer to Nigit. She nodded toward a table where Ty Bennet smoothed a hand over Goth Girl's black lace veil.

Zack Marks, the deer killer, sauntered by wearing a bright orange vest and Army-green pants. I would've thought he'd just murdered something, except he had a plastic Public shopping bag (and one from Piercing Pagoda—weird), which meant he'd been to U.P. Mall. He waved his new buyPhone at me and I waved back.

My mom emerged from the tiny room next to the cash register where she took care of stuff like who qualified for reduced lunch prices. She raised a hand and I waved to her, too. (My arm was getting tired, like Miss America's must.)

Blake was noticeably absent. Her cronies glared at me from their position a few tables away, except for Xander, who avoided my glance altogether. He had one earbud in, half listening to his buyPlayer while Blake's friends took turns talking and glowering in my direction.

DING DING DONG DING.

Conversation quieted across the cafeteria and heads turned toward the sound of the BFA.

It was coming from Carrie Sommers's underwear.

Carrie's round brown eyes blinked. She rummaged beneath her cheerleading skirt into the hand-stitched pocket of her bloomers, where she stored her phone. She stared at the screen and did a little tap dance—*shuffle, tap, tap, shuffle, shuffle.* Her head whipped in the direction of our table and her chestnut-colored ponytail followed, her perfect curls tumbling over her shoulder like a shampoo commercial. "Aidan Bailey!" she cried.

No. My legs went rubbery. My insides pinched. Hard.

The Boyfriend App had made weird matches all over Harrison. But Carrie and Aidan? Was it malfunctioning? Carrie couldn't be Aidan's type. Could she?

Aidan glanced at me. The rosy color was gone from his cheeks, maybe because Carrie Sommers was one of the prettiest girls in our class, especially if you liked that bubbly, spirit-fingers kind of thing, which most Harrison guys did. But did Aidan?

Someone whistled. Carrie's cheerleading cocaptain, Martha Lee, yelled, "Go, Carrie!"

Carrie threw back her shoulders and marched in our direction. I had the sudden urge to claw her face with my rabbit's foot's toenails.

Aidan was still looking at me. I stared back, waiting for him to do something—to tell Carrie *NO.* But he didn't. And everyone was watching us. So I went into survival mode. "Wow," I said, faking enthusiasm like Lindsay and I did at our cousin's bridal shower while she unwrapped gifts like dish towels and salad spinners. "Go for it, Aidan."

His dark brows narrowed. But what else was I supposed

to do? I couldn't throw myself in front of Aidan and claim him as mine, like Blake did to me all those years ago. He wasn't mine. I still wasn't even sure what had happened yesterday by the water, or what it meant. Or if it meant anything at all.

Carrie stopped at our table. Her glittery silver eye shadow had spilled onto her cheek and made her look like a disco ball. "Hey, Aidan," she said demurely. "I'm Carrie." As if we all didn't know. "Is this seat taken?" she asked, not-so-subtly tossing a smile to the rest of the lunchroom, like this was a sitcom and Harrison was her live audience.

My body was burning watching them.

Maybe Aidan's shyness was acting up, but he didn't speak, or couldn't. He didn't even move as Carrie leaned over our table with her freckled cleavage on display. She pushed her boobs together and smiled. When Aidan didn't say anything, she glanced over her shoulder as the entire cafeteria stared. *"Pull out my chair,"* she whisper-hissed.

The color came back to Aidan's cheeks. He looked at me again, like he was waiting for me to do something. But I felt frozen, so I just stupidly sat there. And then Aidan did like Carrie said.

Carrie took off her maroon cardigan and lowered herself slowly. Her cheerleading skirt was so short I found myself hoping she'd get an infection from the plastic seat. "Hi, Aidan," she said, drawing out the words like they were original poetry.

"Hello," he said.

Riveting.

Heat bubbled within me as Carrie nodded encouragingly. "Maybe we should go for a stroll since it's warm out?" she suggested. She gave Aidan a meaningful, loaded look like the Bachelorette always does when she feels a connection.

Aidan looked at me.

"The Boyfriend App strikes again!" I chirped in my bridal-shower voice.

Lindsay turned to Carrie and said, "Audrey and I *so* hope this works out. Don't we, Audrey?" She smiled at Carrie. "Feel free to chime in under THE BOYFRIEND APP USERS SOUND OFF section on *FBM*."

I noticed my mom watching from the kitchen. She looked sort of worried, and I suddenly felt embarrassed that she was seeing all of this.

Carrie grabbed Aidan's forearm. Her chin was sky-high as she strode through the cafeteria to encouraging catcalls.

I waited for Aidan to look at me again as they made their way through the glass doors. I battled a hard lump in my throat when he didn't.

chapter thirteen

"Just do it," I said later that evening.

"Yeah. Just do it," Carrie Sommers echoed.

"C'mon, Mindy," Lindsay said. "It's your turn to find love."

Lindsay, Nigit, Mindy, and I sat next to Aidan and Carrie on the sidelines of Harrison's varsity soccer game. I felt like I was drowning when Carrie's eyes traveled over Aidan's perfect face. His curls were black against the night sky, his skin translucent. He was barely looking at me. He was so absorbed in Carrie, I wasn't even sure if he knew I was there.

Floodlights illuminated the darkness, bathing the bleachers and the field in a golden glow. The smell of freshly cut grass mixed with Nigit's caramel latte. Whistles blasted the air and Harrison students shouted the names of players ("Score, Briggs! Score!"). Guys decked in Harrison's trademark maroon-and-yellow uniforms (think: McDonald's) raced across the field kicking the ball like Neanderthals.

Maybe I liked to internet-stalk Xander's lacrosse pics, but I hadn't been to an actual live sporting event since Blake and I used to go to JV football games. Now I remembered why: The back of my legs were freezing through my jeans against the metal bleachers, I didn't understand the rules of the game, I longed for alone time with Hector, and I was hungry because I had missed my mom's ratatouille (and didn't want to waste money on food from the snack bar). Not even the flexing quads of Briggs Lick made it worth it. But Lindsay convinced me this kind of socializing was key for keeping me in the public eye and building momentum for the BFA.

"Just press the OK button, Mindy," Carrie said, smiling and nodding like a professional.

Mindy had filled out the Boyfriend App's survey, and now she just needed to submit it. Her thumb hovered above the phone. She looked at me, unsure.

"Your dream guy might be right around the corner," Carrie went on, like a commercial for her life. She glanced at Aidan. "Mine was."

We were in public, so I smiled instead of puked. But it all felt like confirmation that I'd overreacted to what happened in the spot behind my apartment. If Aidan liked me, he wouldn't go out with Carrie, no matter how gorgeous she was.

"Guys, if she doesn't want to do it, she shouldn't," Aidan said. His jeans were just the right amount of broken in—they showed off the muscles in his legs without being too tight. I tried not to notice Carrie's hand on them.

Nigit clapped Aidan on the back. "Love is in the air, man." Then, to Mindy, he said, "You should do it."

Lindsay sang the first verse of "Can You Feel the Love Tonight."

Mindy still looked flustered, but she finally pressed OK. Then she showed me her phone's screen, where the Boyfriend App's shiny white icon and pink-studded heart floated among the other apps. I smiled at her. I still got a little buzz every time I saw its graphics. "I'm so glad you did it," I said, putting an arm around her shoulders.

"Me too, Min," Carrie said.

Min?

On the field, a cheerleader did a Rockette kick, slipped, and fell into a puddle of mud.

"Pick yourself up, Martinez!" Carrie screamed. "We leave soccer to the JV cheerleaders," she said to Aidan. I tried not to wonder if they'd hung out after school before the game—visions of Carrie chanting *A-I-D-A-N* in private made me want to flush myself down a toilet. I'd wanted him for so long. Carrie had gotten him in one afternoon. Why could some girls do it so easily, and I couldn't? "Soccer is a lesser game than football," Carrie said, hushing her voice like she didn't want to offend anyone with this pearl of wisdom. Her chestnut-colored hair spilled over her snug-fitting green sweater. She'd curled the ends, and they rested happily on her nipples, which were obviously cold.

Aidan's face was still ghostly pale. He was either coming

128

down with the flu, or so enraptured by Carrie's charm that he was forgetting to breathe. "How interesting," he said.

"Friggin' fascinating," I said.

"There are so many hidden layers of cheer hierarchy," Carrie said. "It's a nuanced sport."

Sport? Mindy texted me.

Barf, I texted back.

Then Carrie told us she'd wanted to date someone named Aidan ever since last year, when she watched all six seasons of *Sex and the City* while she was resting her broken toe.

I caught a glimpse of Blake in the parking lot with her mother. Blake's mom had her hands on her hips while Blake gesticulated wildly. They looked like they were arguing. I smiled a little when I thought of the name Blake and I had made up for her in eighth grade: the Pirate Psycho, on account of her mood swings, the gold hoop earrings she wore, and the frosted blond hair that obscured one eye.

The Harrison goalie dove to save a goal and missed. Choked sobs sounded. I turned to see who'd taken the goal too seriously and saw Goth Girl hunched over, clutching her stomach. Wind caught her lace veil and lifted it to expose tears mixing with mascara, marking black rivulets over her cheeks. Ty Bennett descended the bleachers, shaking his head. Goth Girl hid her eyes with ten fingers covered in silver rings.

Cold air hit me like a slap.

"Uh-oh," Lindsay said.

"Another one bites the dust, Audrey," Nigit said. A

cashmere scarf draped his sateen dinner jacket. His white-gloved hand held Lindsay's. "You heard about Kara Neil and Pete DiGordiano?"

What I heard was a hint of satisfaction in Nigit's voice. "Yeah, whatever," I said, trying to sound like it was no big deal. After being matched by the BFA, Kara and Pete engaged in a very public make-out session, after which Kara declared Pete's tongue a "roving fish with no direction" and ended it over text.

DING DING DONG DING.

Mercifully, the crowd's focus shifted from Goth Girl's despair to Annborg Alsvik. Annborg jumped to her feet on the tinny bleacher and held her phone high in the sky. "Boyfriend App! Boyfriend App! Boyfriend App!" she screamed.

Kevin Jacobsen, part-time pot dealer and full-time douche bag, was ascending the bleachers. His hands were tucked into his pockets. He moved and talked slowly, like Matthew McConaughey, but without the looks or southern drawl.

Please, don't let them be matched.

"Kevin Jacobsen?" Annborg cried out. Her accent made it sound like *Kayveen Yacob-son.* "Me your match! Me over here!"

Kevin shaded his red-rimmed eyes and scanned the crowd. His gaze landed on Annborg jumping up and down. Her gauzy white scarf unraveled around her shoulders like a mummy doing a striptease.

Mindy elbowed me.

"Oh no," Lindsay said beneath her breath.

The inevitable happened. The thing I should've predicted. The thing I should've prevented if only there were code that could.

Kevin started laughing. A high-pitched, pot-fueled laugh that built from a cackle into a riot. "Dude. No *way*," he said.

Pink patches spread like hives across Annborg's skin. She glanced around, like someone might help her. No one did.

My fists curled against my jeans. I should've seen it coming.

Programming is perpetually trying to solve riddles, fix problems, and squash bugs. Computer language is so hypersensitive to grammar that you have to get it exactly right or else you'll run your program and all sorts of screwy things could happen because you missed a single parenthesis. But this was different. There were actual people involved now, with their live, beating hearts, and the kind of complicated emotions the app couldn't account for. And then there was *me*. I'd thrown logic aside and played along like the Lindsay-and-Nigit-love-match phenomenon could sweep America. I'd let hope blind me and set me up to fall.

I was the bug in the system.

"I don't feel so good," I said to Mindy. "I'm gonna call it a night."

She gave me a look that asked *Are you okay?* I nodded. She lifted up her car keys to let me know she could take me home.

"I'll be fine," I said. "My mom can pick me up."

"Audrey!" I turned to see Annborg making her way across the bleacher. A lock of blond hair fell loose from her side ponytail. She looked pissed.

Lindsay grabbed my arm. "Just deflect her questions. Use words like *actually* to change the subject, and don't forget to—"

DING DING DONG DING.

Lindsay stopped midsentence. We both looked down into Mindy's lap, where she clutched her buyPhone.

Boyfriend Alert:

WOODY AMES. 8 YARDS SOUTH.

I lifted my gaze. Woody and Blake were stomping up the bleachers. Xander stood a few rows above and watched them climb.

Mindy's eyes went wild with fear. *No,* she mouthed at me. *Please.*

I grabbed the phone. "Don't worry," I said. "I can deprogram—"

But it was too late. Annborg stood over us, cocking her head to read the graphic. "Woody Ames," she read out loud.

"Annborg, *shut up*," I said.

Woody's arm was linked through Blake's as he led her down the row of bleachers where Xander sat with the Martin sisters. Xander moved between Blake and Woody. He patted the seat next to him and gestured for Blake to sit.

Annborg stared at the three of them and smiled.

"Don't say anything, Annborg," I hissed.

But Annborg chose that moment to forget how to

speak English. She angled her phone at Blake, Woody, and Xander.

PING! went the tone that signaled Annborg was recording video.

"Woody Ames!" Annborg screamed. Woody stared up at us. Blake looked up, too. She caught my glance, and her eyes turned into slits. "You matched with Mindy!" Annborg shouted to Woody, pointing at Mindy's head.

A few people giggled.

Mindy's olive skin suddenly looked green. She tried to duck behind me, but Annborg's camera was in her face. Aidan realized what was going on, and put his hand over Annborg's lens. But Annborg just backed up and started filming all of us.

Blake laughed. "Go get her, Woody," she said, her voice soaked with sarcasm. She laughed harder, barely able to contain her hysteria.

My hand found Mindy's and squeezed.

Woody looked at Mindy. "Me and *Es-st-st-stupida*?" he said. "Yah. Freaking. Right."

chapter fourteen

With four days left until Public announces two grand
prizewinners, one mobile application is noticeably absent
from the Top Ten list. Audrey McCarthy's Boyfriend App
hit its stride early this week, riding high on teen sensation
Danny Beaton's Twitter plug. But after thousands of failed
matches and painful rejections, it appears Americans
teens are ready to say good-bye to the Boyfriend App and
recognize it as the too-good-to-be-true marketing ploy
it really was.

Excerpted from http://www.teensblogtoo.com by Xi Liang

It was Tuesday, and *TeensBlogToo* was one of the many blogs
dissing the BFA that Blake and the Martin sisters posted as
their Party statuses, along with a cheery ☺.

I pulled up the blog on Mrs. Condor's PC. Her normally

neutral brow furrowed. "There's still four more days," she said.

The hope in her voice made me feel worse. And after Mindy slept over last night, and I woke up to the sound of her crying, I didn't think that was possible.

I'd spent the morning hacking into Annborg's stupid OMGIuvUBlakeGodBlessBlakeandAmerica website, and taking down the video she posted of Mindy getting rejected by Woody. Blogger software security sucked—it had a new vulnerability detected practically every other week—so I found a vulnerability for the version Annborg used and exploited the login software to hack into the blog and remove the video. Then I changed the password, locking Annborg out so she couldn't repost it. But it didn't matter. Everyone at Harrison had already seen it.

I fidgeted with a tear in my skinny jeans. "My ranking dropped from four to thirty-nine in less than two days. And my cousin says once the PR tide turns, it's nearly impossible to come back," I said, quoting Lindsay's somber pronouncement from the ride to school that morning.

The wood-paneled walls in Mrs. Condor's tiny office loomed close. Even the cuckoo looked concerned with her painted-on red eyes cast down on me. "Ms. Bates says you still have a chance if you make the finals for the Most Innovative App," Mrs. Condor said. It was weird picturing Condor and Bates having a conversation about me. Sort of like how it's weird to imagine teachers existing in any other setting besides in the classroom, teaching you.

But Mrs. Condor was right. Public was announcing

the top two hundred fifty Most Innovative Apps at three. Those would be the finalists considered for one of the two Grand Prizes. So even though my popularity ranking had slipped past the point of recovery, there was a chance Public had noticed it while it was in the Top Ten. Maybe they'd put me into the Most Innovative App finals. Maybe that could redeem me and my friends.

I sank onto the pink cushion. Mrs. Condor twirled a gold stud earring. "You really want this, don't you?" she asked.

No one had ever flat-out asked me like that. I nodded and said, "I want to do something that makes people notice me again, and I want to go to a really good college and not have to work two jobs for three decades to pay it off." I felt so obvious and clichéd, but it was the truth. "Everything was going so well. And then my app bombed. It hurt my best friend, and it matched the guy I like with a cheerleader."

There it was. The first time I'd ever admitted liking Aidan out loud. To another person. And in therapy, no less. The clichés were stacking up around me like dominoes. I wanted to curl beneath Mrs. Condor's desk and hide.

"Have you told this person how you feel?" Mrs. Condor asked.

"I told Mindy how sorry I was like a thousand times," I said, feeling myself get choked up when I thought about her. The way she put an arm around my shoulders last night like I was the one who needed comfort.

Mrs. Condor's perfectly straight blond hair brushed her

shoulders as she leaned forward. "I was referring to the gentleman you like," she said. The way she said *gentleman* in her accent made me think of Aidan taking me to a cotillion in a horse-drawn carriage.

I shook my head.

"And why's that?"

There were a million answers to Mrs. Condor's question. "I can't do that," I finally said.

Mrs. Condor was quiet. I knew she was waiting for me to say something more. But what else was there to say?

"Audrey," she said softly. "When we're afraid of something, it can be helpful to imagine the worst thing that could really happen. It makes whatever we're afraid of less scary." She uncrossed her leg. The hem of her pants caught, and exposed a tattoo on her ankle that read *l.o.v.e.* in lowercase typewriter letters. The next moment it was gone, hidden beneath Banana Republic–looking wool trousers. "What's the worst thing that could happen if you told this friend how you felt?" she asked.

I tried to imagine saying the words to Aidan. I hadn't even said them to my own mirror yet. "He could laugh. Or act weird."

Mrs. Condor didn't look convinced.

"I could lose my friends." Did she understand how bad that would be? Did she have any idea what it was like to be completely alone? No friends, no father. "He could tell our friends that I like him, and that he doesn't like me, which would make everything awkward."

But when I said it out loud, it didn't really sound like

something Aidan would do.

Mrs. Condor tucked a wisp of hair behind her ear. "Sometimes taking a chance is worth it, don't you think?"

I took a breath. It was worth everything.

At 2:52 that afternoon in the computer lab, Carrie gave Joel Norris and his tuba a dirty look. Then she sat next to Aidan. She pulled a butter-colored cashmere sweater over her head to reveal a tiny black baby-doll top that might've been sold in a lingerie section. I fought the urge to roll my eyes. The lab's stuffy heat was making me sweat, too, but I wasn't about to strip down to my Jockey sports bra. (They're more comfortable than regular bras. So sue me.)

"The moment of truth is eight minutes away," Nigit said dramatically. Nigit's parents were doctors, and his lips were shiny with the medicated balm they prescribed him during the cold weather. It made him smell like a cough drop.

Bates wore a row of pearls around her neck and a gold pin on her cardigan. She'd dressed up even more than usual this week, like she was excited about the contest. It made me feel even worse for disappointing her with my fall. "No matter what happens today, I'm pleased with all of you and your creations," Bates said, her warm brown eyes roving the lab and settling on me. My programmer classmates took over the PCs. Lab newbies lined the wall. (They finally realized their place wasn't at our computers. There had to be at least one place in Harrison where the trogs had seniority, and the Dumpster didn't count.) Mindy was at

Creative Writing Club, but I promised I'd text her as soon as we knew the results.

"And I'm thrilled with the way you're supporting one another," Bates went on.

I glanced sideways at Aidan. His big hands were in his lap—nowhere near Carrie's. And he wasn't looking at her, either—even in her Victoria's Secret outfit. Maybe he didn't totally like her yet. Maybe I could take the chance before they got serious.

"It's important to stand by my boyfriend," Carrie announced.

Boyfriend?

Something snapped along my insides like a firecracker. It had been twenty-freaking-seven hours since the app matched them. How could this have happened? What had I done?

I didn't want to look at Aidan—if he was smiling at Carrie, there was a chance I'd start crying. But I had to know. I turned slowly, knowing how I felt had to be written all over my face. Aidan stared back at me, but his eyes were unreadable. And he didn't deny what Carrie said.

Carrie peered over Lindsay's shoulder. "You can put that in your article."

"It's not an article," Lindsay said. "It's a post." She was snuggled on Nigit's lap, staring at the screen. "And I'm not interviewing you; I'm interviewing Audrey."

Carrie's lower lip jutted and she inched closer to Aidan. Her hair was French-braided with a maroon ribbon running through the interlocking strands. I wanted to rip it out. "I just know your app's gonna make it, babe," she said.

Babe?

Aidan fidgeted with his Toyota key chain. "Thanks—"

Please don't call her babe.

"—Carrie."

Aidan's dark blue eyes caught mine again. "You nervous, Auds?" he asked.

Nervous, jealous, upset. So much so that I didn't even attempt speaking. I nodded instead. I squeezed my rabbit's foot and set it on my lap.

Lindsay's fingers clicked across Computer #8 and copy filled the back end of her blog:

At Harrison High School, the eight tech students who submitted apps wait for Public's official announcement. The below photo shows my favorites: Audrey McCarthy, creator of the Boyfriend App, and Nigit Gurung and Aidan Bailey, cocreators of PhilanthrApp. McCarthy, Gurung, and Bailey stand by to see if their entries have made the Most Innovative App finals. If not, they'll have to hold out hope to win the Most Popular App category. I'd like to remind everyone that the Boyfriend App was recently on Public's Top Ten Most Popular App list. I can tell you from personal experience, it deserves another rise in popularity. So go download now!

Lindsay scooted off Nigit's lap and grabbed her buyPhone. "Stand together, you guys," she said, focusing the phone's camera.

Aidan, Nigit, and I arranged ourselves in front of Bates's desk as she moved out of the way. "Stay in the picture, Ms. Bates," I said. Bates flashed the smile I loved—the one that made her look like one of the older models in the J. Crew catalog. Carrie elbowed her way between Aidan and me.

"Carrie," Lindsay said in the saccharine-sweet voice she reserved for saying whatever she wanted, "the lab's temperature is taxing my overactive metabolism, and you're exhausting me. Can you remove yourself from the photo of the contestants and their mentor, please?"

Carrie rolled her eyes and sashayed next to the trash bin. I prayed the fumes would make her clothes reek so Aidan would mistake it for her natural smell.

Aidan moved next to me. His hand brushed my hip, and my skin felt hot where he touched. I looked up and saw his full bottom lip. We were standing so close that if I stood on my tiptoes, I could kiss him.

"*Audrey*, give me a smile," Lindsay said. I turned and she snapped a photo, and then we all sat back down. Lindsay uploaded the photo with her post to *Fashion Becomes Me*. "I'm really proud of you guys," she said softly. She squeezed my shoulder before snuggling next to Nigit. They exchanged a private look and I averted my eyes, feeling myself blush.

Carrie was back, squashing her butt into a too-small yellow plastic chair with Aidan. Students were clustered together in the lab, too, most having chosen to work in pairs. One girl who usually programmed her apps solo sat with her boyfriend. Some guys had girlfriends online and IM'd. Even Joel had his tuba.

I felt worse than a fifth wheel. I felt alone.

I glanced at my phone. Two minutes to go. I said a silent prayer. *Dear Dad, wherever you are. If you could just help me with this one thing. Love, Audrey.*

My prayers always sounded like the Post-it notes my dad used to leave around the apartment. *Dear Audrey, if you could just vacuum your room, we'd all be thrilled. The dust bunnies aren't paying rent. Love, Dad.* The first thing I did after his funeral was search the house from top to bottom to find any leftover Post-its. I found four, which now sat in my top desk drawer next to a hot-pink heart eraser and a seashell.

I couldn't bear to watch how Carrie was adjusting herself in Aidan's lap. It was like she was test-driving her butt cheeks on his legs. So I settled my gaze on the wall of magazine clippings and waited. Articles like "Public Reinvents Publishing One buyBook at a Time" were posted next to "Alec Pierce Takes Public Higher," showing a glossy photo of the Public CEO. His buzzed black hair matched his stubble. It was so thick it looked like war paint over his head and chin, like he had more hair follicles per inch of skin than the average person. Another clipping showed cartoon figures of Alec Pierce and Infinitum's CEO, Jane Callaghan, dueling with smartphones shaped like swords, captioned: *Who phones it in best?*

"I can't really type with you sitting like that," Aidan said in his low voice.

Carrie dismounted. My spirits lifted a little.

One more minute.

142

Lindsay refreshed Public's home page, Nigit's foot jolted and jiggled until I was sure it would fly free of his ankle. Only Aidan looked calm. "Ready?" he asked me. Then he did something that made my body catch fire. He opened his hand and linked his fingers through mine. My rabbit's foot was pressed between our palms, but he didn't seem to care. "Good luck," he said, quiet enough so only I could hear. I tore my eyes from him to stare at Computer #7.

A graphic bolted in bright blue across Public's home page.

Congratulations, TOP 250 MOST INNOVATIVE MOBILE APPS! The following contestants have secured a place in Public's finals for Most Innovative Mobile Application. Click Here to View and Download.

I dropped Aidan's hand. As soon as I did it, a cold feeling hit me, and I wanted to take him back. I suddenly didn't want to see the list. I wanted to stay suspended in this moment, when I still had hope for the Boyfriend App, when Aidan's fingers were still warm linked through mine. It was happening too fast. Nigit was scrolling rabidly over the two hundred fifty app titles and contestant names. Aidan read over Nigit's shoulder while Lindsay scrolled on the computer next to them. I scrolled, too, so nervous I could barely see straight. Names blurred into the next. Bloodsucking Vampires, Caffein8ted, Collegiate, DivaLicious, Jock Planet, Got Breastmilk?, Light the Dark, Orientation, PhilanthrApp.

PhilanthrApp.

"Yes!" Nigit screamed.

Lindsay threw her arms around Nigit. He hugged her snug against him, then sprang from his chair and pumped his white-gloved fist.

"PhilanthrApp," Carrie said, like she'd just figured out how to read. "Wow!"

"Congratulations, you guys," I said. I wanted to hug Aidan, or squeeze his shoulder or something, but Carrie already had her arms wrapped around him.

Lindsay was back in her seat, scrolling again. Looking for the Boyfriend App. "Maybe it's under *T*?" she said. Her green eyes narrowed as she reread the list.

My insides curled into a tight ball. My eyes roved, searching for black letters against a white screen, spelling out my creation . . . all I needed.

Nigit was moonwalking. Carrie was laughing. Joel Norris was clapping Aidan on the back.

Lindsay sighed.

I felt Aidan's glance.

"It's not here," I whispered, unraveling.

Part 2.0

chapter fifteen

"Audrey?"

Bates folded her thin arms across her chest. Her movements were graceful, like an ice-skater.

It was just the two of us. The ventilation system kicked to life for the first time in forever, and a dull hum filled the air along with Carrie, sing-chanting in the hallway outside. Her voice quieted as she made her way down the hall with my friends.

"Yes, Ms. Bates," I said, trying not to sound annoyed.

"This isn't over."

I scrawled X's in blue pen on the side of my Vans. "Then why does it feel like it is?" I asked, not meeting her gaze. I drew triangles around the X's to morph them into stars.

"Every great creative has experienced rejection and setbacks."

Duh, Ms. Bates. She may as well have been reading a

quote from a fortune cookie. "Right," I said, exhaling. I tapped my pen next to the keyboard. I didn't want to be with my friends and I didn't want to be with Bates, either, but being surrounded by computers in the lab made me feel like I could keep breathing. I hadn't felt so still in a place since my dad used to take me for walks around the lakes on Notre Dame's campus. I didn't want to leave—not yet, anyway. "I just want to be alone," I told Bates. I felt worse for being rude, but I couldn't help it. "I'm sorry," I added.

Ms. Bates slid her Infinitum laptop into a black leather carrying case. "I'll be in the lounge across the hall if you need me." She peered through the door's plastic partition into the hallway. She didn't look at me while she said, "If you want to win this thing, dig deeper." She turned the bronze knob and the door opened with a *click*. "Look within. And then build a better app."

Hours later, I sat with my knees to my chest, my fingers alternating between the keyboard and hugging the toes of my sneakers. The vents were still blowing cold air and it was the first time I needed one of my hoodies in the lab. I was wrapped in the one Lindsay found for me at Farrah's Finds for seven bucks that was a few washes away from disintegration. It was dark gray with black wings silkscreened across the back. It made me feel like a girl who rode a motorcycle. It made me feel brave.

Without the other trogs, the lab felt soft and slow, ready to rest for the night. I checked my phone. It was quarter to seven and I needed to make the last bus at 6:50. I logged off my computer and slung my backpack over my shoulder. In the hall, dim light spilled across the linoleum.

"Audrey?"

I looked behind me. Lindsay sat outside the lab, leaning against a bank of steely gray lockers. Had she been waiting for me this entire time? "I didn't see you," I said.

Normally she'd tell me to stop being obvious. Instead she said, "I thought you might need a ride," like it was no big deal. Like her butt hadn't gone pins-and-needles from sitting on a rock-hard floor.

In the parking lot, we folded into Lindsay's Acura. She didn't bother trying to get me to talk during the ride. We were about to pull onto Route 31 when she veered left.

"Lindsay?"

"You're going to have to trust me," she said. She took a right, and then another, until we were cruising along a small side street I didn't recognize. Tiny ramshackle houses sat close to the curb. We passed a yard filled with a dozen broken-down bicycles. Another had plastic flamingoes next to a Santa Claus. A dark-haired little boy in denim overalls zigzagged through the flamingoes pushing a Radio Flyer wagon.

My parents used to talk about the kind of house they wanted to buy once we'd saved enough money. But I liked our apartment: Houses felt too personal. In an apartment complex, there's the anonymity of uniformity. Houses publicized how much money a family had by their niceness, and revealed what kind of people lived inside with paint-color choices, cars, decorations, and flower beds.

These houses told a different story. They looked like abandoned children, left in playgrounds with dirty faces and skinned knees.

Lindsay curved around a bend. Heavy black wires looped in half circles from telephone poles. The car slowed as we neared a tiny bumblebee-colored house: Black shutters hung crookedly on chipped bright-yellow paint. Sparrows lined a thin tree branch that arched like a finger over the driveway. Lindsay pulled behind a light yellow rust-covered Buick that made her 1995 Acura look new. The Buick's hood was open. Jumper cables were attached from its engine to a pickup truck. Tiny sparks shot from the cables as the car's battery got a jump.

A wooden sign next to the bumblebee house read: MADAME BERNESE: WORLD-RENOWNED FORTUNE-TELLER AND READER OF CHAKRAS.

My chakras clenched. "No way," I said.

Lindsay stared through the front windshield. "I've never asked you for anything, have I?"

I combed my brain. I'd asked Lindsay for plenty: rides to school, clothing hand-me-downs, to test-drive the Boyfriend App. And there was plenty Lindsay did that I didn't need to ask for: the way she'd supported the Boyfriend App with her PR tactics, for instance. But there was nothing she'd asked me for. Ever. And now that I thought about it, there wasn't much I'd really done for her, either. Except maybe embarrass her.

I shook my head.

"Well, I'm asking now," she said. She turned off the

ignition. A tiny red stiletto charm jingled on her key chain against a miniature Statue of Liberty. She always said it reminded her of her future. "I want you to win this thing, Audrey. I want us both to get chances at something big." She swiveled in her seat to face me. "You have what it takes—you always have."

I wanted more than anything to believe her.

"You're the one with the brilliant brain," she said. "And I know we need a miracle—you said it yourself. But there isn't anything more I can do. You're going to have to make this happen."

A pit bull emerged from a gap in a boarded-up shed. It nosed a piece of trash along the chain-link fence. Lindsay gestured toward the yellow house. "Madame Bernese is the one who guided me to start *Fashion Becomes Me*," she said. "And that blog saved me. It's the thing that got me into FIT. So all I'm asking is for you to spend a measly five minutes with the woman, 'kay?" She grabbed her zebra-striped purse from the backseat. "My treat," she said as she climbed from the car.

I kicked at a rock on the driveway and followed her. What else could I do?

Lindsay punched a black button next to Madame Bernese's sign. A shrill buzz sounded from inside the house. I held my breath. I just needed to get this over with, like a tetanus booster.

The door opened to reveal the same little boy we saw tugging the wagon in the neighbor's yard. He must have sprinted through the back when he saw us pull into the driveway. He stared up at us with round, dark eyes.

"We're here to see Madame Bernese," Lindsay said, smiling like it was great news.

The little boy stared through the screen until a woman appeared behind him. Her chubby curves were draped in magenta swaths of fabric, and her head was wrapped in a teal scarf.

Lindsay clasped her hands in a prayer position and bowed like we were in a kung-fu movie. Madame Bernese returned the gesture and beckoned us inside. The little boy hid behind her skirts until she whispered in his ear. He took off running down the hall, and I heard the unmistakable clatter of a porcelain cookie jar.

Madame Bernese gestured to a room off a dimly lit hallway. Lindsay sat on a chair next to the door and made a shooing gesture for me to follow Madame Bernese. I gave Lindsay a look and she gave me a worse one back. I convinced my feet to move and stepped behind Madame Bernese into the tiny room. The scent of sage and patchouli filled the air as she shut the door behind us. My eyes adjusted to the darkness. I made out maroon walls covered in gold-framed pictures of people who looked like the Lakshmi photo Lindsay had uploaded to her blog on her first date with Nigit. The people (saints, maybe?) had knowing, placid expressions and wore head scarves and clothing like Madame Bernese. Some were praying. Others held their hands up like they were giving a blessing (or at least that's the blessing move Father Doyle did on Sundays).

Madame Bernese still hadn't said anything. The patchouli

smell was making my throat feel choked, like the time I had acid reflux and thought I was dying of a heart attack. She pointed to a metal folding chair next to a round table covered in tarot cards. Thank God there wasn't a crystal ball.

"Um, hi," I said, feeling like one of us should say something. I sat in the chair and flinched when the metal creaked.

But Madame Bernese only nodded as she sat opposite me. Her eyeballs looked too big for her eye sockets, like they might pop out and roll across the table like marbles. Pink powder shimmered on her cheeks. "What bring you here today?" she finally asked. Her accent was French, or something, and it made the words sound like *Wha bring you eere today?*

"My cousin thought you could help me."

Madame Bernese lit an ivory candle surrounded with black lace that belonged in a fire-safety video. The flame shot to life and lit the lower half of her face. She stared at me until I blurted, "There's this contest." What did I have to lose? "And I want to win it."

Madame Bernese closed her eyes. She kept them jammed shut for so long I worried I'd offended her with my non-spiritual request, or that she'd fallen asleep. I stared at a watercolor painting behind her of a person with golden light emanating from the crown of his head. I AM THAT I AM was inscribed on the bottom. I was about to clear my throat and say something more about the contest when Madame Bernese's eyes shot open.

"Look within," she said, her hands clamping on the metal table.

Why did everyone keep telling me that?

"There is more," she went on, the words oozing like toothpaste . . . *Thayerrr ees mooore*. She opened her palm and raised her hand above the table. "Dig beneath surface. Find what is hidden." Her voice was soothing and creepy at the same time, like she was trying to put me in a trance. I focused on the golden-light painting—I was *not* about to let some lady in a head scarf and chandelier earrings put me in a trance.

Madame Bernese blinked and shook her head. The peaceful expression on her face was gone. She looked bored.

"That's it?" I asked, not meaning to sound as unimpressed as I was.

Madame Bernese shrugged. "Sometime it come fast. Simple." She tucked a dyed-red strand of hair beneath her scarf. "You want more?"

"Some concrete guidance would be nice."

Madame Bernese closed her marble eyes again. "It's time to let it shine, that light of yours; it's all within you. Let the truth reveal itself."

What she said felt so familiar I was momentarily stunned. It was like my mind recognized the message on a deep soul level, like I'd been waiting to hear someone say it my entire life. For a split second I was in awe, until I realized Madame Bernese was quoting a Danny Beaton lyric. "Thanks," I grumbled. "Haven't heard that one before."

Madame Bernese arched forward. Then she quoted the

next verse: *"Be the light. Enter the realm of truth."*

"I think I've got it from here." I shoved my chair from the table and stood. "Thanks."

For nothing.

Lindsay waited outside the door at a mosaic side table with a crystal sword in the center. The little boy sat on the floor with a set of jacks. I didn't wait for Lindsay to get up. I pushed through the front door and stepped onto the lawn.

The cars in the driveway were still turned on, their engines rumbling with the transfer of electricity. Sparks jumped from the cables into the darkening sky. It was that purple-and-navy time of night, just after the sun has set, but hasn't abandoned you completely, still gifting glints of light across the shadows. It was the after-dinner and before-bed time when the world seems easier, more at peace with herself. It was the time of night my dad used to take me to the grotto by the lakes at Notre Dame—a hollowed-out stone cave formation lit with hundreds of glittering candles. Usually we just knelt on the wooden kneelers and said prayers. But when we talked, the cave made normal speech sound sacred.

I breathed the cold night air, imagining the slivers of golden light on the horizon seeping through me. A car engine groaned and sputtered in the distance. Wind gusted through the trees, making the skinny branches tremble. A white-haired woman emerged on a falling-down porch down the street and lit a cigarette. A guy pushed through the screen door and tried to take the cigarette away. I squinted as they argued. The guy looked so much like

Xander. I watched him throw up his hands and retreat. His large frame lingered in the doorway before disappearing inside. *Was* that Xander?

No. He couldn't live there, in that falling-down place. I shook my head to clear it.

Where was Lindsay?

I felt like such a kid, stranded at some house where I didn't belong, completely alone. No car. No boyfriend. No college. I blinked back tears and checked Public's home page on my buyPhone. The Boyfriend App had fallen further: number 189. Now the tears pushed past the barrier of my lashes and streamed down my face, coming faster until my shoulders were shaking. I wrapped an arm around my stomach and tried to squeeze away the gulping noises my body was making. It wasn't fair. None of it was fair. My fingers tightened around my phone. I felt my arm cock back like I was throwing a softball pitch.

"Audrey?" Lindsay called from the porch. "What are you—?"

I didn't realize what I was doing until my phone was already flying through the air.

CRACK!

My buyPhone slammed into the car battery. The sparks went wild and the screen lit up. The phone jolted and buzzed, and then dropped onto the driveway.

I cursed my temper. I moved to the phone and saw the impact with the battery had fractured the screen. The reflection of my pale skin and messed-up pixie-girl haircut stared back at me through a spiderweb of fault lines in the plastic. Why hadn't I spent the money on a case? I knelt and felt the cold asphalt through my jeans. The back had popped off. I tried to jam it together, but it wouldn't close.

I should've been freaking out about how I was going to afford a new phone. I should've been rehearsing how I was going to explain to my mom what I'd done.

Instead, I felt a great sense of warmth and inner calm. And the strangest buzzing noise was coming from my buyPhone.

Bzzzzzzzzzzzzzzzzzzz.

"Audrey?"

I wanted to fix the phone. But I sat there staring at it instead, like it was the answer to all my prayers.

"Audrey?"

I turned to see Lindsay alone on the porch. She looked so beautiful. Standing there with her platinum hair shining and her khaki-colored jacket cinched perfectly at the waist.

Bzzzzzzzzzzzzzzzzzzz.

The noise was so loud I could barely think straight. And I couldn't stop staring at Lindsay. It was so sweet of her to bring me here to Madame Bernese. So what if the silly woman didn't have a cure for my college scholarship problems? It was the thought that counted, and Lindsay was always thinking of me. I had the sudden urge to embrace my cousin and tell her just how fond I was of her, how appreciative. I had to get to Lindsay, to tell her how I felt. I loved my cousin *so* much. I jumped up and accidentally kicked my phone beneath Madame Bernese's Buick.

The buzzing stopped.

I blinked and cocked my head. My thinking suddenly became sharp again, like it did in the computer lab after those first sips of Mountain Dew. I glanced at my cousin. Whatever fleeting affection I'd felt had vanished, and now I wanted to kick her for bringing me to Madame Fraud and making me smash my phone.

"What is *wrong* with you?" Lindsay asked, putting a hand on her hip. Her crystal cocktail ring looked like an ice cube.

"What's wrong with *you*?" I shot back. I felt weird. Like how they explain coming down from a high in those Don't Do Drugs or Else You'll Die videos from health class. "This was the stupidest idea ever. I can't believe you fall for gypsies and crazy crap like this."

Lindsay's mouth dropped. "You are so ungrateful!"

"Madame Bernese quoted Danny Beaton," I said. "Am I supposed to be grateful for that?"

"You're hopeless," Lindsay said, looking disgusted. "And I'm tired of trying to help you live up to your potential."

"Good! I don't want your help." I felt words crawl through me, ones I wouldn't be able to take back. "I just want you to leave me alone."

"*Fine,*" Lindsay said. "Go back to being *alone* all the time. You and your computer. Quite a life you have together." She didn't look mad anymore. She looked profoundly sad as she crossed the driveway and put her key in the car door.

"Wait," I said. I wanted to tell her I was sorry. I wanted to tell her I needed her, that I'd wanted nothing more than her friendship since we were little kids. Instead I said, "I

158

can't find my phone." The wind died down until it was only a whisper in the maple trees. I pointed at Madame Bernese's Buick. "Can you shine Loulou de la Falaise under there?"

Lindsay rolled her eyes. We knelt on opposite sides of the car and Loulou de la Falaise illuminated the gravel beneath. "Got it," she said, grabbing my phone where it rested next to the front tire.

I stood and glanced at her over the hood. If I was going to apologize, I needed to do it now. "Lindsay, I'm really sorry," I started to say. But her eyes were half-closed, as if she was meditating.

Still clutching my buyPhone, she raised her eyes to meet mine with a piercing stare. "No," she said. "*I'm* so sorry. You know how much I love you."

"I shouldn't have said that, though," I said. "I guess I've been stressed, and I wanted to win the scholarship so badly, and I let the pressure get to me and I . . ."

Lindsay crossed in front of the car. She stopped inches before me, scratching at her ear. "It's my fault," she said dreamily.

Well, that wasn't true. And her behavior was starting to make me wonder if Madame Bernese was burning something stronger than patchouli.

"I just love you so much," Lindsay said, taking my hands in hers. I'd never seen her be so affectionate. And then I heard it.

Bzzzzzzzzzzzzzzzzzzzzzzzzzzzzzzz.

The noise was back. It had to be coming from—

159

I grabbed my phone from Lindsay's grip and threw it again, hard. It landed fifteen yards away next to a half-dead-looking brown-and-green shrub.

Lindsay took a step back, and screamed.

chapter sixteen

I clapped my hand over her mouth.

"What just happened?" she said into my palm.

I looked at the yellow house and thought of the buzzing. "Bumblebees," I lied. "Wait here. And don't scream again."

Lindsay didn't protest. She stood next to the Buick with her arms crossed over her chest, shivering. The white-haired woman across the street had finished her cigarette and was beating a Navajo-style rug on the porch railing with a rhythmic *thud, thud, thud.* I was breathless as I crossed the lawn and knelt beside the phone.

Bzzzzzzzzzzzzzzzzzzzzzzz.

It wasn't an ordinary sound. It was like a combination of a high-pitched squeal and a vibrating buzz. I moved closer, but then jumped back just as a burst of complete and utter euphoria flooded my body. It felt like the endorphins that kick in after running for fifteen minutes and pushing past the pain, mixed with the sugar high and caffeine jolt from Mountain Dew, blended with the zing I felt looking at Xander's lacrosse pics, combined with the warmth that swirled through me when Aidan's hand held mine, and the rush I felt when his lips touched my cheek.

My mind was working a million miles a minute. Something was wrong with me—at least, temporarily. A strange noise was coming from my phone and it was making me heady and delirious. It was tricking me into feeling something I otherwise wouldn't—the way I felt when I looked at Lindsay standing on Madame Bernese's porch.

I stared at my buyPhone. It stuck up straight in the air, the bottom half nestled in the dirt next to the dead shrub.

I had to be mistaken. I'd seen too many science-fiction movies, and now my imagination was getting the better of me.

I crept forward until I heard it again.

Bzzzzzzzzzzzzzzzzzzzzzzzzzz.

Blood swirled in my knees until they knocked together. A rush of tenderness and well-being covered me like a quilt, and I didn't think I'd be able to pull myself from its grip. It felt so *good*. I fell to my knees in front of the phone like I'd seen old ladies do at church in front of holy statues.

I was sure now. It was unmistakable.

I was falling in love.

There was no one in sight to become the object of my affection—only Lindsay and the white-haired woman across the street, but my back was turned and I couldn't see them. Without an object, the falling-in-love feeling was general, nonspecific: a warming that crept from my toes to my fingertips. Pulling myself from the feeling was like stretching saltwater taffy—I resisted until I snapped, stumbling backward until I couldn't hear the noise anymore. I tried to catch my breath, but now that the feeling was gone, I wanted nothing more than to have it again. I stood there, trembling, both scared of the feeling and craving it.

I crawled over the cold earth as the buzzing got louder and the feeling grew stronger, making my thoughts cloud and swirl together. Images of Aidan filled my brain. His broad shoulders. Full bottom lip. Aidan lowering me to the ground, his hands touching my bare skin, kissing my mouth.

The images sped up, blurring together until I felt like I was going to pass out.

Focus.

I steadied my hands against the shrub. Tiny thorns pricked me and I saw blood on my fingers. I dug into the wet dirt, unearthing my phone and setting free the pungent smell of fertilizer.

Bzzzzzzzzzzzzzzzzzzzzzzzzzzz.

Aidan. His navy-blue eyes staring into mine. Aidan. Aidan. Pulling me against him, his breath warm on my neck.

Almost there.

I brushed mud from my buyPhone and pressed the oval button at the top, shutting down the screen. The buzzing noise stopped.

A motorcycle revved behind me as I sank to my knees. I heard it zoom down the street as I collapsed against the shrub. My thoughts raced. It was real. It was happening. Something in my phone was activating a physical response that mimicked love—not only in my body but in Lindsay's, too. She'd held my hands and looked dreamily into my eyes—not exactly par for the course in our relationship. Something was seriously wrong—or seriously *right*—with my buyPhone.

Lindsay eyed me from the driveway.

There was no way to explain the places my mind was going—somewhere absurd and fantastical and possibly too good to be true. It was a hunch I wasn't even sure I could put into words. I moved across the lawn on shaking legs.

"Let's get out of here," I said to my cousin. My fingertips itched. I needed to get home to my own computer. Fast.

In my bedroom, Hector's blinking green light was salvation. I locked the door and stared at the screen. I took out my phone and set it next to the computer. I heard my dad's voice.

A problem is solved one step at a time. So what's the first step, sweetheart?

My buyPhone lay cracked open, its guts beckoning me to look further. I bent down, squinting, sure that I saw a JTAG port, even if the dimensions weren't standard. I'd fooled around with JTAG on Hector before and built a USB-to-JTAG adapter, so I wired up a cable and some clips to connect to the buyPhone's JTAG port. My breath caught

164

as information poured from my phone into my computer. Public must have been arrogant enough to assume no one could open up a buyPhone without making it inoperable.

I searched until I found it: software that created a non-linear response aliasing into the voiceband of my phone, creating the strange buzzing noise. Public had labeled the software *Inaudible Frequency BuyWare*. So something must have happened when I broke my phone to make the noise audible—either the jolt of electricity from Madame Bernese's car battery, or the impact on the driveway, or, most likely a combination of the two. Now software Public had meant to be inaudible was audible. Something secret wasn't so secret anymore.

Now I *knew*.

I found a backdoor into the BuyWare software and scanned recent activity and databases. The BuyWare was only being activated on certain phones. It would make the most sense if BuyWare was installed on all buyPhones, because that way any phone sold could make the buzzing sound. But for whatever reason, BuyWare was only being activated on phones that belonged to added users. That meant only those phones were letting off the sound. I tapped a finger on my mouse. Added users would include spouses and children.

I found the encryption key that allowed for secure transfer of data from users' buyPhones to Public. Text files of information poured from my phone into Hector. Data flashed across the screen as more and more files were copied over. My mouth dropped as I scanned the data.

BuyWare was monitoring the users' every move, from their whereabouts to websites visited. That data was filtered into a program that rated each user's degree of what Public labeled *susceptibility to BuyWare*.

I hacked into the database to find the numbers with BuyWare most recently activated: 917-555-6731 belonged to Kim Lee, age seventeen, location coordinates: 40.741237,-74.007085T. Susceptibility: High. 619-555-2381 belonged to Colin Hoggatt, age eighteen, location coordinates: 32.727631,-117.244137. Susceptibility: Midrange. 630-555-3201 belonged to Megan Lucke, sixteen, and so on. . . .

I kept hacking until I was sure: Every phone Public targeted with BuyWare belonged to a teenager. And activation history showed a more aggressive activation of BuyWare on the teens with higher levels of susceptibility.

I entered the coordinates of BuyWare activation and found locations across the continental US from Seattle to Miami. BuyWare was being activated even as I hacked, but I couldn't find a pattern. It was activated more frequently in big cities, but, of course, that was to be expected. I pulled up the visuals for location coordinate 40.717764,-74.045077, where BuyWare was currently being activated on six separate phones. The location coordinates showed me the corner of Montgomery Street and Grove Street in Jersey City, New Jersey, where, sandwiched between Kanibal Home Boutique and a restaurant called Tacqueria, lived a Public store.

Adrenaline pulsed through me as I checked the other coordinates. Every location where the BuyWare software

166

was activated boasted a Public storefront, or a private residence. I set my phone to listen for data being transmitted on the correct frequency, allowing me to find the IP address at the tens of thousands of private residences where BuyWare was live and unleashed. I used my encryption key on Public's server to connect from Public to each user's buyPhone. From there, I installed a small application that would install a backdoor on the users' computers the next time the phone was connected to it.

The first connections came in seconds later. Every private residence where BuyWare was activated found the users either downloading music from buyJams or browsing Public.com.

I ran my hands over my face. Public was unleashing the software on teenagers in the virtual and physical vicinity of their products.

Could this be real?

The key lay in the sound. If an inaudible sound frequency could truly stimulate some sort of falling-in-love/craving/wanting response, then there was one major reason for Public to unleash the sound while the teenagers were in their stores, or surfing Public.com, or purchasing from buyJams. And that reason was to make teens buy their products.

I entered the idea into Google. Articles dated as far back as the sixties blamed music for making people crazy, making them euphoric, making them angry. Newer posts linked music on buyJams with mood-altering properties. Everyone knew music could change their mood, but apparently, so could inaudible sound frequencies—they were used for all kinds of purposes from dog training to healing diseases. I scrolled hundreds of articles until one caught my eye. "Nikhil Gurung: The Brain in Love."

Nigit's father?

I clicked on a small blurb in the *South Bend Tribune*: *Local neurologist receives grant from private investor to study sound waves' potential effect on oxytocin, dopamine, and other mood-altering neurotransmitters in the human brain.*

Huh. Not exactly something Nigit mentioned during lunch.

I Googled Nikhil Gurung and found articles he'd published, medical conferences he'd attended, committees he'd chaired, and a syllabus for the course he taught as a premed professor at Notre Dame. Seven pages of Google results later, I found a page on ClinicalTrials.gov:

ClinicalTrials.gov Identifier NC304921
The Effect of Sound Waves on Release of Adrenaline, Oxytocin, and Dopamine
Status: Terminated.

There were no results reported.

That was weird.

But Nigit's dad had to know something—anything.

I opened the search to Dr. Gurung's home page at Notre Dame. His email address was listed next to his office hours. On Tuesdays and Thursdays he held office hours from six to nine p.m.

It was 8:44.

My dad and I used to run from our apartment to Notre Dame's campus. Four minutes, if I sprinted.

I grabbed my coat from where it lay on an upended computer-security manual. "Just going for a run around the campus!" I called to my mom. "Be back before nine thirty."

My mom looked up from a cookbook called *La Cuisine*. I caught her light eyes widen. I hadn't been back to Notre Dame since my dad died.

"Be safe," she said as I flew out the door.

chapter seventeen

I kept my motorcycle-girl hoodie over my eyes until I could barely see the grass beneath my feet, until it halved the scenery that triggered my memories. Washington Hall: the old yellow-brick theater where my dad and I went to shows. LaFortune: the student center where we got watered-down hot chocolate. The Basilica: the mammoth, arching church where the three of us went for Sunday mass up until the day before he died (the church my mom tried to reserve for his funeral until she was told they didn't allow non-alums).

I pushed forward, my breath on fire as I sprinted across South Quad. Lampposts cast golden light across the green-black grass. I skirted between two burly redheaded twins tossing a football, and passed a girl on a bench whistling a Rihanna song. A skinny boy in a navy sweater with a shamrock handed out flyers to the students who trickled in twos and threes along the sidewalk.

I cut across the courtyard. I pushed groaning wooden doors into O'Shaughnessy Hall, where dim yellow light illuminated a long oak table, and climbed the stairs. I opened my palm and read numbers scrawled in blue ink. *203.* I swung left and nearly trampled two students poring over a laptop, downloading music. *209. 207.* A girl stood in the doorway of room 205 and whispered into her cell phone about having nailed her *Romeo and Juliet* audition. I felt a pinch of envy. Something about seeing the students I saw in town in their real college life made me want it even more.

203. DR. NIKHIL GURUNG. OFFICE HOURS. 6–9. Bingo.

My hand was sweaty on the knob. I pushed open the door and took in the small Indian man sitting at a white table with a green briefcase and an Infinitum laptop. I'd never met him before, but I would've recognized him anywhere. It was like the same makeup artist who Benjamin-Buttoned Brad Pitt had worked her magic on Nigit: The man in front of me was the fifty-year-old version of his son.

"Dr. Gurung?" I said, closing the door behind me. "I'm Audrey, one of Nigit's friends."

Dr. Gurung's wrinkled face split into a smile. His deep-set, intelligent eyes matched Nigit's, and his lips had the same light pink rose-petal color in the center. "What a pleasure," he said, his words heavily accented. "How can I help you, Audrey?"

"Um, well," I started, stepping closer. I pulled a pen

and tiny pad of paper from my jacket pocket. "I was wondering if I could interview you for an extra-credit AP Chem project. I'm proposing a theory that the neurological changes in the brain when we fall in love are much like the brain experiencing drug addiction."

Dr. Gurung raised an eyebrow. "Go on," he said, looking impressed even though I came up with the theory after a few Wikipedia clicks.

"Take dopamine," I said. It was one of the neurotransmitters he'd supposedly studied with his grant. I sat across the table from him. "Our brains secrete dopamine when a person is in love, but also when they're using cocaine. Dopamine is responsible for creating the reward pathways in the brain seen in drug addiction. One could argue the brain's secretion of dopamine leads to behavior modifications: wanting *more, more, more* of something."

If my hunch was right, if it was BuyWare's inaudible sound frequency that created the euphoric response, it stood to reason that Public was unleashing the software to create a dopamine reward pathway by stimulating the falling-in-love feeling in the teenager's brain. This would make teens crave more buyPhones and Beasts. More high-tech gadgets, souped-up headphones, and accessories. More buyPlayers and downloadable music.

More apps.

"Brain research supports your theory," Dr. Gurung said. His face was open and friendly, and his dark eyes actually twinkled, like an Indian Santa Claus. "Dopamine receptors are expressed by many neurons in the brain, including in the amygdala, the primitive 'reptile brain.' And teenagers like you are most susceptible, because teens use the amygdala to interpret emotional information, while adults use the prefrontal cortex."

A shiver passed through me. Teens were more susceptible to dopamine, which meant they were more susceptible to Public's software. I thought about the way I felt in the Public store: itching with desire for more and more of their stuff. Or how I got when I was downloading music, when I needed *just one more song.* Alec Pierce and his crew knew no one would notice if a teenager's behavior changed with a hormonal response to Public software. Craving new Public gear, or more music, would be brushed off as normal teen behavior.

I tapped my pen on the metal table, and said, "So we know drugs can stimulate dopamine and make us feel like we're falling in love. But I was wondering if anything else could. Like, say, sound waves, or maybe an inaudible sound frequency?"

I was still staring at my notepad, trying to look relaxed even though my heart was racing. It took me a second to realize Dr. Gurung wasn't saying anything. I glanced up to see his features harden. When our eyes met, he looked down at the table at the white space between his dark hands. *"No."* He cleared his throat. "I do not believe hormones can be triggered by sound."

My heart slowed. It wasn't what I expected. "I thought you would know, because of the study you did, the one I saw in the paper, on the internet."

Dr. Gurung's face was a stony mask. "My research showed that sound frequencies had zero effect on hormonal changes in the brain."

"But the paper said you proposed a theory that—"

"I found nothing."

Okay. "Well, I guess that answers my questions," I said, making my voice sound cheery. "Can I just borrow your computer for a sec?" I took a breath. I had to do this. He'd left me no choice. "I'm meeting my friend at Lisa's Café and I totally forget how to get there from here."

I made up a fake place so he wouldn't offer directions. Dr. Gurung frowned, but he turned his laptop around.

I angled it so he couldn't see the screen. "Gotta love Google maps," I said.

I entered a URL that linked me to a backdoor application. (A backdoor is a separate program that listens for connections—it's the back way into a computer. And I'd hosted it on a server I'd already compromised to make secure, so it couldn't be traced to me. At least, not by anyone unfamiliar with network security.)

Dr. Gurung leveled his gaze on me over the top of the computer.

I smiled at him. Then I downloaded the backdoor application, extracted it, and installed it on Dr. Gurung's laptop. I disabled his firewall and antivirus software to make sure nothing was detected. I disabled the security notifications on his laptop, too, so no one knew the firewall and antivirus software was disabled.

I did all of this in less than sixty seconds.

"Thanks again for all of your help," I said, turning the computer around.

Dr. Gurung forced a smile I wanted to believe was real. "I wish I could have been of more assistance," he said.

I crammed my notepad into my jacket pocket and made my way to the door. "You've helped me more than you know."

chapter eighteen

A regular person has to earn trust to pull a secret from a reluctant source. A regular person has to cajole, beg, bribe, blackmail—or worse—to get coveted information from an unwilling party. A regular person tries to solve conspiracies and cover-ups with doors shut in her face, impenetrable walls of silence, untruths to throw her off course.

A hacker does not.

The itch to get to Hector got worse the faster I ran. My lungs burned as I sprinted the final distance across the parking lot and into the courtyard. I was so consumed by my desire to hack that I didn't process the rusted Toyota Camry beneath the carport.

"Audrey," a low voice said.

The hair on the back of my neck woke up like it always did, and I knew it was him.

I turned. Aidan stood silhouetted beneath an iron lamp lighting the sidewalk to our apartment complex. The shadow that spilled into the light copied his pose—hands shoved into his pockets, his body arched slightly forward, shifting his weight between his long legs.

Had he been waiting for me?

"I just got here," he said quickly, as if he could read my mind. "But I started worrying it was too late and I'd piss your mom off if I rang the buzzer." He sounded unsure, like that wasn't the whole truth, but I didn't press him. I didn't say anything—I was too freaked out. A part of me wanted to get to my computer so I could figure out what was hidden. The other part of me wanted to go to Aidan, to lean into the crook of his body and forget about what I knew. Both choices scared me.

Aidan stepped from the light until we were both shrouded in darkness. I could feel every step he took toward me. My body felt like a magnet; the closer he came, the more I wanted him. I tilted my chin to take in his mussed hair, his alluring features. He leaned closer and I could barely breathe. I tried to remind myself that he was with Carrie, but it was hopeless. I wanted him to kiss me more than ever.

His voice was quiet when he said, "I just . . . I wanted to say I think your app should've made the finals." His hands left his pockets and went to my arms. My whole body lit up. "I wanted to tell you that in person."

I felt his words, how much he meant them. I also felt something else, something he wanted to—

"Audrey?"

My mother's voice. The window was open.

Aidan backed away as she stared at us.

"It's late," she finally said.

I wanted to tell her I'd be right up, but the look on her face told me she meant *now*.

"Can we talk tomorrow?" I said to Aidan. He gave me a small nod and then made his way to his car. "Thank you for saying that," I whispered. I wasn't sure if he heard me.

I didn't want to stand there and watch him go. So I turned and tore up the steps to our apartment. There was one thing I knew would take away the sting.

I made small talk with my mom and avoided her questions about my impromptu voyage to Notre Dame. Then I turned the light off in my bedroom so she'd think I was sleeping.

My fingers dangled above the keyboard. I pushed Aidan from my mind and tried to focus. With the backdoor application, I had full remote access to *everything* on Dr. Gurung's computer—emails, files, photos, you name it.

Don't use what you know to hurt people.

My dad's words curled through my mind like smoke. But if my theory was true, and Dr. Gurung was hiding something, it wasn't breaking my dad's code to uncover it.

My fingertips touched down. I opened the program on my computer that connected to the backdoor running on Gurung's computer. I was staring at his desktop open in a window on mine. I needed to be careful—with the way I was remotely logged on through the backdoor, it was possible Gurung could see me messing around on his desktop if he happened to be staring at it right then. So I waited to touch anything until the dead of the night when I figured he had to be sleeping.

The waiting was agony.

At 2:38 a.m., I started with his Word docs. It took me forever to sort through his files. (He wasn't bad with encryption, but it was an older algorithm and easy to break.) I finally found what I thought were notes from the study. I read through countless pages where Dr. Gurung described the reactions of the fifty mice he used as test subjects. I had to Google some of the medical terms, but I got the basic gist.

For his experiment, Dr. Gurung had placed the mice in two separate cages, each equipped with levers that the mice could push. In Cage A, the lever released an ultrasonic chord progression—the sound Lindsay and I must have heard coming from my buyPhone. Dr. Gurung believed the sound activated a burst of adrenaline, followed by oxytocin, and then dopamine in the mice brains.

In Cage B, there was a random sound frequency. A placebo.

In Cage B, the mice didn't care about the lever. They hit it a couple times, and when nothing happened, they moved on and did regular mouse stuff.

In Cage A, the mice went ape for the lever. As soon as they hit the lever, Dr. Gurung noted an immediate increase of blood pressure and heart rate. Moments later, the mice engaged in mating behaviors. (Sometimes cuddling and nesting, but usually hooking up.) Then the mice came racing back to the lever and hit it again, starting the cycle all over.

The mouse orgy lasted for days. Meanwhile, the mice had decreased appetite and decreased sleep (similar symptoms to humans in love). And they had an increase of obsessive behaviors like hitting the lever until their paws bled, and getting it on until they collapsed from exhaustion.

Dr. Gurung deduced that the mice were indeed experiencing a burst of adrenaline, followed by oxytocin and dopamine (the exact neurological changes the human brain experiences while falling in love, or lust).

I ran my hands over my pajama pants. It was true. Inaudible sound frequencies stimulated a cocktail of neurotransmitters to amp up the users, flood them with love and well-being, and keep them coming back for more. So why would Dr. Gurung hide the study results? And why was the study terminated if the results so obviously proved the hypothesis?

I opened Dr. Gurung's email and searched for *ADRENALINE/OXYTOCIN/DOPAMINE*. Dozens of emails popped up, but nothing suspicious. Mostly answers to questions posed by his students. I searched *NEUROTRANSMITTERS* in his deleted-items folder. Like so many people do, Dr. Gurung deleted his emails but never trashed his deleted-mail folder. Then I came across something big:

From: robertdawkins@R.DawkinsTech.com

A chill passed over my skin. *Blake's father* was involved?

To: nikhil.gurung@InfinitumMail.com

Nikhil,
I'm writing with the opportunity of a lifetime. I'm
working with a private investor interested in funding a
study of the possibility of sound-triggering the release
of neurotransmitters in the brain. I told them you're the
only neurologist they should consider.
Please keep this information confidential, of course.
What do you think, old roomie?

Robert

I tried to breathe, to steady my thinking. I read on
and on, discovering that it was Public Corporation's CEO
Alec Pierce who funded the study. The study's secondary
investor, Robert Dawkins, roped his college roommate
(conveniently, a neurologist) into conducting the study.
When the doctor found the results Public needed, Public
pulled its funding. So did Robert Dawkins.

I scrolled back up and reread one of the emails from
Robert Dawkins to Gurung.

You know what will happen if you don't cooperate.

It sounded like blackmail.
Public had access to hundreds of top-notch neurologists

across the country. Maybe I'd watched too many movies, but something told me whatever blackmail-worthy information Robert Dawkins had on Nikhil Gurung was the reason he was selected to complete the trial—so that he could be effectively shut up once he'd handed Public the sound frequency that triggered the love hormones.

And there was nothing I could do about it. Hacking into private, secure accounts was illegal. I couldn't reveal what Public had done to Nigit's father without exposing my trespassing.

My hands arched above the keyboard. Maybe there was a way to get Public back for what they did to Nigit's dad. For what they did to teenagers. Maybe there was a way to reverse-engineer the software and turn the tables, to outsmart *the brightest minds in the country*, as the Public reps called themselves in press releases.

Just because I didn't dare reveal Public's technology didn't mean I couldn't use it to beat them at their own game.

chapter nineteen

Days later, sunlight streaked through my bedroom window and made the textbooks, computer manuals, and old socks scattered across my floor look like they'd caught fire. The bottle of Mountain Dew on my desk was empty. Public Party was open on my computer, telling me Carrie Sommers commented on Aidan's post about a brand-new zero-day vulnerability that left a computer system highly susceptible to exploit.

So glad ur getting in touch with ur vulnerability, babe!

On my *War of the Worlds* calendar (a gift from Nigit) I'd marked today's date with red ink: DANNY BEATON CONCERT. INDIANAPOLIS, EIGHT P.M. PUBLIC ANNOUNCES WINNERS, NINE P.M. My window was still cracked, the fresh air pumping into my lungs.

Outside, Roger's butt was up in the air. His head was hidden beneath a Volkswagen Jetta and wrenches were scattered on the gravel around a yellow toolbox.

Ernie, my neighbor's Labradoodle, raced across the parking lot and nosed Roger's bare leg. He kicked crazily, rolling from beneath the car and shouting a slew of swearwords while the dog's owner came running with a leash.

My world outside looked the same—or, at least, a variation on a common theme. But inside my room—no, inside *me*—something had ignited.

I clutched my buyPhone and glanced at the BFA 2.0 icon on my home screen. Once you understood the science, Public's BuyWare was remarkably simple software. The ultrasonic chord progression had gotten messed up when I smashed my phone, becoming both audible and continuous. Public had been using the software in controlled, short, inaudible bursts—intensifying the user's desire for Public products, but not enough to make them go head-over-heels in love like Lindsay and me when my phone emitted one continuous buzzing chord progression. For the BFA 2.0, I'd altered the program so that instead of the buyPhones emitting the ultrasonic chord progression using the sequence Public did (one-second bursts every thirty seconds), the phones would now emit one continuous progression. I figured this *had* to be the way to get the maximum love effect.

Instead of GPS automatically triggering the ultrasonic chord progression when the user was in the vicinity of a Public store, I compiled the code into an app format so that after download, User A could activate a hormone burst in User B by pointing her phone at him and his buyPhone and pressing a button on the screen marked IT'S ON.

I'd programmed the app so I could manually enter a guy's number and activate his phone. But I needed it to work for a girl who didn't know her dream guy's cell number. That's how I came up with pointing the phone. Once User A's phone was oriented in a direction, the antenna would identify the closest phone within forty feet.

Public was using BuyWare when users laid eyes on their products either in an actual store (which they tracked by using the phone's GPS) or in a virtual store. (As soon as a user logged in to his or her account on buyJams or Public.com, the BuyWare on his or her phone was activated. Public took the chance that—like most people—the user's phone was nearby while he or she was browsing Public or downloading music on buyJams.)

And my and Lindsay's reaction to each other had happened when the phone emitted the buzzing sound while we were the object-in-sight. So if my theory was right, User A (Lonely Girl) had to wait until the precise moment of eye contact with User B (Dream Guy) to elicit the love reaction. Activation timing worked like a phone call: Dream Guy's phone was activated with one touch of the IT'S ON button, and he experienced the hormone surge until Lonely Girl pressed IT'S OVER. He was in love with her for as long as she wanted the connection to last.

Now all I needed to do was test it.

My mind raced through experimental options and imaginary outcomes on the ride to school. Lindsay prattled on about tonight's Danny Beaton concert, debating what time we needed to leave South Bend to get to Indianapolis by eight, avoiding the topic of Public's contest altogether. She still thought I was crushed and hopeless. Still down on my luck.

Not exactly.

I kept both hands in my hoodie's pockets—one clutching my rabbit's foot, one clutching my buyPhone. As we pulled into Harrison's lot, I knew everything could change—if I let it. If I had the guts to let loose Public's sketchy software (for love, not consumerism—I wasn't violating my dad's rule if I was creating *love*), everything could be different. My app could create happiness. It could catch on like wildfire and win the contest and fix everything.

"Are you even listening to anything I'm saying?" Lindsay asked as she pulled next to Nigit's Prius. The car sighed as I stared blankly. "I overheard Jolene say Blake's dad got them front-row seats for Danny Beaton, too," she said, turning off the ignition. "Can you believe that? They're like two thousand dollars a ticket. My metabolism is cranking up when I think about the grossness of them sharing the front row with us tonight."

I cobbled together some words of reassurance as we trekked across the parking lot. My buyPhone felt like a scandal in my pocket, like I was transporting the Ebola virus, or fertilized endangered panda embryos, or Oscar results. I whipped it out to make sure the keyboard was locked for the thousandth time.

"Are you all *right*, Audrey?" Lindsay asked. The tribal

wooden beads she wore looked heavy enough to give her a neckache.

I nodded. We crossed the front lawn and entered Pothead Cliché World, where Kevin Jacobsen played Hacky Sack with his red-eyed friend Greg, who permanently kept Visine in business. Nerves pricked my skin. As long as Kevin Jacobsen had enough brain cells left to activate the dopamine reward pathway, he was the perfect target. He hadn't realized I was alive during the four years we'd gone to school together. If the BFA piqued his love interest, I'd know it was for real. Well, for real in that it could create a false emotional response. Maybe that wasn't so real. Maybe I shouldn't be doing this.

My phone was warm in my hand. There were a hundred reasons not to do it. But I'd already lost everything I wanted—what if this was the only way to get it back?

I unlocked the screen as we passed the *Eros Sleeping* statue. Lindsay was still going on about Blake & Co. crashing our front-row Danny Beaton party. "Lindsay, shut up for one sec, okay?" I whispered, pointing my phone at Kevin. Better to do it now while there were no teachers around in case I'd botched the ratio of ultrasonic emissions. "Hey, Kevin!" I called.

Kevin pulled himself from the thrill of the hacky sack. His buyPhone's outline was visible through his thin cords. His eyes passed over me, looking disappointed that I was neither (A) hot, nor (B) holding a bong.

My fingers trembled over the button. Then I pressed it.

IT'S ON

187

A green light ignited in his pants. One quick, barely visible flash.

Kevin blinked. His eyes glazed over, but that was typical.

Come on, Boyfriend App the Second. Work.

"Yo, man," his friend Greg said, cackling. Greg stood three feet away from Kevin—far enough that he wouldn't be susceptible to the sound waves coming from Kevin's phone. The more I studied the software, the more safeguards I found. Public wasn't stupid. The sound waves traveled just far enough from the phone to reach the user. At the distance a parent would stand from their teenager in the Public store, the sound waves would be ineffective.

Kevin's hand curled open, dropping the hacky sack like someone injected him with cyanide. My heart went wild in my chest as he took an unsteady step toward me. *"Audrey,"* he said, his eyes never leaving me as he stumbled across the courtyard. He stretched his arms out like I was a rare Costa Rican pot leaf. "You're so out of this world, girl," he said, moving to embrace me. He smelled like a nauseating mix of aftershave, cigarette ash, and pot. His hand gripped the side of my hoodie. His face moved closer until he and his goatee were inches from me and I could make out a tiny nick where he'd cut himself shaving. Holy *crap*.

I jumped backward, pressing IT'S OVER.

"What the freak?" Lindsay said, glancing between Kevin and me, the gold triangles on her top catching the sunlight. "Is this a joke?"

It worked.

My blood was on fire. Kevin stared at me, looking like he'd drunk a bottle of Nyquil and had no idea where he was (a familiar look for him, but this was worse than usual). "Dude!" he finally said, looking over his shoulder at Greg. "What'd you put in that stuff?"

Greg laughed that high-pitched laugh particular to potheads, the one that sounds like a witch's cackle combined with a car breaking down. "It's good, right?" Greg said.

Kevin was laughing now, too.

"Morons!" Lindsay shouted as she yanked me toward school.

My limbs twitched as we crossed Harrison's front lawn. An *app* had made a guy lust after me. This was no magazine-quiz matchup. Everything felt electric—like I could see/smell/hear/touch/taste like never before. The dewy grass that stroked my Vans sent a chill to the bones of my feet. Xander's choking motorbike in the parking lot was a chorus of punching, angry snarls assaulting my eardrums. I took in the orange-tinged maple leaves about to fall like I was seeing them for the first time, and they struck me as incredibly sad—like they were protesting their death with their beauty.

I swore I even smelled new notes of dough in South Bend's permanent Bread Smell.

I'd done it. I'd uncovered Public's dirty little secret with my most productive hacking to date. I'd tweaked the software and created an app. *The* app.

Hello, world. Hello, contest. Hello, college scholarship.

My grape Bubblicious got a second wind, zinging like a party in my mouth.

Hello, *boys.*

Here comes Audrey McCarthy.

Trog.

Hacker.

Sex object.

Inventor of the Boyfriend App 2.0.

chapter twenty

I could barely think straight as we pushed open the doors to Harrison. Boys crossed the foyer with backpacks, handbags, duffel bags . . . wearing fleece jackets, puffy down jackets, a random corduroy blazer . . . blond boys, dark-haired boys, redheads . . . tall boys, short boys, round boys, skinny boys . . . boys with freckles . . . boys with glasses . . . boys with tattoos . . . a boy with a Mohawk . . . a boy on a cell phone . . . a boy on crutches . . . a boy on a skateboard, getting yelled at by a teacher.

So many boys. So many possibilities.

"If you're going to wear flats, the hem of your pants should practically skim the floor," Lindsay was saying as we pushed through the students and stopped in front of her locker. "Tailoring is a lost art, like archery."

Sean DeFosse—captain of the debate team, early admission to Northwestern shoo-in—stood a few feet away, admiring his cherubic face in a mirror. He'd said hello to me last week for the first time since freshman year, but since my app fell from the Top Ten, he'd barely registered my existence.

I mentally entered him into my Test Group Database. Sean DeFosse = Subject #2.

Lindsay twirled the combination lock and opened her locker with a *clank*.

"Hey, Sean," I said, cocking a hip bone forward and grinning like I was posing on the red carpet in my ripped black skinny jeans.

Lindsay's expression switched from *hemlines* to *what the heck?*

I couldn't stop smiling as I waited for Sean to acknowledge my presence. I *never* would have randomly said hi to some hot guy before. But the app meant I didn't have to freak out about what said Hot Guy would think when someone like me said hi—because said Hot Guy was now just User B. The Boyfriend App 2.0 meant I didn't need a witty line to follow up my greeting; as User A, I didn't have to *do* anything. I just had to press a button, stand there, and *be*. It must have been the way Blake felt every day of her life. She was the Original User A: Just being herself was enough.

"Yeah?" Sean said. But what he meant was: *Is someone like you seriously talking to someone like me?*

It made me laugh.

IT'S ON

Sean's dark brown eyes widened. His grip tightened on the strap of his leather satchel.

"I just think that satchel is *so* girly," I said, pointing at his bag. "Don't you?"

Sean dropped the satchel onto the floor. He half kicked and half punched it into his locker. "It's dead to me," he said, running a hand through his blond hair. His hair was thick, and parted on the side, like he'd studied a brochure featuring men who work at banks.

Lindsay shut her locker and stared at me like I'd gone insane. Maybe I had. I suddenly couldn't stop laughing. This was what it felt like to be popular. To be desired. To belong.

It felt like *power.*

"*Audrey,*" Sean said, like my name was music and the hills were alive with the sound of it. "You're seriously so smart. And *beautiful.*" No one had ever told me I was beautiful other than my mom and dad, and even though Sean was hopped up on hormones, it still felt amazing.

"I try, Sean," I said, attempting to hold my ground as he stepped closer. I wasn't used to guys getting up in my grill like this. The air between us felt hot and sticky, like a piece of chocolate melting in your pocket.

Sean pushed Lindsay aside. Her mouth dropped so far her head lowered with it.

My fingers hovered above the IT'S OVER button, my nerves threatening to take over as Sean hooked a finger in the pocket of my jeans. His mouth went to my neck like we were in *Twilight* and I freaked out, my body going rigid. "Um, sorry, Sean, I—"

A crowd formed. Lindsay's friend Princess Di mouthed

OMG. Annborg squealed something in Swedish. Charlotte Davis crashed through the other kids in her wheelchair and snapped a photo.

My thumb pressed IT's OVER.

Sean's lips went lifeless on my neck. He staggered back and knocked into Lindsay. "What the—?" he said. He looked at me like I'd poisoned him, and maybe he was right. He stumbled down the hallway, zigzagging like he was still a little love-drunk.

"Audrey," Lindsay whispered.

"I'll explain later," I said quickly. Lindsay opened her mouth to say more, but I cut her off. "Now you have to trust *me*, okay?" Her green eyes blinked, rapid-fire. "I want you to be prepared to announce the Boyfriend App 2.0 at lunch." My mind was flying. I needed to upload the app to Public's site and have it ready for download. "I'll fill you in on the details later," I went on. "Just get your blog readers and followers hooked for a big announcement coming at noon."

Lindsay gave me a slow nod. Everyone around us was staring.

"He tried to make out with her," I heard Carrie's cocaptain, Martha Lee, say into her cell phone. At this rate, the news that Golden Boy Sean DeFosse had made a move on Trog Girl Audrey McCarthy would circulate through school within hours.

Which was exactly what I wanted.

chapter twenty-one

Contestant Number 21082: Audrey McCarthy. Harrison High School. South Bend, Indiana. THE BOYFRIEND APP 2.0: MAKE YOUR DREAM GUY FALL IN LOVE WITH YOU. Available for Download. Users: 1. Click <u>Here</u> for More Information.

It was live.

My current popularity ranking was 21,081, one spot above the guy who didn't download his own app.

I'd spent the morning in the computer lab after begging Ms. Bates to write me a note excusing me from morning classes. She finally caved—with the exception of my session with Mrs. Condor, which Bates insisted I go to because *mental health is a priority, especially for creative innovators,* which sounded like the title of a book.

Pick u up for lunch? Mindy texted at noon.

In lab. C u soon.

U have explaining to do. Why is everyone talking
about Debate Team Boy trying to make out w u?

I hated lying to Mindy, but I couldn't give her the
full lowdown on the BFA 2.0 without admitting what
I'd done. As we made our way to lunch, I gave her the
G-rated version of how I created my new app. Her doe-
eyed expression was placid, even though I was sure she
knew I was keeping something from her. I switched gears
to a short story she wrote, and I was going on about how
talented she was when a hand landed on my arm.

Aidan said my name, and his low voice made my breath
hitch. He and Nigit hadn't been in the lab that morning—
Channel 9 was interviewing them about their app making
the Public finals. "I was wondering if I could talk to you
about something," he said, out of breath like he'd just run
the mile in gym. Dark stubble kissed his skin. I'd never
seen him unshaven. "Um, privately," he said, glancing at
Mindy.

Mindy smiled at me over Aidan's shoulder and left us
standing there.

The air felt overoxygenated. Between Aidan's stubble
and the hormone-inducing golden ticket in my pocket,
there was zero chance of me carrying on an intelligent
conversation.

"You didn't chat me back last night," Aidan was saying
as I imagined using the BFA 2.0 on him. Being kissed by
him. *Really* kissed.

He waited for me to say something. He tugged at the
neckline of his light blue button-down when I didn't.

Unless it was ninety degrees, I rarely saw him in anything other than fisherman sweaters. The button-down, the stubble, the contest: How much could I take?

"I messaged you around midnight?" Aidan said, like a question, and I could practically feel his arms around me. I imagined him leaning forward, crushing my lips with his. I imagined him under the influence of the app, how hot and heavy we could get together, just like I'd always dreamed about it.

"Are you okay, Auds?"

I took a step away from him. It wouldn't *really* be a kiss. It would be fake. I'd be tricking him. "I—I'm fine," I said.

Harrison kids were staring at us, but Aidan didn't seem to notice. Or if he did, he didn't care. "Maybe this isn't the time or the place," he said. "But I need to talk to you about something important. It has to do with your app."

Aidan was a genius programmer. What if he'd somehow figured out what I was up to?

"I appreciate that you've paired Carrie and me," he went on.

I'm sure you do.

"And I don't want to undermine your work, but I—"

"Aidan!"

Carrie appeared out of nowhere, like a rash. And it was a game day, which meant she was decked in her cheerleading finest. "Hi, babe," she said, smashing a pom-pom into her violin case.

Aidan dropped his hand from where it touched the top of my arm. I wanted to grab and reattach it. I wanted his touch under my sweatshirt and against my skin. I wanted him all to myself.

Carrie turned. "Audrey!" she said, as if I'd materialized from thin air. "OMG. Martha told me about Sean DeFosse kissing you!" She gasped like the Blessed Mother had appeared. "You should totally go for him."

Aidan's mouth went taut at the corners, like something was wrong. He was the one hanging around with Carrie. So what did he care if Sean DeFosse had kissed me?

"Later, then?" he said. "We'll talk later."

His broad shoulders tightened beneath the thin blue cotton of his shirt. Was I right? *Did* he care?

I wanted him to more than anything.

Carrie linked her arm through Aidan's and they left me standing there alone, again.

I took in the students who passed—some ignoring me, some considering me. My phone buzzed with a text from Lindsay. U coming to lunch? My readers r ready.

12:10 p.m. Five minutes after the start of lunch, which meant the cafeteria would be filled.

I strolled into the lunchroom. Lindsay waved from our table (next to the Dumpster), where Nigit held up a 1980s poster of Michael Jackson standing on top of a car. Carrie was sitting next to Aidan for the seventh day in a row, pushing me to the edge of sanity. The rubbery smell of pasta and meat mixed with something sweet—red Jell-O, maybe?—and I scanned the kitchen for my mom: She was covering for one of her staff who called in sick that morning. Her plastic-covered head was over a tin of turkey.

She ladled gravy onto kids' plates.

I passed Sean DeFosse's table as his friend punched his shoulder and said, "There's your girlfriend!" His buddies erupted in laughter, pointing at me like I was Hester Prynne if Hester were trog trash and not just a sex kitten.

Briggs Lick sat at the table next to ours with his cousin, Andy, and the Perez twins, Marisol and Mara.

I could practically see Briggs's thigh muscles through his navy Adidas warm-up pants. His biceps were so taut he could make drinking a Capri Sun look manly.

Nerves raced through me. Coaxing in the form of my dad's Post-it notes echoed through my mind.

Dear Audrey, you can do this. Think: college scholarship. Think: grassy, rolling quads. Think: men who appreciate smart women.

They did in college, right?

Conversations chattered around me. No one seemed to notice I was standing there in the middle of the cafeteria, still as the flagpole.

Do it.

I locked my knees. "Briggs!" I shouted. My voice was high-pitched, scared. The tables surrounding me stopped their conversation to stare, but Briggs was too far away to hear.

I felt sick. I'd set something in motion and it was now or never.

"BRIGGS!"

I was a banshee.

"BRIGGS LICK!"

The foghorn that blared for fire alarms.

"BRIIIGGGS LIIIICCCK!"

Cyndi Lauper hitting a high note.

I was alive and I was screaming. Louder than Carrie screamed from the top of the pyramid, louder than Claire screamed when you told her that her bike wasn't actually a horse, louder than any high-school girl has ever screamed in any cafeteria in the fifty United States of America.

Everybody shut up.

If a pin had dropped, you would've heard it. But a pin didn't drop—did it ever in these situations?—so there was nothing except deafening silence. My shaking legs made it nearly impossible to walk. Briggs stared at me, but so did everyone else, and I needed to get closer so I didn't accidentally activate a different buyPhone in the direct line of mine. This was about Briggs. Briggs Joshua Lick II: my first French kiss, soccer hottie/jock superstar, bona fide make-the-girls-squeal Harrison Heartthrob, who just happened to be single at the present moment.

Briggs stared at me with the side of his mouth cocked into a snarl. He *still* looked hot, even snarled and confused.

My thumb hovered above the IT'S ON button when I heard it.

"You call this crap *food*?"

Jolene's shrill voice echoed across the cafeteria. I whirled around. Jolene stood in the lunch line with her cream-colored plastic tray set on the metal bars in front of her. Her blond ponytail hung halfway down her back, the ends flipping into curls. One hand was on her hip and the other gestured with a palm toward the ceiling. "What's the matter? You don't need to understand English for this job? I said: *Do you call this disgusting crap food?*"

Jolene was talking to my mother. And Blake and Joanna stood on either side of her, laughing. My mother held her silver ladle in midair, unmoving, like someone had pressed pause on a television screen. I flashed to her at home, in the kitchen, humming while she stirred hollandaise sauce. Fingers wrapped around my heart and squeezed. A curl escaped beneath my mother's hairnet. Her green eyes blinked and she glanced between Blake, Joanna, and Jolene. Then Blake reached forward with a closed fist and slammed the ladle, sending gravy flying across my mom's face.

A collective intake of breath snapped across the cafeteria.

Fire started in my feet. It rose like bile into my stomach, burning my lungs, climbing up my throat, pooling in my mouth.

"*Mom,*" I heard myself whisper.

She raised her hands to wipe her face, but it just made things worse, smearing the brown liquid across her cheeks. She looked furious as she rubbed her eyes with tight fists. She took a step back, and I could tell by the way she was blinking it was stinging her eyes and she couldn't see.

The blaze burned inside me until my entire body felt hot. Stillness settled over me. There was only the feeling of fire, and it roared so loud it quieted my racing thoughts, until suddenly, I didn't want Briggs Lick.

I wanted to get to Blake.

I wanted Xander Knight.

chapter twenty-two

I forced myself not to go to my mother.

Her coworkers surrounded her, fussing and pressing wet rags against her face. I overheard her assure them she was perfectly fine. She stepped into the small office next to the register—probably to call the Battery: I knew she'd report Blake, even if she knew the Battery would find a reason to excuse his darling niece.

Good. I didn't want her seeing this.

My legs carried me one foot in front of the other across the cafeteria, my body bathed with hundreds of eyeballs. Carrie's cheerleading friends covered their mouths. Kevin Jacobsen and the potheads gazed with watery eyes but unwavering focus. Annborg and the foreign-exchange students nudged one another, some of them unsure what had been said but sure *something* was about to go down. Sean DeFosse's friends weren't laughing anymore as I stopped inches from Xander's table.

I looked down at Xander, registering how light-brown-instead-of-black his lashes were, and the patch of stubble on his jaw he'd missed shaving. "Hi, Xander," I said, my voice a whisper. I liked the way it felt saying Xander's name out loud, the way it tasted in my mouth. So I said it again.

"Xander."

His eyes locked on mine.

I made out the tip of his buyPhone protruding from his right pocket. He blinked at me, looking unsure. I felt the weight of the cafeteria as I took out my phone and angled it at his pants.

IT'S ON

Xander's palms hit the table—*hard.* His muscles flexed as he pushed back, his chair screeching.

My heart pounded.

He leapt to his feet and came at me. His palm went to my cheek and his fingertips trailed the skin along my jaw.

"Xander?"

Blake's voice. Ringing across the cafeteria.

Xander's eyes never left mine. His hand dropped to my collarbone. *"Audrey,"* he whispered.

I tried to catch my breath, but his hands were at my waist now, pulling me against him. He covered my mouth with his and suddenly we were kissing. We were *kissing.* Xander Knight was kissing me. I was kissing Xander Knight. And, okay, so maybe the kiss didn't live up to everything I'd fantasized about during freshman year, but it was a *kiss,* and I hadn't been kissed in so long, and it felt so good.

204

"Stop it!"

She was close—I guessed about ten feet away—but Xander was so busy kissing me like I'd never been kissed— like no one had ever been kissed, not even the contestants on *The Bachelor*—that he didn't seem to register the sound of her voice. His lips traveled from my mouth to my neck to my collarbone. I tried to keep up with him, but it was like making out with a ten-mouthed beast from Xion: His hands were clawing me everywhere, and wherever his hands weren't, his mouth was.

I let out a crazed scream—partly for effect, partly because I couldn't help it. Xander's hands went beneath my butt, lifting me so my legs straddled his waist. He looked at me and I looked at him—staring into the gold-flecked hazel eyes I half pretended to obsess over with Mindy.

"XANDER DAVID KNIGHT!"

But it was like Blake's voice only spurred him on. He jumped onto the lunch table cradling me in one arm and lowered me onto my back. I stared at his handsome features, but I couldn't focus on him. Aidan's face flashed through my mind. He was only a few tables away.

"I love you, Audrey McCarthy," Xander whispered into my ear. "I always have."

I didn't want Aidan to get the wrong idea—even if he was with Carrie. But I needed to do this.

"Say it louder, Xander," I begged.

"I LOVE YOU, AUDREY McCARTHY! I ALWAYS—"

Blake's fist connected with Xander's mouth. She jumped

205

onto the table and tried to tear Xander from me. "You are nothing without me, you impoverished tramp!" she shrieked at Xander. "Get off her!"

Xander's hands were flailing as she dug her fingernails into his bicep and all I could think was: *Xander Knight is poor?*

"I love her!" Xander shouted, diving back on top of me like a fumbled football.

Gasps sounded across the cafeteria. Then the cheering started.

I squirmed farther beneath Xander to avoid Blake's fists, scared she was going to *Single White Female* my eyeball with her stiletto. Her black stockings snagged on the corner of the table as she drew her knee back and nailed Xander's crotch.

"Ow!" Xander grabbed his injury and rolled off me.

I was still on my back—not a wonderful position now that Blake was hovering over me. "I will *end* you," she said through gritted teeth. She cocked a fist.

Lindsay's tribal beads flashed turquoise and yellow balls in the space between Blake's fist and my face.

"Not while wearing knockoff Gucci, you won't," Lindsay said. She jumped. Her arms cinched Blake's waist and the two of them went flying off the table. I dove after them. Jolene and Joanna raced toward us with Aidan and Nigit close behind. Everyone in the cafeteria was on his or her feet. I was trying to pry Blake's grip from Lindsay's hair when I heard it.

"Attenshayn, Harrison soodents!"

I whirled around. Mindy had climbed onto our lunch table. Her patent-leather Mary Janes *clickedy-clack-clack*ed across the table like tap shoes. She lifted her chin and brushed her caramel waves off her shoulder.

"The Bo-friend App 2.0 is now availabill for download! Every girl can gayt her dream guy like Ohdrey McCarthy!"

A roar exploded across the cafeteria.

"Go, Mindy!" Carrie shouted, which prompted her cheerleading teammates to shout Mindy's name, too.

Lunch aides scrambled through the standing ovation to break apart Blake and Lindsay, who rolled across the linoleum. Aidan and Nigit tried to keep Joanna and Jolene from jumping on Lindsay's back. Xander recovered from Blake's knee and crawled across the floor in my direction. "Down, boy!" I shouted as he pawed my legs.

"Cheer, cheer for Audrey!" Carrie screamed. No matter how jealous of her I was—I could've kissed her in that moment. Everyone was suddenly screaming my name: "Audrey! Audrey! AUDREY!" I turned and glanced over the heads of my clapping, cheering classmates. My mother stood in her same position behind the lunch line. She wasn't wearing her hairnet now and someone must have helped her wipe her face clean. Her light green eyes caught mine. She ran a hand through her hair. She shook her head slowly and gave me one of her *What am I going to do with you?* looks.

Then she started clapping.

"Break it up!" Hot Gym Coach shouted as he raced across the cafeteria in his maroon-colored Umbros. The lunch ladies got between the Martin sisters and Lindsay, and HGC manhandled Blake and Xander. "Sit! Now!" he shouted. "Martins, Gurung, Fanning, Bailey, McCarthy!" He managed to line all eight of us up on opposite sides of a lunch table. "Who started this?" he demanded. His tan hands were clenched and rugged from doing athlete stuff like coaching or rowing a canoe. *"Audrey?"*

Of course he blamed me with Blake sitting right there, her pouting lips so glossy I could practically see my reflection.

Blake pointed at me. "It was Abby, Taylor," she whined, still breathing heavy. I'd graduated from Aubrey to Abby. And *Taylor*? Who called a teacher by his first name?

HGC shot Blake a look, but she faked a whimper and he melted.

Aidan's blue button-down was ruffled from intercepting Blake and Co.'s attacks on Lindsay. He caught my glance. A smile played on his lips.

Nigit's white glove was smeared with a raspberry-colored lipstick that matched Joanna's mouth, and I recognized the eight tiny indentations on his index finger as teeth marks. He looked freaked out—probably because he'd never been in trouble in the history of his educational career. Jolene sat next to her sister, staring at me beneath a puffed, swelling eye socket.

"Blake attacked my aunt Marian!" Lindsay said, smacking a hand on the lunch table. Her wooden necklace had broken, and now only a few multicolored beads remained around her neck, like a half-eaten candy choker.

HGC restrained Xander, who was practically panting. I waved my fingers suggestively and Xander lunged again.

"Enough, Audrey!" HGC said, slamming his forearm against Xander's chest.

I glanced around Xander's flailing body to see nearly every girl in the cafeteria bent over her buyPhone. (This time, I'd coded the app so only female users could download it.) Annborg Alsvik was reading the Boyfriend App instructions out loud: "Point your phone at your Dream Guy. As soon as he makes eye contact with you, press the IT'S ON button. To end his obsession with you, press IT'S OVER." She translated this for another foreign-exchange student who only knew how to say *hello*, *good-bye*, *cheese*, and *Beyonce*.

The next second, Annborg's voice was drowned out by a girl screaming, "What's up now, Briggs Lick?"

CRACK!

chapter twenty-three

I turned to see Briggs Lick's porcelain lunch plate in two jagged pieces next to his feet. He sprung from his chair. He darted across the cafeteria, dodging kids and chairs like he was on the soccer field.

The student government president (I forget her first name—but her campaign buttons read ELECT RIC-hardson) clutched her buyPhone with both hands and pointed it at his crotch.

Briggs raced toward her. Then he stopped, standing tall before Richardson. He ran a hand over her smooth black skin, and pressed his lips against hers. Richardson arched back and kicked her heel up like an actress getting kissed in a movie.

Girls. Freaked. Out.

In a wave of chaos they jumped from their chairs and scrambled across the cafeteria, forming amoebalike clusters around the hottest guys. Water-polo boy Wes Clark, who smelled like chlorine, but had modeled as a child in California, flattened himself against a window as a dozen screaming girls vied for eye contact.

"Wes!"

"Over here, Wes!"

Theresa Rexford (who everyone called T. Rex on account of her name and her masculine voice) secured eye contact with her booming "WES CLARK!" and stood there, her mouth shaped like an O, as Wes swam through the crowd and Frenched her. Sara Oaks, a mousy-haired girl who was always apologizing for things out of her control (like the weather, or a zit) pointed her buyPhone at viola player Robby Timson, who sat alone with wide eyes primed for Apptivation. "Sorry, Robby!"

Across the cafeteria, Wallflower Amanda Thompson fainted as Key Club vice president Max Laudano came at her with outstretched arms. (Thank God he caught her: I didn't need Lindsay to tell me a fainting injury would be bad press.) Goth Girl made eye contact with a Phish Head, and moments later they were making out on the lunchroom floor. Barron Feldman's IBS meant he ran to the bathroom whenever he was nervous, but he seemed to be holding it together, even with the hormone flood apptivated by Lindsay's friend Princess Di. Barron unwrapped Di's head scarf and performed some kind of scarf show by rubbing it around the small of her back before he kissed her.

The eight of us stared at the mayhem, unbelieving. HGC actually looked scared. Blake scrambled for her buyPhone.

"Put that away, Blake," HGC said, restraining Xander with both arms.

"Not on your life, Taylor," Blake snarled. "What've you done this time, Angela?" she asked as she downloaded the Boyfriend App.

Something in her voice made me shudder.

Aidan nudged me and pointed to our lunch table, where Carrie stood on a chair and pointed her phone at Gary Cary (why do parents do that?), a male cheerleader on her squad. Gary knelt to one knee. At first I thought he was proposing (which would mean she'd be Carrie Cary if they got married), but then he flipped both palms up and Carrie climbed on board. He threw her into the air, where she executed a backflip with a twist, landed expertly in his arms, and closed her eyes while he kissed her.

My mouth was open—so was Carrie's—as I glanced at Aidan. I raised my voice so he could hear me over the chaos. "I'm sorry! I didn't mean to hurt you!"

But Aidan was smiling. He leaned in so close I could smell him: a perfect mix of fresh air and Ivory soap. "I don't really like Carrie," he said into my ear. "I went with it because I didn't want to make your app look bad. But I've tried breaking up with her, like, seven times, and she always interrupts with a story about cheerleading." He grinned. "It turns out cheerleading *is* a nuanced sport."

I started laughing and couldn't stop. Aidan cracked up, too, and then we were both doubled over, clutching our stomachs, until a whistle blared. I glanced up to see the Battery in a crap-colored brown suit blowing a whistle like

212

we were animals in a zoo.

"Harrison students!" the Battery screamed. "Sit down! Right now!"

But no one listened.

Zack Marks, the deer killer, ran by with his camouflage shirt unbuttoned to reveal his peach ballet leotard. "I'll hunt you forever!" he said as he jumped into the waiting arms of the basketball player with stitches. They dropped to the floor and started making out.

"Audrey McCarthy started this," HGC told the Battery.

I pressed IT'S OVER and deapptivated Xander—I didn't want to get him in trouble now that the Battery was here. He slumped into a seat and looked dazed.

The Battery glared at me. "What's going on here, Audrey?"

I straightened. "Well, you see," I said, gesturing at the mania surrounding us. "I've created an app."

"Cut the crap!" HGC said. I was just close enough to see his hairline hinted at premature male pattern baldness. "She's antagonizing students," he started. But right then Glenda (our eighty-year-old librarian's aide) scuttled through the cafeteria and cried out, "Taylor!"

Glenda was holding her buyPhone. I smelled her lilac scent as she got closer, and saw the Boyfriend App's graphics bounce across the screen.

I held my breath. Just because Public had been targeting teens who were more susceptible didn't mean the software wouldn't work on adults.

Glenda pointed her phone at Hot Gym Coach.

No. Way.

HGC's muscular forearms twitched. His eyes went wide as he watched her shuffle in her long, flowered skirt. "Glenda?" he said. Lime-colored barrettes clipped Glenda's white hair into mini ponytails. HGC shoved aside the Battery like he was a chess piece in the way of his victory, and sprinted at Glenda. He took her wrinkled hand and pressed it against his chest. Glenda's pointy fingernails were painted that color every old lady wears—shimmery mauve—and she dug them into his soccer jersey and said, "Yes, Taylor?" like this was all totally normal, like this was the way our gym teacher always asked about how to find a reference book.

HGC scooped Glenda into his arms and kissed her smack on the lips.

"Coach?" the Battery said, his mouth agape.

HGC and Glenda made out as color drained from the Battery's face. "It's a wonderful app you've created, Audrey!" Glenda called over HGC's shoulder between kisses.

Mindy was suddenly at my side, linking her arm through mine. "How did you do this, Oh-drey?" she said, laughing. Her dark eyes looked lit from within. I hadn't seen her like this since we were kids and there was no Blake making fun of her, no exasperated teachers asking her to *please repeat the sentence correctly.*

The Battery turned. "Audrey, I want you to tell me right now what—" But he stopped midsentence when he saw Charlotte Davis riding her wheelchair at us. Joel

Norris was balanced on the armrests, kissing Charlotte's collarbone. Charlotte veered left and they crashed into the Battery. The impact folded him into the wheelchair, too, and then the wheelchair sped across the lunchroom with the Battery trying to tear apart Joel and Charlotte.

"See ya later, Bawh-tery!" Mindy shouted. We were laughing as we elbowed our way back to our lunch table, until we saw Blake pointing her phone at Nigit.

"No!" I screamed.

"You're just in time, Augusta," Blake said to me, her tweezed eyebrows arching like accent marks. She smirked at Lindsay, Mindy, and me. "Eye for an eye, right, girls?"

Nigit's head snapped up. His white glove shot to the ceiling and he dance-moved toward Blake.

"Nigit!" Lindsay screamed.

Blake laughed in Lindsay's face as Nigit pawed at her. I was trying to pry Nigit's phone from his grip, when Annborg Alsvik said, "Over here, Blake!"

Blake's body contorted into one of her *Vogue* poses and she fixed her eyes on Annborg with a smoldering, camera-worthy stare. But Annborg wasn't angling her phone up like she did when she took Blake's picture. She was pointing it at her. And the Boyfriend App's graphics were flashing across the screen.

"I love you, Blake!" Annborg screamed as she pressed a button.

Blake's arms dropped to her sides. She took one giant lunge forward and tore Annborg's light pink cardigan down the middle. Little pearly buttons popped from the cashmere and clacked onto the floor. Annborg started screaming, "God Bless Blake and America!" over and over. Blake ripped Annborg's red-rimmed glasses from her face and threw them on the floor, stomping them with her heel. She clamped two hands onto Annborg's shoulders and kissed her on the mouth.

Nigit tried to claw between Blake and Annborg, but an alarm sounded, followed by torrents of water pouring from the ceiling. Mascara ran over Lindsay's cheeks and water beaded on her chemically-treated hair. Aidan was suddenly at my side, drenched and pulling me to safety beneath a table. Water gushed over the sides of the table like a sheet, hiding us from the surrounding turmoil. I snuggled next to Aidan. My heart pounded in my throat like I'd swallowed our little drummer boy Christmas ornament. He leaned closer and for a second I swore he was going to kiss me. But then he put his hands into my wet hair and made it spiky, laughing. "What did you *do*, Auds?" he asked, his navy eyes shining. His hands dropped to my shoulders, warming my skin. I inched closer. Could I do it?

I was impossibly nervous, way more so than making out with Xander in front of my entire school.

Aidan looked at me with wide eyes. A drop of water fell from his thick lashes. He opened his mouth like maybe he was going to say something, but then Goth Girl slid beneath our table. The sprinklers had washed makeup from her face and she was barely recognizable except for her dog collar. Aidan made room for her to hide with us as water puddled in the plastic seats and slicked the floors.

Whoever had activated the sprinkler system was soaking the lunchroom, soaking the students, soaking the buyPhones . . .

Deactivating the Boyfriend App.

chapter twenty-four

"*Sugar, you're the one, our life is fun, in the sun, come on let's run . . . away!*"

Claire's tiny fingers interlocked with mine. My jade polished nails mixed with her red ones like Christmas M&Ms.

"*Do you wonder, how it will be, girl, when the lights are off and it's just you and me . . .*"

Danny Beaton's lyrics reverberated through the speakers until my body felt like it was being attacked with music and sound. I could just make out the dyed blond tips of his brown fauxhawk over the warm bodies that danced and jostled us. I saw a similar hairdo at the edge of the stage, and when we got closer, I saw it was a lion, not really doing anything, just sitting in a cage and licking its paws. Light on the back wall of the stage gave the effect of a rainstorm, and illuminated two bodies grinding behind a curtain, like shadows making out. Lindsay and I rolled our eyes at each other above Claire's head when unicyclists sped across the stage juggling My Little Ponies with their tails on fire.

"It's devastating not documenting tonight for my readers!" Lindsay shouted over the music, looking up at the giant TV screens above the stage. In some multimillion-dollar partnership, Danny Beaton's concert was being broadcast live on YouTube. "Poor Loulou de la Falaise. When I think of how she's coping with the water damage . . . even if she does dry out, will she be the same?"

I checked my phone. (I'd stuffed it into the quality water-resistant fabric of my Jockey sports bra, so it made it through the sprinklers unharmed.) Twenty-three minutes until the winners would be announced.

The Battery had called off the Public app contest for Harrison students after the BFA 2.0 debacle in the lunchroom. Nigit tried to argue I was the only one who should be disqualified. (Thanks, Nigit!) But rational thought (the very thing Public tried to strip from us with their software) said there was no way the Battery could forbid us to compete in a nationwide competition that wasn't even dependent on being enrolled in high school.

"It's you and me . . . together we will be . . . never apart . . . one heart . . . one soul . . ."

I handed over my phone so Lindsay could update her blog. We'd spent the three and a half–hour car ride with Lindsay dictating Twitter and *FBM* updates for the Boyfriend App, and recounting the G-rated version of today's events to Claire, who'd already heard murmurings

219

among her elementary-school friends with older siblings. We'd rabidly checked my standing on Public's website during the ride, too. My numbers were climbing, but I was still in the thousands, not even close to getting into the Top Ten—let alone the number one spot.

"Danny!" Claire screamed as we neared our front-row seats. She practically panted at the sight of him. A uniformed usher shined a light down our row and I caught Blake's dark figure silhouetted. Her low-cut V-neck top showed off a black sequined bra. Her hair was pulled into a ponytail that started near the crown of her head, and made her look like Cleopatra.

Claire stopped short. "You said she wasn't going to be here," she said to Lindsay, her voice terrified.

"What?" Lindsay called over the music.

"I said our life is fun and when we run . . . away! We'll be together, forever . . ."

Danny Beaton's red-and-white striped shirt hung loose over tight-fitting jeans tucked into high-top sneakers with flashing lights. He gyrated across the stage as backup dancers in black bodysuits clawed at his legs. The lion took a dump in its cage.

Claire's palms were suddenly wet against mine. She tried to push back the way we came and it took both Lindsay and me to restrain her sixty pounds of fury. "She's here!" Claire screamed, pointing down our row. Her body was a live wire twitching against our grip. Lindsay and I exchanged a glance. *Joelle Martin,* Lindsay mouthed.

Lindsay smoothed a hand over Claire's light hair. We'd

spent an hour braiding it just right—two French braids that crossed her head and wound into a bun in the back with little wisps sticking out: exactly like the picture she'd ripped from *Teen Vogue*.

I glanced down our row. Just beyond Blake, Joanna and Jolene hoisted Joelle up to get a better look at Danny Beaton. Joelle's honey-blond hair matched her sisters'—as did the hostile look on her face when she turned and locked eyes with Claire, and then mouthed, *Freak*.

Claire buried her head against me.

"Forever we'll be together, forever in any weather, forever isn't far away!"

Forever *was* far away by definition—but who was I to argue with Danny Beaton? I crouched until I was Claire's height. "I have an idea," I told her. "Do you trust me?"

I stretched out my hand and she took it.

Nerves flooded me as we maneuvered through the darkness to our seats. Maybe the Boyfriend App was meant for this one thing—this one night where Lindsay, Claire, and I could make something amazing happen—*a chance at something big,* Lindsay had said that night at Madame Bernese's.

I glanced at Claire's wide green eyes—the ones that matched Lindsay's, the ones that matched mine. Lindsay and Claire were my family. They mattered way more than any contest or scholarship. If the Boyfriend App could give Claire one big—*huge*—night, then it was worth it.

"We're going to shine our light . . . we're going to shine what's inside . . ."

Darkness fell as Danny Beaton sang the opening verse to his hit song. The audience went wild as a single spotlight bathed him in violet-colored light.

"I need my phone!" I yelled above the music.

Lindsay handed it over. We were so close to the stage I could see bodyguards dressed in black behind the maroon-colored velvet curtains. Stage managers carried clipboards and talked into radios. I made out the rectangular outline in Danny Beaton's pocket. (Part of Danny Beaton's deal with Public was that he Tweeted from his buyPhone between songs.)

"Everyone has a light . . . inside . . . and they have to let it shine."

The violet color onstage morphed into a shimmery, golden haze.

I pointed my phone at Danny, but I couldn't do anything until he made eye contact. Dozens of screaming girls filled the front rows. I wasn't sure how I could . . .

A glittery pink color flashed in the darkness a few seats down our aisle. It was the color I'd created by blending hot pink with fluorescent white, and I'd recognize it anywhere: the Boyfriend App's heart graphic.

"And when you let it shine . . . you're divine . . ."

Blake lifted her buyPhone and smirked at me. It was covered in a shimmery gold case I recognized as an exclusive for the buyPhone 17.5—just released this week. The Boyfriend App's graphics flew over the screen.

Blake was laughing as her fingers danced across the keys. She pointed her phone at Danny.

No!

"So, girl, you've got the key . . ."

Danny dance-stepped closer to Blake. He twirled a half circle and sang with his back facing the audience.

"Just be yourself . . . no one else . . . it's who you're meant to be . . ."

He clapped a hand against his thigh and spun around. He was moving back in my direction when a black sequined bra hit him in the face. I turned to see Blake yank her V-neck top up to her chin and flash her boobs.

No freaking way.

Danny didn't miss a beat. He linked a finger through the bra strap and twirled it above his head. He was turning toward Blake and her fully loaded buyPhone when another bra hit him smack on the forehead. It was enormous and beige—a total Mom Bra. I turned to see a forty-something lady screaming her head off, topless. A hot-pink string number sailed through the air, followed by a padded white one, and then a navy mesh one. Blake had ignited a Bra Riot. They fired at the stage from all angles—big ones, little ones, lacy ones, satin ones, black ones, white ones, and a neon-yellow one.

Blake still pointed her phone, but she was stomping her silver platform sandal, too, and looked pissed. Danny twirled the bras around his fingers and improvised a new dance routine, crooning, "Whoa, ladies!" into the microphone between verses. Girls screamed at the top of their lungs and jumped up and down. I'd never seen so many boobs.

I slammed my hand against my pocket. Something

scratched my fingertip. I grabbed the warm tuft of navy fur and cradled my rabbit's foot in my palm. The Notre Dame logo caught the hazy light from the stage and I remembered his face—the way it softened as he passed the rabbit's foot into my open hands. The way his smile made me feel like I was everything.

This will bring you luck.

I wound my arm back and threw it. The navy crescent arced through the light—a dark moon sailing through a golden sky. Danny opened his palm and his fingers closed around the logo key chain. The rabbit's foot danced in the spotlight. He glanced down at his hand. His face broke into a smile before he caught my gaze.

IT'S ON

Danny's feet went rubbery and he stumbled mid-dance move. He looked down at me with wide, blinking brown eyes. The music screeched to a halt.

I raised my fingers and gave a little wave.

Hi, Danny, I mouthed.

Danny jumped from the stage and nearly knocked me to the ground. A shocked *whoosh* sounded across the stadium. Cameramen rushed down the stairs and into the audience. Their creaturelike black lenses attacked us from all sides, leering in our faces.

Claire stood frozen, staring at Danny. Lindsay's mouth dropped, staring at me.

Danny's hands wrapped around my waist. Sweat glistened over his face and beaded his peach-colored stage makeup. I was close enough to see the white microphone

224

bud in his ear, and the silver St. Bernadette medallion on his leather rope necklace. My heart pounded as he pulled me to him. The audience erupted. I turned my head before he could kiss me, and spoke into his ear. "See the little girl next to me?"

Danny turned to Claire, his breath coming in ragged gasps. The audience was cheering louder now. Stage managers barked into their headsets. Big guys dressed all in black barreled down the stairs on the side of the stage and closed in on us.

I ran my fingers through Danny's fauxhawk. "I want you to take her onstage and sing the rest of this song to her," I said. "And if you sing it better than ever, I *might* consider kissing you."

"But I can't sing it better than ever," Danny said, devastation washing over his face. "I'm lip-synching."

Oh, Lord. "Just lip-synch your best. 'Kay, Danny?"

Danny glanced at Claire. It was the first night my aunt Linda let her wear "makeup," and her little lips were painted pink from the $1.99 strawberry gloss Lindsay and I found at CVS.

He reached out his hand and Claire took it. Her green eyes were saucers staring up at him. The audience screamed. Danny hoisted Claire onto the stage and her image was broadcast on six YouTube-logoed television screens hanging from the rafters. The world was watching, which meant so were Claire's third-grade classmates.

Lindsay grabbed my hand and didn't let go. "Go, Claire!" she screamed, jumping and waving crazily.

Danny led Claire toward center stage. He squinted through the lights to see me, and I gave him an approving nod. Claire's pink capri pants were tucked into her glossy riding boots. Her crop was wedged into the top of the right one. Her face split into a grin as Danny twirled her and the music started up again. I looked at the television screens to see a shot of the audience freaking out and holding up signs like BE MY PROM DATE, DANNY! The camera panned back to Danny and Claire in the center of the stage. Danny's sneakers flashed as he kissed Claire's cheek.

I couldn't stop myself. I glanced down our row.

Blake and the three Martin sisters stared at Claire in disbelief. Jolene whispered something in Joanna's ear and Joanna shook her head. If envy had a face, it was Joelle Martin's. And then there was Blake, who covered her boobs with her top and looked on the verge of exploding.

Danny took both of Claire's hands in his and started singing.

"So, girl, it's time to let it shine, that light of yours, it's all within you . . ."

He got down on his knees like the Bachelor proposing, and sang the rest of the song to Claire while the audience whooped and cheered.

"Let the truth reveal itself. Be the light. Enter the realm of truth."

My little cousin stared at him for the duration of the song like they were the only two people in the world. The closing piano notes tinkled through the sound system. Lindsay and I held hands and hopped up and down with the rest of the audience, screaming Claire's name. Endorphins flooded my system—*naturally*—sans Public software. I'd pulled it off. And maybe the Boyfriend App wasn't going to win the contest tonight—but it changed us. It brought Nigit and Lindsay together. It gave Claire the singular moment every teen and preteen across America dreamed about. And it changed me: It showed me my power to create.

Claire tapped Danny's shoulder. She stood on tiptoes and said something into his ear, gesturing with her tiny hands as she spoke. She turned, pointed at me, and smiled.

Danny moved to the end of the stage and pushed off with one hand beneath him, one reaching out to me. The cameras were on me and I tried not to think about how nervous my face must've looked. Up close I saw one of Danny's eyes had blue mixed in with the brown. I breathed in cologne that smelled like sandalwood. I thought he was going to try to kiss me again, but instead, he lifted me onto the stage. I could barely think straight with the golden light swirling around us, and the deafening screams from the audience. Danny inhaled and his microphone made it sound like a hurricane. He waited until the cheers died down and said, "I've just been informed that the girl of my dreams is the very sexy programmer Audrey McCarthy, creator of the Boyfriend App, now available for download at the Public app store."

My heart stopped.

When it started, it pounded with a wild fury, making up for lost beats.

Danny leaned forward and kissed me in front of all

of Indianapolis, Indiana, the United States, planet Earth. He kissed me as the BFA's heart-shaped graphic flashed in shimmery pink bursts across the dark stadium. He kissed me as Claire stood on the side of the stage and clapped. He kissed me as YouTube reached a record number of viewers around the world. He kissed me as a snarling Blake tried to climb onstage and was escorted from the premises by security. He kissed me as the Boyfriend App exploded in popularity—momentarily shutting down Public's site as hundreds of thousands of people downloaded.

He kissed me as I won the contest.

chapter twenty-five

9:39 p.m.

NewsNow.com

Chaos has been reported around the world as women download Audrey McCarthy's Boyfriend App. Though the exact functionality of McCarthy's app is unclear, no one seems to care once the object of their affection is in their arms.

9:47 p.m.

TechTastic.com

Might anyone be wondering how it is the Boyfriend App functions? Or is our world so consumed with being loved we're willing to forget how and why it's happening? Here at TechTastic, we plan to dig deeper with a test group of buyPhone users. Observation is being assembled, and testing will start tomorrow at 6:00 a.m.

10:09 p.m.

ItaliaNews.net

Translated by Giancarlo Fabrizio

The Polizia di Stato have temporarily shut down parts of Venice's canals due to social unrest. Rumors of a youth revolt have circulated; however, no violence has been reported. Rather, the unrest is romantic in nature. Amorous teens have taken to the streets and waterways in growing numbers, making main traffic pathways impassable. Announcements and alternate routes will be posted as soon as updates are available.

10:48 p.m.

ParisianDaily.net

Translated by Anais Moreau

Pandemonium has erupted in the City of Love as Parisian teenagers swarmed the streets and nightclubs in the early morning hours armed with American Audrey McCarthy's Boyfriend App. PR rep Lindsay Fanning says, "Audrey's creation is poised to change the rules of love as we know them."

Vive l'amour!

11:31 p.m.

TeensBlogToo.com

By Xi Liang

We here at TeensBlogToo wish to rescind last week's criticism of Audrey McCarthy's Boyfriend App. The BFA 2.0

"Get Your Dream Guy" RULES! I can speak from experience: I just made out with the formerly elusive Jason VanDercar on the hood of his Mercedes.
Hotness Factor: 10!

12:09 a.m.
Twitter.com
@DannyBeaton: parts of tonight's concert a blur . . . guess that's what happens when you're #InTheMoment performing. Catch ya later, Indianapolis!

1:11 a.m.
FashionBecomesMe.com
Just now arriving home with my cousin, YouTube sensation Audrey McCarthy, creator of the Boyfriend App, winner of a $200K tax-free college scholarship. Audrey can barely form words! So cute. She shook her head the whole way home (for like three hours) and asked, "Is this really happening?" over and over! Right now she and my little sis are dancing around the parking lot of her apt. building (see pic below) singing "Ignite the Light."

In an exclusive interview with *Fashion Becomes Me*, Audrey says, "Thank you so much to everyone who downloaded the Boyfriend App. I am so grateful."

More fashion coverage from Danny Beaton's concert coming tomorrow . . . stay tuned!

2:32 a.m.

WorldNews.net

"We were just getting started!"

It's a cry heard echoed in different languages across the world as Public removes the Boyfriend App from its server and—even worse—remotely disables the app from buyPhones.

2:36 a.m.

Twitter.com

@AlaskaGirlBrrr: WTF, Public? Finally making out w my Dream Eskimo and you pull the plug on the BFA? Now my DE won't even share his hot chocolate w me. BRRR!

3:03 a.m.

ChannelThirteenNews.com

"I tasted love, and now it's gone," says a tear-streaked seventeen-year-old Florida girl who asked to remain anonymous.

One thing's certain: For lovesick women everywhere, the return of the Boyfriend App can't come soon enough.

4:21 a.m.

Public.com

PRESS RELEASE FROM THE DESK OF ALEC PIERCE, PUBLIC CEO

RE: MOBILE APPLICATION CONTEST

Regarding user concerns over all apps no longer available for download or use on buyPhones: Public has always intondcd to discontinue the use of free apps from our teen creators once the winners were announced. It's the only fair way to enter into negotiations with the winners regarding compensation for apps downloaded. Please check back for more information and the return of your favorite apps after we convene with our winners here at Public headquarters.

chapter twenty-six

The *Today Show* anchor wore a crisp white button-down, green wool trousers, and pearls the size of eyeballs. I couldn't stop staring. It was so weird to see someone my mom watched every day on TV standing *right in front of me* at Harrison High. Just yesterday I'd seen her present a segment on the skin benefits of choline in an egg-yolk face mask, and then the concert happened and here she was, twenty-four hours later, about to interview me.

We stood in front of the HARRISON HIGH SCHOOL letter-board sign as a guy with a big white sheet tested the light against our faces. Snow fell in airy flakes that didn't stick. The Anchor was saying, "I can't believe it's snowing," and I was thinking, *Sometimes it does that.*

"Are we introing the students first?" the Anchor asked a dark-haired man around Brad Pitt's age who introduced himself as the producer, and made a strong case for the word *distinguished*. A makeup artist brushed powder over the Anchor's nose. The Anchor was more wrinkly in person but just as beautiful.

"Students first," the Distinguished Producer repeated, not looking up from his buyPhone. "And then their teacher."

Ms. Bates stood tall next to my mother, wearing a chic black sweater over silk pants and stiletto boots. The Battery stood next to Bates, looking like a telephone pole in his brown suit. He seemed to have forgotten how much he hated me just yesterday.

"We're live in sixty," the Distinguished Producer said to the Anchor and five guys congregating near a dark green van. A twenty-something guy in a T-shirt and jeans carried a long microphone with a fuzzy black thing at the end. He held it a few inches above the Anchor's head as she studied a blue cue card. Then the Anchor took off her leather gloves and tossed them to a nervous-looking college-age girl, who dropped them into the mud and acted like it was the end of the world.

I glanced at Harrison's front lawn, where nearly every student (four hundred in each class: sixteen hundred total) stood screaming and waving homemade signs. I scanned the crowd for Mindy and spotted her on the ledge of the *Eros Sleeping* statue waving a white poster with red bubble letters: HARRISON TROGS DO IT BEST! Blake and the Martin sisters were nowhere to be seen. Xander stood off to the side with Barron Feldman, who held up a sign that said HARRISON LAX PLAYS STANFORD INVITATIONAL 2–MORROW!

WE WILL KICK EVERYONE'S A$$ INTO THE OCEAN! P.S.
PUBLIC PARTY MESSAGE ME (BARRON FELDMAN) IF YOU LIVE
IN CALIFORNIA AND YOU'RE A HOT GIRL BUT NOT PRUDE.

Seriously, Barron?

A bulky camera loomed in front of me. "You'll stare right into this lens when you give your answers," the Distinguished Producer said. The nervous-looking college-age girl handed him a coffee and he winced like it burned.

I tried to practice in my head how to answer the Anchor's questions without stuttering or looking dumb. *Well, I've always loved Public.* No, too fangirl. *I'm thrilled America loves the Boyfriend App.* Too kiss-up. *Well, I amped up secret software already in place by Public—software Public stole from my friend's neurologist father by blackmailing him.* Yeah, right.

The nervous-looking college-age girl was back with a buyPhone. She held it out to the Distinguished Producer and mouthed *Alec Pierce.* "Hello, Mr. Pierce," the Distinguished Producer said into the phone. "Of course we plan to ask her that." The Distinguished Producer's features contracted as he listened to whatever Alec Pierce was saying. "I see," he said. He disconnected his call and stalked across the grass to the Anchor, gesturing toward me. I fidgeted with the hem of my green Old Navy sweater (the one I saved for special occasions because it made my eyes look sort of nice). Then I adjusted the silver necklace Lindsay lent me so it wouldn't catch on the tiny microphone pinned near the strap of my sports bra. The Anchor smiled at me as the Distinguished Producer spoke into her ear, but it didn't look real. She'd probably smiled at hundreds of people she'd interviewed during her career, and she'd probably forget today in a few weeks, when she was back in New York City interviewing someone else. But I never would.

Cold air froze my fingertips. I shifted my weight in my mom's gold ballet flats.

"You kids ready?" the Distinguished Producer asked. He didn't wait for a reply. "Here we go!" he shouted. "Live in five-four-three-two . . ."

The Anchor's voice moved over words like fingers on a piano. "With results that shocked the nation: Public Corporation has announced two grand prize winners: Audrey McCarthy, creator of the Boyfriend App, winner of the Most Popular App. And Aidan Bailey and Nigit Gurung, cocreators of PhilanthrApp, winner of the Most Innovative App." She cocked an eyebrow. "The kicker? All three students attend Harrison High School in South Bend, Indiana."

I glanced at Aidan. His hands were jammed into the pockets of his dark green chinos. He stood ramrod straight with the kind of forced smile first-graders have on Picture Day. Nigit appeared oddly chill in a three-piece suit with an iridescent silver bow tie that looked like a minnow. The red light flashed on the camera angled at us. "Let's meet the tech-savvy students," the Anchor said. "Audrey, can you explain what it is about the Boyfriend App that captivated buyPhone users around the world?"

The first day without my rabbit's foot and here I was on live national television. Blood pooled in my feet. I had the sense of sinking into the cold grass. *Just talk, Audrey. Just make words.* I felt my mouth open—a good start. I cleared my throat and revved my vocal cords like an engine.

"Everyone wants to fall in love," I sputtered. "It's a universal desire." My voice was a combination of a whisper and a croak, but I kept going. "Love is what everyone wants to feel. Including me," I said into the camera's glassy lens. I saw my reflection, and smoothed down a dark strand of hair spiking up straight like it was giving America the finger. "So if there's an app that can get the guy you love to love you back, I think that's an app people will want. Um. So that's why I made it. And now I get to go to college because of it. So I'm really happy." *Rein it in, trog.* "Thank you," I said, like I'd been giving a toast and not an interview response.

The Anchor blinked at me. She turned to Aidan and Nigit. "And how about you, gentlemen? What inspired you to create PhilanthrApp?"

"Helping people is important," Aidan blurted, like he'd been practicing. But then he froze, and an awkward silence followed. I had the sense neither of us had a future in TV presenting.

Nigit jumped in. "And sometimes you might want to help, but you don't know how to get involved. PhilanthrApp takes the guesswork out of how to volunteer. It makes it easy to help someone in need by entering your location and how much time you have to spare." Then he smiled warmly like a professional actor hosting a telethon. Maybe Lindsay coached him?

Screams erupted on Harrison's lawn as a white van with PUBLIC splashed in orange letters pulled in front. The Anchor flashed her porcelain veneers and said, "Perfect timing! It looks like Public has just arrived with sixteen hundred twenty-six buyPlayers and Beast 5.0s—a full twenty-four hours before their official release." She smiled wide into the camera and brought it home. "I can't imagine a better day to be a Harrison High School student."

The cameraman turned to film the side door of the white van swinging open. Kids raced across the lawn. Mindy jumped from the ledge of the *Eros Sleeping* statue and joined the fray that swarmed the van. Three burly guys wearing sunglasses and PUBLIC T-shirts emerged holding cardboard boxes. A skinny, squirrely guy in glasses climbed on top of the van. He barked into a megaphone: "Everyone eligible will receive a buyPlayer and the Beast 5.0! You must sign the release form before receiving your Public products. Please form a single line to expedite this process."

Students cheered. They angled themselves from a clump to a zigzagging line. Carrie Sommers flew through the air doing a full flip-layout thing. The Anchor clapped and said, "Wow!"

"Carrie and Gary Cary are starting to annoy me," I whispered to Aidan as Gary caught Carrie, and they both screamed, "Go, Harrison High Cheer Team!"

Aidan laughed. "I don't think anything could annoy me right now," he said. "Not even cheerleaders." He playfully touched the spot just above my hip and my pulse picked up. His grin turned devilish. "Who thought you'd get into college by getting people boyfriends?" His eyes locked on mine. "You never got matched, though." Then, under his breath he said, "Thank God."

What did *that* mean? I started to ask "What do you—" but Aidan put a finger to his scarlet lips and nodded toward Ms. Bates, who'd just started talking into the camera about how hard her programming students worked and the importance of technological instruction in American schools. I blacked out for most of what she said because I was trying to figure out what Aidan meant. Then Bates looked over at us, and ended with a line about how she was the one that felt truly lucky, being gifted with the responsibility of nurturing geniuses, which made Nigit smile even bigger—he loved being called a genius.

The *Today Show* people shook our hands like we were adults and packed up their equipment. Aidan towered over the Distinguished Producer, who was telling him that his daughters had downloaded PhilanthrApp that morning.

Did he mean thank God I hadn't been matched with someone other than him?

I was standing there like an idiot staring at him. So I turned and started toward Harrison. My face felt hot as I trekked across the grass.

My mom hung back with Ms. Bates as the Battery got the Anchor's autograph on her latest bestseller: *TV Nation: Are Americans Obsessed with Television?* which made me feel like I should write a book called *Math: Does One Plus One Equal Two?*

"Audrey!" Nigit called. He and Aidan raced toward me, and then the three of us ran the rest of the way to Harrison's front lawn. Aviation Boy Ty Bennett saw us first and pumped his fist. "Go, trogs!" he shouted. Harrison turned a collective head and started screaming. "Trogs! Go, trogs! Go!" The back three quarters of the line realized they weren't getting Beasts or buyPlayers anytime soon and raced toward us. I felt claustrophobic as warm bodies crashed into me from every side. The crowd was a living, pulsing thing. I hadn't been hugged so many times in my entire life. Lindsay elbowed next to me and screamed, "Audrey for Homecoming Queen!" Students exploded with hooting applause.

"Will you autograph my shirt?" asked one of the girls with the homemade Danny Beaton INDIANAPOLIS OR BUST! T-shirts. "Um, sure," I said as she handed me a purple Sharpie. President Richardson yakked on about me joining student government: "We could use a forward thinker." The basketball player with stitches leaned down until our noses were practically touching. "Audrey McCarthy is my homegirl!" she screamed, yanking my fist high in the air and possibly dislocating my elbow. Charlotte Davis gave me a smile, and then resumed canoodling with Joel Norris next to the *Eros Sleeping* statue. (Sans the BFA 2.0, which meant they'd graduated to becoming a real deal.)

I'd lost sight of Aidan. Nigit sat on Gary Cary's shoulders looking simultaneously thrilled and terrified. He clutched the sides of Gary's head like it was a video-game control stick and steered him through the mob. "Who's your daddy?!" he shouted to the crowd, squeezing Gary's head like his life depended on it. Gary grinned even as his face turned shades of purple.

Harrison was chanting, "Trogs! Trogs! Trogs!" and Nigit was screaming, "Your daddy got you buyPlayers!" when Blake, Joanna, and Jolene emerged from a side door. Blake's eyes widened. She secretly hated crowds. I saw a flash of her vulnerability, and an old instinct flickered, telling me she needed me. But I reminded myself she didn't—not anymore.

I watched her steel herself and push toward the Public van. There were still fifty or so kids waiting in line. Blake marched to the front and tried to cut in front of Goth Girl, who was next up for a Beast. Joanna and Jolene elbowed behind Blake. Goth Girl screamed something in Blake's face, and Blake drew back like she'd been slapped.

"No cutting!" boomed Theresa "T. Rex" Rexford.

Blake flushed a raspberry color. She lurched forward and grabbed the megaphone from the squirrely Public guy. "My father is the reason Public even exists!" she screamed into the megaphone. (Gross overstatement.) "You all have me to thank." (Grosser.) "Not the skanky trogs!" (Grossest.)

The Public guy yanked back his megaphone. Xander materialized at Blake's side. I figured he was going to defend her honor. (Their statuses were Single on Public Party, but maybe they'd patched things up?) Instead, he whispered something into her ear. She glanced up and caught my eye. Something flashed over her face, but I couldn't read it. She let Xander guide her away from the crowd. Jolene and Joanna still stood near the front of the line, looking nervous and—for the first time ever—kind of pointless. They considered the screaming fray, then raced after Xander and Blake. Harrison students screamed louder as Xander kicked open the door to the school and disappeared inside.

My phone vibrated in my pocket. I ducked down and covered my opposite ear. "Hello?" I shouted, my head knocking against my classmates' legs.

"Audrey McCarthy? This is Tag Adams, Senior Vice President of Consumer Relations at Public." The voice was low and the connection was staticky. I pressed my phone harder against my ear. Goth Girl was shouting: "The Beast is mine!" in the background.

"Hi, Mr. Adams," I said.

"Call me Tag. I'm calling to personally congratulate you. Public is so excited about the Boyfriend App that we've bumped up your prizewinning visit by two weeks. You'll be leaving for the Public offices in Ecru Point, California, tomorrow."

Tomorrow?

"All information will arrive over email," Tag was saying. Then he rambled on about rooming accommodations. "We'll be hosting you right here on Public's campus. We don't want to let you out of our sight, Ms. McCarthy." He laughed, but it sounded strained. Then he said good-bye and hung up.

I stared at my phone. That was totally weird. Or was I being paranoid? Maybe that was California humor?

Tag's words swirled in my mind as the crowd pushed me toward the Public van. My imagination played images of big computer screens and hordes of techy-looking Public trogs running around making discoveries and testing new products. I mean, okay, so I'd found some really bad stuff they did. But they were *Public*. They were geniuses!

Lindsay stood on the granite ledge of the *Eros Sleeping* statue. "For just twenty-nine ninety-nine you can get a custom Beast case with the inscription 'TROGS RULE OUR SCHOOL,'" she was saying, taking orders on Loulou de la Falaise, who had spent the night drying out in a bowl of rice. "All proceeds will go to technology instruction in underfunded high schools, a cause dear to me and you too, I'm sure," Lindsay said, sweeping a hand dramatically over her heart.

My phone pinged with a text from Aidan. escaped into The Books. u still out front? Some dude named Tag just called me. u ready for cali tomorrow?

yes! I texted back. Then I typed, glad we'll be 2gether. I almost deleted it. But instead I took a breath, and hit SEND. I stared at the screen until Aidan texted back: should I be ready for you to use your app on me?

My fingers tightened on my phone. Did he seriously just write that? I was so panicked I didn't know what to respond.

Lindsay always said: *When in doubt, play it cool.*

So I texted him back: haha u wish.

But I didn't feel very cool. I felt insanely nervous. Was I reading him wrong, or were things changing between us?

244

* * *

That night when I got home to Hector, I couldn't ignore my suspicion any longer. A part of me didn't want to know. The other part had to.

I waited until midnight to remotely log on to Gurung's computer through the backdoor application. I opened his email, and just in case he was surfing around, I backed it up into a file and copied it onto my computer to minimize suspicion. It was safe that way. Or, at least, safer.

I searched *Nigit* and *contest*. Two emails matched.

> From: Alec.Pierce@Public.com
> CC: robertdawkins@R.DawkinsTech.com
> To: nikhil.gurung@InfinitumMail.com
>
> Nikhil,
>
> You can only imagine how thrilled I am to see your son Nigit has submitted a mobile application to Public's nationwide contest. With a college scholarship on the line, it pleases me even more to tell you I'll be seriously considering your son's application for the grand prize.
>
> Alec
>
> From: nikhil.gurung@InfinitumMail.com
> To: Alec.Pierce@Public.com
> CC: robertdawkins@R.DawkinsTech.com

Alec,
I don't need your consolation prizes. Leave my son out
of this.
Nikhil

I felt like I'd swallowed something cold. Nigit and
Aidan's win was orchestrated by Alec Pierce. Their
scholarship was built on lies.

But then again, maybe so was mine.

chapter twenty-seven

"I still can't believe they chartered a private plane for us!" Lindsay squealed, sinking into a beige leather seat. "This is so *Dynasty*." She snapped a photo of Nigit, who pointed his white-gloved index finger at a box of chocolates that waited on our tray tables and said, "Wassup!" He jumped into his seat. "And the lax jocks have to fly commercial," he said. "That's freaking priceless."

The Harrison lacrosse team was playing the Stanford Invitational this weekend, and Robert Dawkins had arranged their tour of Public headquarters. The South Bend papers ate that up, printing stories like: "ROBERT DAWKINS EXPANDS YOUNG ATHLETIC MINDS." I hadn't realized minds could be athletic.

The plane's engine growled beneath us. I'd never flown before and I was trying not to freak out. (Neither had Lindsay, but she showed up looking like a travel pro in a pink terry-cloth jumpsuit and huge sunglasses, like a famous person from L.A. She even put a fake toy dog in her carry-on bag and called it Fifi. It looked real until you got right next to it.)

Icy rain shattered the plane's wings like Tic Tacs. "The best thing about flying private is that we can brave weather like this," the peppy flight attendant said.

"My last flight to Dubai emergency-landed on a tropical island because of weather *just like this*," Lindsay lied, putting a hand to her forehead.

The flight attendant nodded sympathetically. Lindsay winked at me. Then the flight attendant showed us an oxygen mask and how to use it.

Great.

My mom squeezed my hand. She'd gotten up at five to deep-condition her hair, and she looked radiant. I tried to focus on how happy she was, how proud. But my nerves were running the show. Something wasn't right.

Nigit checked the time on his eBay present from Lindsay: a plastic watch with Michael Jackson in his iconic red jacket and white gloves, his outstretched arms the hands of the clock. "Finally, Dad," he muttered to himself, staring out the plane's window. The flight attendant opened the door and Nigit's father boarded. Sweat trickled over his brown, wrinkled skin even though it was freezing outside. Salt-and-pepper-colored stubble crossed his face. His dark eyes looked fatigued, and they held mine for a moment too long before breaking into the same fake smile he gave me during his Notre Dame office hours. "I'm sorry I'm late, son," he said, lowering into the seat next to Nigit.

It was totally weird that he didn't acknowledge me, but I wasn't going to be the one to say something about our meeting.

The flight attendant pointed to Dr. Gurung's green leather briefcase. "Can I store that in the overhead compartment?"

"No," Dr. Gurung said quickly. He clutched the briefcase to his chest.

The small print said each winning app entry was allowed two guests to accompany them to Public's headquarters. I'd picked my mom and Lindsay, and Aidan and Nigit split theirs: Aidan picked Mindy because his mom couldn't leave his little sister home alone, and Nigit picked his dad.

"Water, please," Mindy said to the flight attendant. She'd said more words in the past two days than in the past two years, like something had broken loose and couldn't be contained anymore.

"Do you want to sit next to Aidan?" my mom asked, smoothing a hand over the cream silk blouse she usually saved for church.

"Uh—no," I said, hoping he hadn't heard her. She smiled like she knew something.

Across the aisle, Aidan's head was bent over a brochure with BROWN UNIVERSITY splashed on the cover. It was cracked open to a photo of students sitting on a grassy quad next to a stone building. There wasn't any writing on the page; Aidan was just staring at the picture. I liked watching the way his fingers curled and settled on a stack of textbooks pictured next to a student wearing a Brown sweatshirt.

He looked up at me and smiled. He picked out one of his chocolates and said, "Five bucks if you can guess which kind this is."

I guessed wrong, but he split it with me anyway. My hand felt warm when he passed it into my palm.

An alert sounded on the flight attendant's buyPhone and she excused herself behind a velvet curtain. I popped the chocolate into my mouth as two men wearing dark suits emerged from the cockpit.

"Good morning, ladies and gentlemen; I'm your pilot," said a guy who looked less like a pilot and more like a guy Lindsay would post photos of on *FBM*: tall, trim, and wearing an expensive-looking suit. I would've felt better if he at least had a pin with wings. He didn't introduce the other guy. Instead, he said, "We'll be arriving in Ecru Point at noon." The other guy closed the door to the plane. I heard the flight attendant say into her phone: *"Everyone is onboard."*

In California, everything felt different. And we hadn't even gotten off the airplane. The sun glinted—on the runway, on the grass lining the runway, on the shining heads of the guys unloading our luggage from beneath the plane—like I'd only seen it do in South Bend on hubcaps and other metally stuff on the hottest August days.

My nerves still felt shot as I powered on my phone. This was Brad Pitt's home state. On the off chance I saw him, I needed the Boyfriend App to be fully loaded. (Just because Public had disabled the Boyfriend App on everyone else's phone didn't mean I couldn't still use it: I had the original code.)

The nervous feeling got worse as the Public logo came to life on my screen. I tried to chalk it up to first-time-flying jitters, but I knew it was something else.

"California women, I can't get enough of you!" Lindsay sang in a dead-on Danny Beaton impression.

"You are the cootest, most ad-ur-able, ladies, whoa-oh-oh," Mindy joined in—not quite as good, but just as enthusiastic.

My mom returned her pearly blue rosary beads to her purse. She'd clutched the beads the entire flight. My favorite part was when they draped over the Fabio-haired shirtless man making out with a courtesan on the cover of her romance novel. My dad would've thought that was hilarious.

We peered out onto the runway. Our tiny window had gotten dirty in the air, and now there was grime on it, like looking through a forgotten fish tank. "Your father and I always talked about taking you to Disneyland," my mom said. She twirled the silver Claddagh ring she never took off her fourth finger. "He'd be so excited we made it to California. And he'd be so proud of you."

"Thanks, Mom," I said, happy she was here with me. And I felt my dad, too. It calmed my nerves thinking of him.

My phone pinged with message alerts. I opened a text from Blake.

Trog. I need to talk to you about something big. B.

I didn't have time to freak out or obsess over what she could possibly want, because there was another text from the same area code Tag Adams had called from.

WE KNOW WHAT YOU'VE DONE. ARRIVE ON THE TOP FLOOR ALONE. TELL NO ONE.

For an eternity, I couldn't think: There was static where my thoughts used to be.

Public.

"Auds?" Aidan's voice. "Are you coming?"

I shoved the phone into my jeans with trembling fingers. Aidan and Mindy were staring at me. My mom was talking to Dr. Gurung about how proud she was. The flight attendant was texting. Lindsay and Nigit were kissing. The door to the plane opened to more Guys in Dark Suits waiting outside, wearing sunglasses and pissed-off expressions.

A metal staircase cranked and clanked along the runway to the door of our plane. My legs shook so hard I could barely descend the steps. My hand instinctually went to my pocket to touch my rabbit's foot, but it wasn't there.

"You're coming with us, Miss McCarthy," the Guy in the Dark Suit said, gesturing to a massive SUV parked on the runway.

This couldn't be happening—they couldn't kidnap me in front of my family and friends. The flight attendant's lip liner twisted the corners of her mouth into a smirk. She'd seemed so nice on the plane, offering me biscotti every fifteen minutes. I didn't even know what biscotti was, and

I'd eaten her stale cookies not realizing she was probably a conspirator. What if she'd drugged my orange juice? What the freak had I gotten myself into?

"No!" I screamed.

Everyone turned. "Sweetie?" my mom asked. Aidan's navy eyes stared. Lindsay pulled from Nigit's embrace, but her bumblebee brooch caught his sateen dinner jacket and rendered them inseparable.

The flight attendant blinked. "Would you like more biscotti for the ride to headquarters, Audrey?"

I surveyed the guys loading luggage into the back of a second SUV. My mom's flowered bag was tossed into the trunk with Lindsay's and mine, and I realized Public was splitting the seven of us into two cars. "Oh." I exhaled. "I'm fine. I just meant I wish we could all go together." I forced a smile. Mindy's lips pursed, like she didn't believe me, but she followed the Guy in the Dark Suit's directions anyway. She boarded the second black SUV with Dr. Gurung, Nigit, and Aidan. "It's like we're on *Entourage*," Nigit said, shimmying inside. "And I'm definitely Johnny Drama." Dr. Gurung's face darkened as our eyes met. He slammed the door behind him.

"Listen, sweetie, I know you're probably nervous," my mom said as we clamored into the backseat of our identical, colossal ride.

You have no idea.

Lindsay eyed me. I wanted to tell them—to warn them—but the Guy in the Dark Suit was inches away in the driver's seat. I was about to text Lindsay before I thought better of it: Public could easily access my phone's data activity.

"We're en route," the Guy said into his earpiece. He turned toward the three of us. "We'll be arriving at Public's headquarters in seven minutes." I saw my reflection in his sunglasses. My skin looked even paler in California and my hair was spiking all wrong.

Lindsay pressed a black button. Air-conditioning blasted our faces. "My overactive metabolism wasn't made for California," she said. The sides of our hands touched and I tried ESP: *Lindsay. I'm in trouble.*

We passed planes lining runways like hulking gray birds ready for takeoff. "You're going to do great today, Audrey," my mom said.

"Indeed," the Guy in the Dark Suit said. I saw him smirk in the rearview mirror. "Public is very much awaiting your arrival."

chapter twenty-eight

The SUV crunched over gravel. Yellow wildflowers lined the side of the road next to a farmer's market. The Santa Cruz Mountains loomed in the distance. Clusters of redwood trees arched into the sky on either side of us, like they were standing guard. We curved onto a paved driveway and my heart seized as I took in Public headquarters glistening on the horizon.

Looking inside the circular glass tower was like watching a video game: Floor-to-ceiling windows made it see-through, and miniature people milled about inside. There weren't actual floors stacked on top of one another—the tower was constructed with one sloping floor that spiraled to the top. I'd read online the slope was so gradual you could barely detect it inside, even though your coworker's desk could be a few inches higher than yours. In person it was like science fiction: an Escher-esque coil with no escape. We neared the entrance and I tried to act like I was okay, like my insides weren't melting in a pressure cooker.

The SUV parked in front of headquarters. Two twenty-somethings wearing jeans stood in front of an ice-cream-truck-shaped vehicle marked: PUBLIC COFFEE CART: GET BUZZED. A sidewalk parted an elaborately landscaped courtyard. Weeping willows shaded two women hunched over their Beasts. Prickly-looking bushes were shaped into computers complete with keyboards. Potted vases held electric-blue flowers. A wooden sign with an arrow pointing to headquarters read: PROGRESS, THIS WAY.

The second SUV pulled behind ours. Nigit, his dad, Aidan, and Mindy climbed out. Aidan shook his head in awe as he took in the building. Nigit went to Lindsay's side. "Can you believe how sick this is?" he asked her.

"Totes sick," she said, nuzzling against him.

My mother's neon-orange fanny pack matched the PUBLIC letters arching over the entrance. "I've never seen anything like this," she said, gazing into the sloping levels of office space. Chrome desks lined the interior. A glass elevator brought busy-looking people up and down the tower.

Dr. Gurung stood off the side. His face was grim when Nigit said, "Cool, right, Dad?"

Through the glass I saw two dozen Harrison lacrosse players waiting on the first floor. Xander saw me, and waved. I waved back, trying to act normal. The lax guys being there just made me more nervous.

My mom snapped a photo of the life-sized stone statue

of Alec Pierce next to the entrance. Alec's stone hand was lifted midgesture like he was in the middle of giving a TED talk. Lindsay climbed onto the ledge. "Take my picture, Aunt Marian!" She reached her arms around Alec and put her hands on his stone butt cheeks. "Mwah!" she said, and kissed his stone lips.

"Please don't be inappropriate, Lindsay," my mom said. But I could tell she was trying not to smile.

A man with a pink Mohawk walked by with his buyPhone pressed against his ear, eating a sandwich. I smelled salami.

The Guy in the Dark Suit pressed his fingertip against a print detector on the side of the building. The doors swung open and we entered the glass matrix.

"Hey, trogs!" Barron Feldman called, sounding oddly reverent. Then some of the other Harrison guys said, "What's up?" like we were all friends. They wore collared shirts and khaki pants, like someone had given them a uniform. I'd never seen Xander in anything other than a T-shirt or lacrosse jersey.

I felt Aidan watching me as I noticed Xander. Heat rose to my face, and I looked away.

On our right, water gushed down a wall behind a receptionist who looked like a supermodel. Goldfish the size of hamsters swam in a sparkling black glass pool surrounding the reception desk. Pennies glinted beneath the surface. The receptionist looked up from her computer and smiled without showing her teeth. "We'll begin your tour momentarily," she told the lacrosse players. She exchanged a glance with the Guy in the Dark Suit. "You will wait here," she told our group. "Except for Miss McCarthy," she said, looking at me. How did she know which one I was?

"Good luck, sweetie," my mom said.

My throat constricted. *Calm down, trog.* It wasn't like they were going to murder me—I'd watched enough primetime to know you didn't bring the person to your place of work to commit the felony.

A woman with long red hair emerged from behind the water-wall like a mermaid. Next came a short guy in a salmon-colored button-down. His sunburned skin matched his shirt, except for the white area surrounding his eyes in the shape of sunglasses. The mermaid went behind the reception desk. The sunburned guy strode in our direction, extending his hand. "I'm Tag Adams," he said, smiling. His canine teeth were too long, like a wolf. He shook our hands. "I'm pleased to tell you that you'll each have the opportunity to meet Alec Pierce today," he said.

"Are you freaking serious?" Nigit asked.

No one had ever said anything about meeting Alec Pierce in the contest-prize description.

The lacrosse guys overheard Tag and mumbled among themselves, sounding impressed.

Tag nodded. "And you'll meet him first, Miss McCarthy," he said.

Everyone had to be wondering why I was meeting Alec alone, right? I prayed someone would speak up. Say they wanted to come with me.

No one did.

Aidan was standing next to my mom, who was smiling at me. I cleared my throat. "I don't feel so good," I said to my mom, quiet enough so just she and Aidan could hear.

"Do you want me to ask if I can come with you?" she whispered.

I shook my head. I couldn't involve her in this.

Aidan reached behind his neck. His long fingers grabbed the piece of twine I'd noticed in the spot behind my apartment. He took it off over his head and I saw a silver computer charm hanging from the twine. It took me a second to remember why I recognized it—I'd given it to him freshman year when he transferred into Harrison. I'd told him, *The trogs know where it's at. Come hang out with us in the lab.*

I looked up and met his eyes. I saw how nervous he was—like he was telling me something when he passed it into my hands. I brought the twine over my neck and ran my fingers over the silver computer. We stared at each other. We didn't speak. We didn't need to.

"I'll be okay," I told them softly.

The mermaid woman gestured to a square of plush white leather sofas. "What can I get you?" she asked our group.

Lindsay was asking for *Something to cool my metabolism down, please. A slushie?* when the glass doors to the elevator opened. I followed Tag. A cleaning woman wearing an outfit that looked like a Wimbledon uniform boarded the elevator alongside us. I stared at Aidan as the doors closed.

The cleaning woman's bag of eco-friendly, organic cleaning supplies reeked of eucalyptus, and she smiled (probably because she was the only one who didn't know I was being taken hostage by Public). I held the computer charm in a tight fist and tried to take deep, calming breaths, but the eucalyptus burned my nose hairs.

Tag smiled back at the cleaning woman as she got off on the third level. The elevator doors closed. Tag wouldn't look at me.

The elevator moved quickly and soundlessly. The glass windows made it feel like flying into the sky on one of those amusement-park rides that rockets up, only to free-fall you back down to the earth until you want to throw up. We soared above the redwoods. I took in the desks and Public employees at their computers as we shot past them. The Santa Cruz Mountains were blue and hazy in the distance, and a memory struck me: I saw my dad's broad hand holding mine as we hiked a trail on the Mini Mountain Campground in New Carlisle. I was only ten, and panic-attacking about mountain lions, and my dad taught me some Survival 101 about widening your arms and making yourself as big as possible to scare one off. *Know your opponent,* he'd said as we climbed higher.

On the top level, the elevator opened to a circular floor three times the size of our apartment. Sun poured through the glass onto the marble floors. Model airplanes like the kind Amelia Earhart would fly hung from the ceiling next to modern ones. The airplanes circled a spaceship-looking dome. A putting green with real grass sat in the center of the room with a flag over the hole that read PAST, PRESENT, FUTURE: CREATE BIG. White sand filled kidney-shaped traps on either side of the grass. A glass shelf circled the room, showcasing wooden plaques and a golden statue that looked like an Oscar.

Even grander than the showcase was a supertall Alec Pierce in plaid pants and a short-sleeved baby-blue golf shirt. His back faced me, but I knew it was him by the overcrowded hair follicles on his head and forearms. His right hand clutched a putter way shinier than the ones they give you in mini golf. A candle burned on his long chrome desk. I couldn't smell the scent—only the smoke.

"Alec Pierce: Audrey McCarthy," Tag said. Then he disappeared into the elevator, leaving me alone with Alec.

Alec turned. Sunlight backlit his body and stubble shaded his face. His eyes were black like an oil spill. He smiled. I shivered. He moved slowly to his desk. He pressed a button on his keyboard and the massive computer screens that hung from the ceiling illuminated. Data scrolled. I recognized conversation after conversation:

u goin 2 win the contest? 200k?

We need to get the Boyfriend App into the Top Ten . . . we need a miracle . . .

U have explaining to do. Why is everyone talking about Debate Team Boy trying to make out w u?

The computer screen flickered and I felt like I was going to be sick.

I know you want to know more but I can't tell you more right now. I just need you to trust me.

It was the text I sent Lindsay the morning after the Danny Beaton concert. They were tracking every move I made.

Alec pressed another button and the computers faded to black. The smoke smell made the air between us hot and thick. We were quiet until Alec gestured to a miniature pool of water next to his desk.

"The salt water's good for my eczema," he said.

A tiny black fluff-ball dog emerged from beneath the desk. The metal tags on his collar caught the sun streaming through the window.

"We have a situation here, don't we, Audrey?" Alec ran a hairy-knuckled hand over his stomach like he'd eaten too much. "I'm hoping we can come to an amicable agreement that benefits both of us."

Pins and needles prickled my legs.

"You've stolen software from my company," Alec said. His voice grated over his words like a train covering tracks. "Software I'd rather the world know nothing about." Yellow lights flickered on a vintage pinball machine and reflected off the glass. "Oh, and Audrey," Alec said, chuckling to himself like this was all a game, "I've deactivated the BuyWare on my phone, so don't get any ideas about using it on me." He pushed a piece of paper and a fancy-looking ballpoint pen across his desk. "I've done a lot of thinking about how to right this situation. And I've come up with something I'm confident will work for both of us."

A blue-green vein bisected Alec's throat. I imagined seawater coursing beneath his skin.

"You're going to sign this document swearing never to reveal or use the software you've uncovered," he said. "And in exchange, I'll grant your college scholarship. The world will eventually forget all about the Boyfriend App. It will be like this conversation never happened."

My heart clenched and then released.

Alec shoved the paper closer. "Sign it."

I was so used to being unsure that I almost didn't recognize the emotion surfacing in me now. Ever since my dad died, uncertainty about who I was and what the future had in store felt like a mystery, like the rug had been pulled from beneath me, leaving me unsteady, reeling. But I didn't feel that now. I felt strong. Public wasn't going to hide who I was and what I could do. How could I take Alec's money and keep quiet when I'd always wanted software to be free and open? There was supposed to be truth in technology, not lies and secrets and cover-ups. Even though I was scared, everything my dad and I believed in made this the easiest decision I'd ever made.

"No," I said.

Alec's face remained perfectly calm, perfectly still. But a red color spread across his cheeks and forehead.

I said it louder. *"No."*

His eyes were so black I couldn't distinguish the pupil from the iris. "If you don't agree to my terms, things will be made extremely unpleasant for you and your family," he said.

I didn't even flinch. "Things have already been *extremely unpleasant* for my family and me," I pointed out. The person we loved most had died way before his time. How much more unpleasant could things get? "And the truth isn't meant to be covered up."

I battled the aching sadness that crept through me. There was nothing else to say. The only collateral I had against Alec Pierce and Public would hurt people I cared about and break my dad's rule. *My* rule. If I fought back, if I let on that I knew Alec funded a public-health study and then blackmailed Dr. Gurung into keeping the results quiet, then Nigit and Aidan would be involved, and Alec would find a way to take away their scholarships, too. He'd find a way to keep them quiet—he'd threaten them like he was threatening me, like he'd threatened Dr. Gurung. Nigit's parents could pay for his college. Aidan's couldn't.

Alec pressed a black button. "Send them up to get her," he said into an intercom.

I braced myself. For security, for the FBI, for whoever was coming to take me away and lock me up for illegal hacking and software pirating. I was guilty of it; that was for sure.

We never go down without a fight, my father used to say when we watched Notre Dame football on TV, making us a part of them. *Even when we're outmatched.*

I yanked my buyPhone from my pocket.

Alec's black eyes were wild. "Call whoever you like. Who do you think the world will believe? Public, or a thieving high-school student? How do you think the law punishes a person who steals multibillion-dollar property?"

Shut up, Alec.

I tore across the room and hung my head over the ledge into the center of the spiral. BuyWare could be activated by targeting individual cell numbers, and the original Boyfriend App stored every contact number registered. I copied and pasted the lacrosse team's digits. I tried to keep the dizziness at bay as I stared hundreds of feet down to the first floor where the Harrison lacrosse team waited with my mom and my friends. I spied Aidan sitting on the edge of a sofa drinking a Coke. Maybe it wasn't the worst idea to activate him, too—Aidan's smarts plus the lacrosse brawn. Unbeatable.

I added Aidan's number. Nerves shot from my feet to my fingertips.

"Hey, guys!" I screamed down into the spiral. Everybody looked up.

IT'S ON

The lacrosse guys jumped to their feet. Xander moved first. He sprinted past the wall of gushing water and the mermaid-receptionists. "Audrey!" he yelled.

Aidan watched the team tear past him. "Audrey?" he called back up at me. "You okay?"

I shook my head. And then Aidan started sprinting, too.

Alec's seawater vein throbbed. He was saying something about me regretting the day I messed with his institution, but he was drowned out by a single word echoing up the stairwell.

Audrey! Audrey! Audrey!

"What the—?" Alec said beneath his breath, moving to the spiral and taking in the dozens of guys circling the sloping floors and screaming my name.

"Security!" he blared into his intercom.

Aidan's dark head of curls mesmerized me as he rounded the spiral. Xander glanced up. His hazel eyes blazed—just like in the cafeteria. He lunged forward, and the rest of the team followed, banging into fancy chrome desks and tipping over cartons of writing utensils. Public employees screamed and bolted out of the way of the herd. One skinny guy seemed to miss the point, and cheered instead: "Go, lacrosse players!" And then when Aidan passed him: "Go, hot techie guy!"

Woody Ames knocked into the man from outside with the pink Mohawk. His paper coffee cup crushed between them. A Public employee who looked like Usher dove on top of his keyboard to save it from the Mohawk-man's coffee spillage.

The Guys in Dark Suits were back—materializing on different levels of the spiral—but there were only eight of them, and there were two dozen lax players, plus Aidan. The Guys could only tackle one player at a time, and each time they released one, he'd spring to his feet and start the climb again. I heard Xander's voice shouting some kind of battle cry as the Guy in the Dark Suit who drove my mom and Lindsay chased him. Xander turned to see how close the Guy was and crashed into a mammoth printer. By the time he scrambled to his feet, the Guy in the Dark Suit was too close. I was sure he was going to get him when Aidan stopped short and jutted his leg in front of the Guy's feet. The Guy went flying into a skinny Public employee and they smashed into bright orange beanbag chairs.

Aidan's eyes were wild. Xander high-fived him, and they ran along with the rest of the team around the final level of the spiral. My mom and Lindsay sprinted a few levels below. "Sweetie?!" my mom screamed.

Alec slammed the button on his desk over and over. "Security!"

Woody Ames darted in front of Xander. "Audrey," Woody said, reaching his arms forward like he was either going to hug or tackle me. But then Xander shoved Woody into a marble stand topped with a miniature version of the Alec Pierce sculpture from outside. "Not again, Woody!" he shouted as Woody and the sculpture crashed. Alec Pierce's nose broke off and rolled down the sloping floor. "I know you did it with Blake, scumbag," Xander said as Woody groaned and rubbed his shoulder.

"*Te amo*, Audrey!" screamed Xander's teammate Ken Hanks, who pronounced words like *enchilada* in a Spanish accent even though he wasn't Spanish, like Alex Trebek does.

Xander came closer, panting. His arms went around my waist. But then Aidan was suddenly next to me, too. He smelled like a heady mix of sunblock and grass. He shouldered Xander out of the way and pulled me close. "Give it a rest, Knight," he said levelly. He seemed shockingly calm for someone whose hormones were being stimulated by an app. "She's not your girlfriend," he said.

Xander stood his ground. "Oh, and she's *yours*?"

Aidan stepped toward Xander. He still had me pressed against his side. He was a few inches taller than Xander, and he looked down at him and growled, "Why don't you ask her who she wants?"

I could barely breathe. It felt *incredible* to be pressed against him. I reached up and touched the line of his jaw—I didn't care that all the other guys could see me do it. I'd wanted to for so long. And now I could go for it without worrying about what he'd do, because of the app.

Aidan looked at me with more heat than anyone ever had before. My heart thrummed in my chest. His arms tightened around my waist and my legs went weak. And then he tilted his chin and I couldn't think anymore.

His lips touched mine and we melted into each other. His lips were so soft. They opened, and his kiss grew stronger and more insistent until I felt his body tighten against me. I couldn't catch my breath. It didn't matter how many times I'd fantasized about making out with him—it was so much better than anything I could've imagined. I wrapped my arms around his neck and returned his passion until I could hardly stand up. I was like a rag doll in his arms.

It's not real.

The words broke into my thoughts uninvited, like an accusation.

I pulled away. "Aidan," I started. I could barely speak.

It's not real.

My heart felt twice its size. I couldn't think straight.

The only thing I knew was that I needed to get out of there, and fast.

I opened my mouth to tell Aidan we needed to go, but he was already scooping me into his arms. I heard my mom, Lindsay, and Mindy on the outskirts of the crowd, asking me if I was okay. Then the lacrosse players closed in on us and pushed Aidan and me away from Alec. Aidan held me snug against him. He gazed longingly into my eyes, and I tried to remind myself over and over that it was all fake. It was about to be over as soon as I pressed a button.

I looked over Aidan's shoulder and caught Alec's glance.

Know your opponent.

The Public security team was scrambling through the mayhem when Alec called them off, and even though I'd just had the best kiss of my life and my mind was spinning, I was suddenly very sure of something: Alec wasn't going to turn me in to the authorities because doing so meant implicating us both—me for hacking, him for using hormone-inducing software on unsuspecting teenagers for financial gain.

His oil-spill eyes caught fire. "You'll regret this," he promised.

chapter twenty-nine

For immediate release:

PUBLIC DISQUALIFIES
HIGH-SCHOOL STUDENT FROM PUBLIC APP CONTEST
Theft of Intellectual Property Leaves Public Corp "No Choice"

Public is saddened to announce the disqualification of
Audrey McCarthy from their nationwide mobile application
contest. Upon review, it has been brought to our attention
that Audrey McCarthy stole intellectual property for the
Boyfriend App from fellow classmate Blake Andrea Dawkins.
An anonymous source provided us with the following email
messages from the Public Party archive:

Blake Dawkins: "What's up, trog? Maybe you

should use your computer skills to get yourself
a boyfriend. Hey, a Boyfriend App! That's an
awesome idea for the Public contest. I'm gonna
get working on it stat."

In an exclusive statement, Dawkins told Public: "I never wanted to say anything because I felt so bad for her. She hardly has any friends, let alone an original idea."

The grand prize for Most Popular App has been awarded to runner-up Aurora Baker, creator of SmittenKitten, an app that delivers baby cat photos to your buyPhone daily. Aurora joins Aidan Bailey and Nigit Gurung, creators of PhilanthrApp, as the gifted students receiving two hundred thousand dollars in college-scholarship money.

"We are incredibly disappointed here at Public," says CEO Alec Pierce. "We'd like to take this moment to remind all innovators: Take steps to protect your creative work from pirates like Audrey McCarthy with our latest apps, CopyrightIt and PatentApp."

My eyes were so swollen I could barely see the road. Every time I shut them, they burned, so I tried focusing on the yellow lines emerging through the fog while Lindsay drove. The air-conditioning attacked my skin. Claire clutched a Ziploc full of celery and chattered on about the horse club she started. Lindsay was silent.

We'd been in South Bend for less than forty-eight hours,

271

and Alec Pierce had already made good on his promise. He'd figured out a way to hurt me without revealing his own wrongdoings, and still left me unable to defend myself without exposing the things I'd done wrong, too. I couldn't tell my mom he'd manipulated Blake's Party archive. And I couldn't tell Lindsay or Aidan or Mindy or Nigit: not without involving them in something dangerous— something that could get worse if I didn't keep my mouth shut.

I'd tried texting Aidan a million times. But he wouldn't text me back. I was freaking out at what that could mean. He could be mad because I apped him. Or what if he was done with me because of what he and everyone else thought I did?

My stomach dropped when we pulled into Harrison. The white Public van was back, chugging through the parking lot.

Lindsay and I pushed through the front entrance and heard the Battery's voice cackle over the loudspeaker: "Attention, Harrison students. In lieu of homeroom, report immediately to the gymnasium, where Public employees are standing by. Due to recent events, all Harrison students must return their Beast 5.0s. Please have your student-identification card ready as you return your device."

A groan vibrated through the halls. My cheeks burned. I tried to move faster, but my foot snagged on Wes the Water Polo Boy's water polo ball. Lindsay caught me moments before a full-on face-plant. *"Chin up, Audrey,"* she whispered as she pulled me to my feet.

Goth Girl looked disgusted, but I couldn't tell if it was directed at me or if it was just the way her black lipstick sloped south. Nina Carlyle, the Olympic hopeful, snickered. The basketball player with the stitches stopped midconversation to gape.

Martha Lee clutched her Beast (already covered in stickers like GET ME TO THE TOP OF THE NEAREST PYRAMID! and a cartoon cutout of a cheerleader who looked like a drunk Barbie doing a split). "It isn't fair!" she screeched. *Tell me about it, Martha.*

The worst was Briggs Lick, who shouldered past me and said, "Not cool, Audrey."

Lindsay's grip on my arm tightened. "Just keep going," she said.

Blake stood at the entrance to the gym. She'd dressed up in shimmery gold pants with charcoal heels. A tight white sweater hugged her C-cups.

I supposed all of this was what her "something big" was. Not that she was going to tell me—but maybe getting me to call her or meet up was part of the plan. It wasn't clear. And now it didn't matter.

"We should have known it was your idea," Mara Perez was saying, twisting her curls into a banana clip while her twin agreed: "Totally."

"Something this good had *Blake* written all over it," Carrie Sommers said, gesturing like a skywriter etching Blake's name in cottony clouds. She reddened when she saw Lindsay and me.

"Are your lips chapped from kissing Blake's butt?"

Lindsay asked Carrie. But her voice didn't sound as confident as it normally did. She had to know everyone was against me. And now, *us.* "You don't have to do this," I whispered.

Blake caught my eye. A flash of doubt passed over her face. It was a rare look for her, but it was one I knew how to spot. But then she sniffed and transformed her expression. "Here they are," she said with fake pity. "The Cheater and her publicist."

Harrison kids clutched their Beasts and turned toward me. "Why you do it?" Annborg asked. There was a picture of Blake taped to her Beast.

"Yeah," Ken Hanks piped in. *"Por qué lo hiciste?"*

Don't say anything, don't say anything.

"Poor Aubrey, she has nothing to say to defend herself," Blake said, taking a dainty sip from a massive Starbucks that cost more than my T-shirt. "Cheaters suck."

Kevin Jacobsen held his Beast with two hands and bounced his hacky sack on top. "Yeah. Cheaters suck!" he echoed, *heh-heh-heh*ing a laugh that turned into a cough.

"And trogs suck," Joanna Martin said, standing so close to Blake her blond hair made them look like a black-and-white cookie.

"Trogs suck!" someone else joined in.

"But trash sucks the most," Jolene Martin growled.

Aidan and Mindy were nowhere to be seen, but I breathed a sigh of relief when Nigit emerged wearing a skinny tie over a black shirt and green velvet pants. "At least you can all keep your buyPlayers!" he shouted. He didn't meet my glance. Instead he pulled Lindsay and me around the corner.

No one followed us. The three of us stood there alone, staring at one another.

"Audrey," Nigit finally said, his face earnest. "How could you do it? How could you break the biggest rule of trog ethics?"

I opened my mouth to talk, but I couldn't make words. There was nothing I could say. I thought about saying how none of this was what it seemed. But what if Nigit started digging around and found something?

Lindsay was staring at me. Waiting for me to explain. When I didn't, she said, "I'm sure Audrey has a reason."

Now they were both waiting, watching.

"I—I don't," I said.

Nigit looked totally conflicted, and Lindsay just looked devastated. I wanted to scream the truth—I could feel it trying to claw its way from my throat.

Nigit turned to Lindsay and said, "I'm sorry, Linds. I can't be aligned with questionable morals in the creative space."

Blood drained from Lindsay's face. "What's that supposed to mean?" she asked, her voice shaky. She stared at Nigit like it was just the two of them standing there alone in the hall.

Nigit didn't say anything.

"She's my family," Lindsay said.

Nigit blinked like he didn't know what to do. He glanced between the two of us, looking more nervous by the second. Then he turned and walked away.

I couldn't bear to look at Lindsay, so I stared at the space between my sneakers. But Lindsay's hand gently lifted my chin. Then she touched the gold Ganesh charm that rested against her collarbone. "Let's get out of here," she said. She pulled me into the girls' locker room past a pink thong tacked to the bulletin board with a handmade sign that read: LOST YOUR PANTIES? As soon as the door shut and we were alone, she burst into tears and slid down a full-length mirror. "You didn't have to do that," I said, kneeling beneath a poster showing how to do the Heimlich maneuver. "You don't always have to stick up for me." I put my arms around her, but she just cried harder. Her tiny shoulders shook against me.

"He'll come back around," I tried. She was the one who always knew what to say, not me.

"Why did you do it?" Lindsay asked, choking on the words.

The thick smell of chlorine seeped from the pool. It made it even harder to breathe. "I can't explain. Not right now." My lungs were so tight I could barely suck down air. "Probably never."

Lindsay shook her head. "I don't understand you," she said, running a hand over her mouth. Mandarin-colored lipstick smudged her palm.

Footsteps sounded behind us.

"Girls?"

I scrambled to my feet. The skin around my mom's green eyes was puffy like a marshmallow. "Mom? What happened?"

276

My mom stood there in her wrinkle-free khakis and the California T-shirt she bought in the airport. She gave me her trademark *Everything's fine* smile, which freaked me out even more. "Principal Dawkins fired me today."

"Mom," I said. It came out like a squeak. And then I couldn't stop the tears I'd been fighting. I felt them hot on my cheeks.

Lindsay was on her feet with her arms around us.

"This is all my fault," I said, barely able to get the words out. How could I have been so stupid to think I could take on Alec Pierce and Public?

"We'll be okay, sweetie," my mom said. But I knew better. Each month we had between sixty and seventy-five dollars left after her paycheck for our savings account. Thirty-six months since my dad died meant a little more than two thousand dollars saved. We were *not* okay.

The loudspeaker cackled like static. "Will Audrey McCarthy please report immediately to Mrs. Condor's office?"

I steadied myself against a dingy gray locker. I felt like someone was carving a hole in me deeper and deeper. I texted Aidan: Please answer this text. He had to have heard the announcement. Can you meet me outside the girls' locker room? Walk me to mrs. condor?

I waited outside the locker room with my mom and Lindsay. But Aidan never showed up.

I cried so hard I could barely see straight. To get to Mrs. Condor's office, Lindsay, my mom, and I had to pass the gym, where the Public people were confiscating everybody's Beasts. So I held my breath and sang a song my dad had taught me about a wealthy guy named Taffy over and over in my head. *Just ignore them, Audrey,* he would've said. So I did. I hummed the lyrics so loud I barely registered the gaping stares, barely registered the accusations. I hummed so loud I barely registered Xander Knight pushing through the crowd toward Lindsay and my mom and me until he caught my elbow and leaned in close.

"I'll take you," he said.

But I didn't want him. Where was Aidan?

chapter thirty

Xander stared sideways at me as we walked through the hall. A worn blue rope was tied around his wrist. His vintage Coca-Cola T-shirt was stretched at the neck and sleeves. Whenever he moved closer, I moved farther away. Even if he was under the influence of hormones, Aidan had asked me to choose.

It wasn't even a choice.

Harrison felt hollow with nearly everyone in the gym. We passed the computer lab and I looked inside, hoping to see Aidan. But it was empty.

Xander cleared his throat as we entered the G Wing. "Do you remember when we were eleven, and I pissed myself at recess and started crying, and you told everyone that a dog came up to me and peed on my pants and that's why they were wet?"

"I remember," I said. I smiled until I saw the serious

look on Xander's face.

"Everyone believed you," he said, fidgeting with the blue rope bracelet. "Because you were the kind of girl that everyone wanted to believe in."

I swallowed.

Xander's face darkened. "I called Blake last night," he said. "She hasn't been right lately, and I still care about her, even if we're not together." He slowed his steps. "Her dad came into her bedroom while we were on the phone and told her to get off. But when she said good-bye to me, she didn't hang up." He glanced over at me. "I think she did it on purpose. Because I heard some stuff. And now I know you didn't steal that idea from Blake." His face was lined with worry. "I realize she's done bad stuff to you, Audrey. But I heard her protest this time, like she didn't want to go along with her dad and Alec's plan to make it look like you stole the idea from her." Xander's eyes narrowed on me. "But you of all people know how convincing her father is."

I imagined Blake's dad storming into her room. Telling her that disobeying him wasn't an option.

Xander picked up our pace again and said, "Blake did a lot of nice things for me." He sounded apologetic, like he wanted me to know why he'd been with her for so many years. But I was the last person he needed to explain it to.

"Like buy lacrosse stuff when my parents couldn't afford it," he said.

I thought about the clothes she'd let me borrow. How she'd practically thrust them into my hands, told me how her favorite thing about shopping was finding stuff I'd like, too. I remembered how funny she was when we'd go to the mall and dare each other to do stuff, like in Ann Taylor when Blake asked the superconservative saleslady if they carried chocolate-flavored edible thongs. Or when she dared me to goose the mall security guard. I did it to hear her laugh.

I was quiet for a while, lost in my memories of her.

Xander kept going. "Blake was the one who encouraged me all the time, always saying lacrosse could get me into a good school. She practically signed me up herself for that lax camp that got me noticed by Stanford. It sounds stupid, but I wouldn't have gone after scholarships without her. I would've settled for something less." He looked at me. "It doesn't mean the other stuff she did was right," he said.

"No, it doesn't," I said.

We were rounding the corner when Xander said, "I don't know what happened to all of us—why we changed." His golden-brown eyes stared somewhere down the hall. "Maybe if we're lucky, we'll change again in college. Maybe be more like we were when we were younger. Especially you."

Sunlight streamed in rectangles across the linoleum as we walked.

The girl I was then—the braver girl, the one who wasn't so scared of bad stuff that she had to carry around a rabbit's foot—that girl had a father. I didn't know if I could get her back, even if I wanted to. "Especially me," I said in a whisper. Maybe he was right. I wanted him to be right.

Xander took my hand and pulled me against the wall

281

next to a water fountain. He leaned close, and I thought he was going to whisper something. But then he pressed his lips against mine. I was jerking away when sneakered feet squeaked around the corner.

"So then how can we prove she didn't do it?"

Aidan's voice.

I pulled from Xander's kiss, but I wasn't fast enough.

Aidan and Mindy stood side by side with matching wide eyes. Color drained from Aidan's face. I suddenly felt sick. "Aidan? Xander was just taking me to . . ."

Aidan backed away. He mumbled something beneath his breath and nearly fell trying to get around the corner.

"Aidan, wait!" I called, my heart pounding.

Mindy raced after him.

The door swung open. Mrs. Condor's dirty-blond hair was freshly trimmed and her pool-water eyes telegraphed: *You're safe now, Audrey.*

I stumbled away from her. "Aidan!" I called again.

I wanted to be the person Xander remembered—but for Aidan, not for Xander. Aidan was the one who took me as I was right now—broken or fixed, right or wrong. He was the one who'd been by my side since the first day we met.

I moved around the corner, but he was gone.

Mrs. Condor motioned me toward her office. I took a breath—I could explain to Aidan later, as soon as I saw him. (*"Aidan, Xander kissed me due to years-old sentimentality. Or maybe he actually likes me now. I don't know, and—shockingly—I don't care, because I like you."*)

Ms. Bates materialized in the doorway behind Mrs.

Condor. *What the heck?*

"Um, Audrey? I'm gonna *go*," Xander said, suddenly looking mortified.

I wrapped my arms around his shoulders and he tensed beneath me, like he was nervous. "Thank you for what you said," I whispered. I wondered if he knew how much I meant it.

Mrs. Condor closed the door behind Bates and me. There were three metal folding chairs in front of her desk, and we sat. The empty chair was obviously the Battery's throne. I needed to get this over with. I needed to find Aidan.

Bates checked her sleek silver watch. "I'm sure he'll be here any minute."

Mrs. Condor was smiling, and despite myself, I felt calmer. (The woman was good.) "Audrey, this is an intervention."

Oh my God.

"I want to welcome you, and remind you that everything you say in this room today—no matter who is present—is confidential," Mrs. Condor said, sitting behind her Compaq and her framed family photograph/L.L.Bean catalogue picture.

Ms. Bates's light brown eyes were blinking at me. Shame heated my face when I looked at her. Bates thinking I'd cheated was a knife in my stomach.

A knock rapped the door and Mrs. Condor opened it. Nigit's father wore a flannel jacket over blue hospital scrubs and clay-colored Crocs. His short hair looked unwashed and his shadow of stubble was darker than in California.

Ms. Bates stood and said, "Nikhil Gurung: Erika Condor."

I was so stunned that all I could think was: *Mrs. Condor's name is Erika. Her friends call her Erika.*

The chair's legs squawked against the floor as Dr. Gurung sat. He gripped his green leather briefcase, his eyes wild.

No one spoke.

Finally Ms. Bates turned to me. "I know how talented you are," she said slowly. "And sometimes I think I've only seen the tip of the iceberg in terms of your capabilities as a programmer." She tucked a strand of smooth white hair behind her ear. "And I know you didn't steal an idea from a classmate. Which leads me to believe something very strange is going on between you and Public. When Dr. Gurung approached me regarding your meeting at Notre Dame and his concerns, the two of us pieced together what we think you may have done."

My heart seized. All three of them stared.

"What did you find on those phones, Audrey?" Bates's voice was gentle, but her grip tightened on the side of the metal chair. I stared at a freckle on the back of her hand shaped like a convertible. When I didn't answer, she said, "Public is powerful. If you don't let us help you, they'll never stop hounding you."

I glanced up to see everyone's eyes on me. The three of them knew my secret, but they didn't seem mad, and they hadn't called the FBI—*yet.*

"I'm nervous, too, Audrey," Dr. Gurung said (nervously). He opened his briefcase and his hands moved over papers with black-and-white graphs and labels like TEST GROUP and CONTROL GROUP. He went on to explain how Public funded his study. (I practiced my theatrical skills and made a surprised face.) When he finished, he took a long breath. "I took money from Public to stay quiet when I should not have. It was a mistake, and they've made me pay. Don't let them do the same to you."

The metal creaked as I leaned forward. If I was the only one who could stop Robert Dawkins and Public . . .

I took a breath and told them everything.

When I finished, the cuckoo shot out from the wall and chirped. Mrs. Condor's face was still professionally neutral, but Dr. Gurung had edged to the front of his seat. And he was looking at me with one part awe and one part horror, like I'd stolen a famous painting.

Bates crossed a black-stockinged leg over the other. She was the one I couldn't read, and she was the one I cared about. Her expression gave away nothing—it was as if I'd been telling a story about a boring weekend trip to T.J.Maxx to pick out a cardigan.

I stared at her, waiting for her to say something, to tell me everything was going to be okay. When she smiled, there was a faraway look in her eyes, like her thoughts were somewhere else.

"We need to talk with Janie Callaghan," she finally said.

She couldn't be serious. "Jane Callaghan?" I said. "As in

the CEO of Infinitum?" Maybe they'd gone to grad school together and worked with each other in the eighties, but it was three decades later. "Why would she give a crap about one of your students?" I asked, too out-of-sorts to watch my language.

"I'm not sure you're grasping what a big deal this is, Audrey," Bates said. "Jane Callaghan is Alec Pierce's biggest rival. Of course she'll care about this." Then she smiled, and I saw that faraway look again. Dr. Gurung and Mrs. Condor were staring at me, but I couldn't take my eyes off Bates. She gazed wistfully at the wall like she was looking through a window instead of 1970s wood paneling. "And Janie and I were once much more than friends," she said. "We were girlfriends."

I clutched the side of my chair. If every day at school were this interesting, no one would drop out.

"If you're willing, I propose we drive to Infinitum's offices in New York City," Bates said.

My heart raced. Mrs. Condor's usually unbiased lips curved into a smile.

"It's the only way to fight back," Ms. Bates said. "Jane will know what to do." She leaned forward. "Meet with Jane. Let Infinitum see your talent."

My body had the fiery feeling for the first time since California.

"I'll do it," I said.

chapter thirty-one

Hours later, we sped along I-90 while Danny Beaton crowed through the radio on a station that called itself "Cleveland's Hottest Hits." The Good & Plenty candies Ms. Bates had brought stained my fingertips white and purple.

My mom was in the backseat with me, alternating between being worried about me and pissed at what I'd done.

Dr. Gurung drove. Ms. Bates sang along to Danny Beaton with a unique technique that involved repeating Danny's lyrics a split second after he did, like an echo. It gave me a headache, but it was Bates, so I didn't mind.

In Allentown, we slept in a Motel 6 with pea-colored curtains and yellow flowered bedspreads. And by *slept*, I mean: *tossed*. And *turned*. I alternately obsessed over Aidan and Infinitum, practicing what I needed to say to both to save myself. The next morning I unzipped my suitcase on the sidewalk so the motel's pet-store smell wouldn't soak into my clothes.

Dr. Gurung's Lincoln Navigator earned its name when we crossed the George Washington Bridge into New York City and darted between cars and taxis on a highway along the water. When we turned onto 14th Street, the car bounced over uneven pavement mixed with cobblestones. "The Meatpacking District has experienced a transformation," Dr. Gurung said as we narrowly avoided a mom wearing stilettos, pushing a baby carriage.

I didn't see any meat or packing, so I figured he was right.

On Washington Street, I snapped a photo of an Asian guy with long hair taking pictures of a six-foot-tall girl wearing platforms and slouchy green trousers. I sent it to Lindsay with the caption: *fashion shoot?* The girl was contorting her body into uncomfortable-looking positions I'd only seen on *America's Next Top Model* reruns at Lindsay's. If there were one thing that would cheer my cousin up, it was a photo she could upload to *FBM*. She hadn't answered her phone since yesterday and it felt weird doing this without her.

We passed a restaurant with picture windows looking in on people drinking wine (at lunch) and parked the car in a garage that cost three times more per hour than I made babysitting.

No one spoke as we followed Dr. Gurung along the street with his map. A cold gust of wind carried a napkin marked THANK YOU FOR COMING. It came to rest against a milk crate. A lady stood on top of the crate and sang a gospel song into a microphone that didn't work. I took in the delis next to glass-front boutiques and a store that served cocktails while they blew your hair dry. The scent of honey-roasted peanuts and hot dogs wafted from an elderly man's cartlike station, where he cooked and sold food. Another man opened a cloth drape filled with glossy fake designer bags. "Louis. Gucci. Chanel," he said, hushing his voice like we were in on a secret.

A taxi honked and two girls carrying big leather bags slipped inside. Another girl with bangs and sunglasses rode a bicycle with a dog in a pink wicker basket. A canvas satchel that read WHOLE FOODS draped over her back with a baguette sticking out.

I loved it here.

I forgot to be nervous until Dr. Gurung held open sleek glass doors marked INFINITUM. I let go of a breath I didn't realize I was holding.

At least the building was a rectangle. I smoothed a hand over the jeans Ms. Bates assured me were *perfectly fine attire for a budding innovator.*

At the reception desk, we paused before a guy and a girl dressed in head-to-toe black. The girl pursed her tiny lips and made short, quick movements like an exotic bird. "Smile for the camera," the guy said, snapping pictures of us for security purposes and inspecting our licenses.

I'd never seen my mom look so nervous. And Bates was wearing mascara in addition to her trademark red lipstick. Only Dr. Gurung looked like himself—unshaven and sleepless.

An elevator took us to another lobby with shiny black leather couches.

"Can I get you some mint tea infused with flower essence?" a man with a goatee asked.

We all declined.

"Jane's expecting you," he said. "Right this way."

The man opened the door into a room with a long wooden table, where a dozen people sat in front of Infinitum laptops. They didn't smile.

I glanced at Ms. Bates. I thought we were only meeting with Jane Callaghan. All these people staring at me made me feel like I might throw up.

The woman I recognized as Jane Callaghan strode across the room. I felt like I should bow to her or something, but instead I smiled like this was normal. Like Tuesday was the day I always spent in New York City convening with geniuses.

"Welcome to Infinitum," Jane said, shaking our hands. "You must be Audrey." Her dark eyes sparkled. "And you must be Mom," she said, like we were at the pediatrician. She turned to Nigit's dad. "Dr. Gurung, I presume. And Hannah," she said to Ms. Bates, shaking her head just slightly. "How are you?" she asked, but the question was entirely different than the way you always hear it. It was weighted with something I didn't understand.

Citrine stones covered the skin at Jane's collarbone and matched her light yellow hair. Her charcoal-gray suit fit her frame perfectly, like she bought a new one every time she gained or lost three pounds. Wrinkles etched the corners of her eyes, and when she smiled at me, I felt like she meant it. "We're ready whenever you are," she said, gesturing for us to sit.

We sat. "Why don't you go ahead, Audrey," Bates said, her voice soft. My mom squeezed my hand under the table.

Blank faces stared. "Well, it sort of happened by accident," I blurted. "I threw my buyPhone into a car battery at this psychic Madame Bernese's house . . ."

A girl in a purple scarf raised an eyebrow. A guy with clear black skin wearing silver eyeliner looked annoyed.

Stay on track, trog.

I cleared my throat. "And after I noticed a strange buzzing sound coming from my phone, I disassembled it and uncovered secret software called BuyWare that Public had installed on their phones—software that released an ultrasonic chord progression to stimulate feel-good hormones like oxytocin and dopamine in the user's brain that simulated falling in love whenever the user was in the vicinity of Public stores or downloading music from buyJams. Public targeted teenagers, who are more susceptible to neurotransmitters triggered in the amygdala, creating a reward pathway in the brain that made the teenager want more music, more Public products, *more, more, more.*"

No one looked bored anymore. So I stood up and paced the room, like I'd seen on TV. "Once I realized the software was in place to induce the hormones, I programmed a mobile application that triggered the ultrasonic chord progression—thereby triggering the hormones—when the

291

user pointed her phone at an intended target and pressed a button to activate the software. I also upped the dosage of hormones triggered far past that which Public utilized. I did this by altering the program so that instead of the buyPhones emitting the ultrasonic chord progression in one-second bursts every thirty seconds, they would now emit one continuous progression that would assault the user and render them helplessly in love until the app user pressed a second button, deactivating the software."

Now a few mouths were open.

Dr. Gurung passed around copies of the research Public had originally funded that backed up everything I was explaining. I circled the table while I prattled on, and only tripped once—on some guy's shiny Infinitum laptop case, for which he profusely apologized. At one point, I gestured to Dr. Gurung. "And then they blackmailed this pillar of our community into keeping quiet." It was a direct quote from a *General Hospital* episode I'd watched with Lindsay, but I felt it was appropriate. When I finished, I sank into my seat.

Jane started the applause. The girl in the purple scarf let out a "Woohoo!" and everyone around the table clapped and cheered. I got caught up in the moment and cheered, too—pumping my fist in the air and yelling, "Power to the people!" which maybe wasn't appropriate, but I got carried away.

"This is all incredibly impressive, Audrey," Jane said once everyone quieted. "I haven't seen programming talent like this in someone so young in years." Her eyes flicked to Ms. Bates, and then back to me. "I won't let it go to waste." She gave me the same unwavering stare I'd seen her give to interviewers on *60 Minutes*. "Hannah has made her primary concern clear: With Public's slander against you, you'll be handicapped for life. I've seen your grades and test scores: They're strong enough to get you into any university in the country," she went on, her voice determined. "You could have gotten there on your own if it hadn't been for Public. I ask that you let me make a phone call to the university of your choice. Infinitum is powerful, too, Audrey. I think you'll be pleased with the outcome."

I felt like gymnasts were performing floor routines on my stomach. Jane Callaghan was going to call a college for me? And get me in? Is that what she meant? I glanced at my mother. I didn't want to embarrass her, but I had to tell Jane the truth. "My mom just lost her job," I said. Lindsay's words echoed in my mind: *Chin up, Audrey.* I straightened. "I can't afford to go to the college of my choice."

Jane's face was impassive. She poured herself a glass of water from a crystal decanter. "I'd like to propose a contract with Infinitum," she said. Her gold charm bracelet jingled as she brought the glass to her lips. "Fifteen hours of programming work per week, completed remotely from whatever university you choose. No excuses. I don't care if you have a busy week with midterms, or your boyfriend or girlfriend dumps you"—she looked at Bates again before returning her glance to me—"or you come down with some nasty stomach bug going around your dorm." She sipped her water. "When you graduate, Infinitum has first option on being your place of employ. In exchange, Infinitum will pay for your college tuition and school-related expenses."

My mother burst into tears. Then she threw her arms around my shoulders. I held my breath. I couldn't take my eyes from Jane.

Jane set her glass on a blue ceramic coaster with a *clink*. "So where do you want to go to college, Audrey?" she asked.

The glossy images of students picnicking on the grass quad at Brown in Aidan's brochure flashed through my mind. I thought of MIT, with its reputation for trogs. Stanford was too close to Public's headquarters, but UCLA was far enough away and still close to Brad Pitt. My imagination played scenes of me studying in an ivy-covered library on the East Coast. Or going to a basketball game at Duke. (Then I remembered I hated basketball.)

My mind spun until it suddenly went quiet.

I thought about lighting candles with my dad in the darkness. His fingers laced through mine watching plays in the theater. The warmth of him next to me when we said our prayers at the Basilica.

I squeezed my mother's hand.

"I want to go to Notre Dame."

chapter thirty-two

It was late when we got back to South Bend and Dr.
Gurung dropped us at our apartment. I watched his SUV
reverse and mouthed *Thank you* to Ms. Bates through the
glass. It was dark, but I hoped she saw me. I hoped she
knew.

My mom and I were giddy and delirious walking up the
sidewalk. "There's just one more thing I need to do," I told
her. "I'll be home before ten, okay?"

She looked like she was going to protest, but then
thought better of it. "Ten at the latest," she said. She kissed
my forehead and went inside.

I started walking the old, familiar route. Rain drizzled,
and red streaks darkened the sky until I felt like I was
walking through drops of merlot.

I took a right onto the winding, picturesque street with
one house bigger than the next. I hadn't been back in so

long that I didn't recognize most of the cars. I wondered if new families had moved in, with kids who played together and forged friendships that wouldn't fracture like Blake's and mine. I hoped so.

The rain fell harder now. I pulled my black hood over my head and took off across the grass. Trees arched above me, blocking the moon and leaving me stumbling blindly over roots that snaked the dirt. A dog barked in a neighboring house and I ran faster.

Rain soaked my clothes. My hands were slick as I pushed the gate. I ran the rest of the way around the circular driveway, darting between Blake's Jeep and her dad's BMW and clamoring up the stone steps.

I rang the bell twice. Footsteps pounded the stairs and Blake swung open the door. A terry-cloth headband pulled her black hair from her forehead. Her jaw lowered and cracked the pasty-green clay mask that covered her face. "Audrey?"

It was the first time she'd called me my real name since freshman year.

"I know you didn't want to go along with your dad's plan," I said, my voice low and rushed. I didn't know how much time I had alone with her.

Blake sniffed, then blinked a few times. It was what she always did when she didn't know what to say.

The night felt too dark. And so did Blake's house. I could just make out moonlight glinting against a mirror at the end of a long hallway.

"Things have changed," Blake finally said, her voice hard.

I tried to make myself sound like her. But my words came out too shaky. "Don't you think I know that?" I wasn't even sure what she meant. *Everything* had changed. Did she mean between us? Or did she mean something had changed since she wrote me that cryptic email saying she needed to talk?

Her fingers gathered the yellow cotton of her night-gown. She inched closer and I felt her soften, just for a breath.

"Blake, please," I said. I stood there waiting for her to say something, wanting her to say she was sorry, that everything that had happened since we were fourteen was a mistake—*her* mistake. But I knew what I wanted was more than she could give me.

"It's complicated," she finally said, lowering her voice to a whisper. "And how am I supposed to trust you when you're the one who betrayed us first?"

I wanted to reach out my hand, like I would've done years before. But all the ways we'd hurt each other felt like a stone wall between us.

She glanced over her shoulder, and I could feel how scared she was. If we were going to talk, it couldn't be *here*. Not with him upstairs.

Blake's hands went to the edge of the door and I worried she'd shut it in my face.

"I need to speak to your father," I said.

Her grip tightened on the door. "Are you sure you want to—"

But right then the bottom half of Robert Dawkins's

body became visible at the top of the stairs. "Not again, Blake!" he yelled. My skin prickled. I remembered his tone like it was yesterday—the one he used when he was in the house with his family and out of earshot of his adoring public. Then I watched what his voice did to Blake. Her entire body went rigid. It made me hate him even more.

"Hello, Mr. Dawkins," I said as he barreled down the stairs like an attack dog. "Care for a chat?"

He froze in the doorway. I wasn't sure who he expected to see—Xander? Woody?—but it certainly wasn't me. I was freaked out he'd say *no*, so I added, "I think you'll want to hear what I have to say."

"Robert?" Blake's mom called.

"I'll be right up!" he shouted. "Go upstairs with your mother," he said to Blake, cold as ice. Blake looked down at her feet like a child. She looked small climbing the stairs.

I stepped into the house. Robert Dawkins shut the door behind me, and then opened another one into a study. Everything appeared leather except the floor. An antique clock so big it could've been stolen from a train station (but was probably purchased from a Pottery Barn catalog) hung on the wall. Hardcover books with titles like *You Belong at the Top* lined the shelves.

He gestured for me to sit. I didn't. He stared out the window with his back to me. Rain trickled down the pane. "What do you want?" he finally asked.

"We both know the answer to that." The words came easier than I thought. I let them hang in the air.

Robert Dawkins turned, and leaned his broad back

against the window. Moonlight silhouetted his silk bathrobe–cloaked frame. His black hair and dark eyes matched Blake's.

My fingers longed for my rabbit's foot. I clenched my fists instead. "I have evidence you covered up the results of a medical study by blackmailing a doctor," I said. "If I release the evidence, your name will be ruined. Just like you tried to ruin my father's."

His face was still, but I sensed fear pulsing in the air between us.

"The study *is* going to see the light of day, Robert," I said. It was the truth. Jane Callaghan was working on a press release as we spoke. "And I have no desire to hurt you or your family." I was so far out of my league that the only thing I knew how to do was make my tone clinical, like actresses do on TV when they want something. It kept the shake out of everything I was saying. "I'll bury the evidence of your blackmail if you publicly take back the statements you made after my father's death, and apologize to my family. We both know my father wasn't careless." I was quiet for a moment. The words were true and deserved their own space. Then I said, "You're also going to tell Blake that I wasn't the one who told you she was having sex freshman year. You'll have to tell the truth again, which I know isn't your strong suit." Robert Dawkins stood stock-still. He wasn't even blinking. I steeled myself, and said, "Oh, and Mr. Dawkins? You're going to get Alec Pierce to cease activation of the BuyWare software on all buyPhones. I'll be watching, and you have twenty-four hours to cooperate before I go public." I leveled my gaze. "Don't test a girl with nothing to lose."

I backed out of the study just as Robert Dawkins's face morphed into a snarl. My hands shoved the front door and I sprinted across the lawn. My legs gave out as soon as I was hidden in the trees, and sobs shook my body.

I knew I was playing with fire, but I couldn't stop now.

chapter thirty-three

Me: I need 2 talk 2 u. Y weren't u in lab?
Aidan: had to get a new phone. bates let me skip
lab. by myself at lunch. nigit w lindsay making up
somewhere.

Nigit had already made up with me, too, profusely apologizing and saying he was an idiot when he should've had my back. It was easy to forgive him. I'd made enough mistakes myself during the past few weeks.

I checked my watch as I entered the cafeteria: nine of the twenty-four hours to go. I zigzagged through the tables. No one said hello, but no one said *You suck*, either. Everyone seemed genuinely sick of anything having to do with me and returned to ignoring my existence.

I sat next to Aidan and lowered my brown-bagged lunch of a baked potato and some tofu wrap my mom assured me tasted good but probably didn't. (I was boycotting the cafeteria food with my mom having been fired.)

I couldn't read Aidan's face. He sat very still. Then he raised an eyebrow, like he was waiting for me to say something. My hands were shaky, so I put them in my lap and wished we were somewhere private, like the secret spot behind my apartment. Why didn't I just tell him then?

Joel Norris played a few depressing notes on his tuba while Charlotte Davis looked on dreamily. Sean DeFosse strode by us with Martha Lee, debating the ethics of animal testing. I waited for them to shut up, but they didn't. So I just started anyway. "A lot has gone down recently," I said, my palms warm against my jeans. "And it's made me realize a few things. I'm sorry you saw Xander kiss me in the hall. It wasn't what I wanted." I held my breath, and then said, "*Who* I wanted."

Aidan's long lashes blinked as he considered me.

"I like *you*, Aidan. I've liked you forever." I tapped my thigh, impossibly nervous. "It's okay if you don't like me. It still doesn't mean I'm going to be with Xander or anyone else." I swallowed. "I've learned a lot about the truth lately, and what can happen when people hide it. And I don't want to do that. So there it is. The truth."

Aidan inched closer. I thought he was going to say something, but right then Joel blasted the intro to a new, equally terrible song that made me question why the tuba even existed. And then Mindy sat down and said: "Well if et e-sn't Public trog verses Infinitum trog."

302

Aidan leaned in and whispered to me. "Later," was all he said.

I felt jittery all over. Now he knew.

Mindy made me give every detail about New York City, and then told us her big secret: The head of NYU's creative-writing program had called her personally to talk about her potential future at NYU after reading the portfolio she submitted. I listened to her voice rise and fall. The way she mixed up the sounds made some of the words more beautiful than the way everybody else said them.

Goth Girl walked by wearing her black veil over her face like she was in mourning. I had the sense everything was back to normal, until Mindy said, "So why heeven't you been oh-nswering texts?" to Aidan.

Aidan took a swig of water. "I just got my new phone like a half an hour ago," he said. "I left the other one on the plane to California."

I gasped. "You didn't have your phone at headquarters?" I managed to sputter.

Aidan shook his head.

"So you weren't apped when you came running up the Public spiral?" *And then pushed Xander away? And kissed me?*

Aidan met my gaze. "I wasn't apped," he said evenly.

My nerves pulsed. That meant—

The kiss.

I thought about the way his hands slid behind my neck. How his mouth had crushed mine.

It was all real.

I took deep breaths as Aidan smiled into his sandwich. He caught my eye. I tried to smile back, but my facial muscles weren't really working right because they were trying so hard not to freak out.

I felt a tap on my arm and nearly jumped out of my chair. I whirled around to see Blake. Her black hair was French-braided and hung over one shoulder. The skin around her eyes looked puffy. She didn't acknowledge Mindy or Aidan. She just said, "Can we talk?"

I let go of a breath. Then nodded.

Mindy glanced between Blake and me. Aidan's hand went to my arm as I stood. "I'm okay," I said. I saw the same intensity in his eyes I saw in California, and I wanted more than anything to be somewhere alone with him. I'd already told him how I felt. Now I wanted to show him.

I could feel him watch me walk away.

Blake and I headed toward the exit. I already knew where we were going—there was an oak tree we used to eat lunch under during the beginning of freshman year. Harrison kids stared at us as we moved between tables, but I didn't care as much as usual.

Blake pushed the door leading to the courtyard. It was cold, and no one was in the yard except for us. A stone trail led from the cafeteria's door to the oak tree. Pebbles lined the square perimeter.

Blake pulled a fuzzy white hand muffler from her bag and put it on. She stood there staring at me with both hands together like she was praying.

I waited for her to say something and imagined what it might be. Maybe how her dad had told her the truth, and how she should've trusted me all along. How she should've known I'd never tell one of our secrets. But instead, she said, "I know how your app worked."

My heart thudded to a stop. How did she know my secret?

Her voice raised in pitch. "And I know what was going on with you and my dad and Public."

My toes scrunched inside my sneakers. "So what?" I asked, because I didn't know what else to say and I was trying to play it cool. And just because she knew something didn't negate what she'd done. "Why did you tell everyone I stole the idea from you?"

Blake pursed her lips, then started talking way faster than usual. "My dad convinced me we'd be ruined if I didn't. That we would lose everything. That I wouldn't get into Notre Dame. Or *anywhere*."

"Big deal, Blake," I said. "I couldn't afford to go to school, either, until—" I held my tongue. I didn't want to tell her about Infinitum. I didn't trust her. "You still shouldn't have done it," I said instead.

"I know that." Her eyes were glassy with tears. I wasn't sure if she was crying or if the cold air was stinging her eyes. I was about to feel sorry for her when she said, "But you *were* getting a little cocky with that app." She smirked. "A part of me enjoyed it."

"*Cocky?*" Was she serious? "I've had nothing good

happen in the past three years. You couldn't let me enjoy a little attention?"

Blake scoffed. "Nothing good? You have Lindsay and your friends who love you. And your overly nice mom who you actually get along with. And you have your perfect straight *A*s." She tried to push her dark braid over her shoulder with her hands still pressed together in the muffler. "And then you have that geek what's-his-name who obviously likes you."

Now she was making me *really* nervous. The whole thing with Aidan felt so new, and I'd wanted him for so long, and some part of me worried she could ruin it.

Cold air swirled between us. Blake leaned against the trunk of the oak tree. But then she looked nervous, too, and straightened again. She lowered her voice. "I'm sorry for what I said about your dad in the bowling alley."

My jaw tightened. I didn't say anything. I wasn't going to lie and say it was okay.

We stared at each other. Blake's eyes were questioning, but I wasn't sure what she was asking.

My phone buzzed. I pulled it from my pocket and saw an email from Blake's dad.

"I need to go," I said. It was too much standing out there together in our old spot. I wasn't ready to have a conversation with her. It felt too foreign.

Her dark eyes watched me back away.

I shoved through the door into the cafeteria. The clinking of silverware and the chatter of voices swallowed me as I opened my email.

To: Audrey.McCarthy@InfinitumMail.com
From: RobertDawkins@R.DawkinsTech.com

Audrey,

Tune into WNDU-TV at 6 p.m.

Robert

Lindsay and her mom rang our buzzer at 5:56. The door was stuck again and my mother said, "If Roger doesn't come fix this thing, I swear . . ." as she cranked it open.

"Namaste," Lindsay said, her body wrapped in a turquoise sari.

Mindy and Nigit were already waiting on the couch. "My princess!" Nigit said, jumping up. He tried to kiss her, but Lindsay's mom smacked his arm and said, "We leave room for the holy spirit in this family." Then, to me, she said, "Six o'clock is a terrible time to ask your friends and family to get on the road with traffic."

"Just sit, please, Aunt Linda," I said, gesturing toward the couch.

Lindsay dunked her hand into a bowl of popcorn. "What are we doing, anyway?" She popped a few kernels in her mouth. "And why are you being so secretive?"

It was 5:59. Where was Aidan?

My mother set the bowl of popcorn on the coffee table. I turned on the television with shaking fingers. An actress bemoaned her cold sore and said, "Get hot again with Vitrex," waving a tube of lip balm. *Any minute now.* The graphics for WNDU shot across the screen. An Asian woman in a khaki-colored trench coat stood in front of the fountain at the Morris Performing Arts Center.

"Everyone sit!" I said.

They sat.

"Good evening, South Bend," the news anchor said. "I'm Julia Parker, and this is the WNDU evening news."

"This is the lady who does the traffic report," my aunt Linda said, nodding like they were friends. "She's very accurate."

A knock sounded.

My mother jumped up. "I hope it's Roger."

I don't.

"Mom, sit!" I yelled.

"Audrey, what in the Lord's name has gotten into you?" my mother said, but she sat back down and stared at the television.

I raced to the door. Aidan stood in his dark green jacket, holding a bouquet of cream-colored roses.

"For you," he said softly, passing them into my arms.

I bit my bottom lip. Something about today already made me want to cry, and what I wanted to happen hadn't even happened yet. "Thank you," I whispered, and led him to the couch. He sat on the end. I squished between him and my mom. I smelled the roses in my lap.

"Today we're live for a press conference with Robert Dawkins of R. Dawkins Tech," the newscaster said.

Aidan's hand lighted on mine.

"Jesus H. Christ," my aunt Linda said, adjusting her Band-Aid-colored stockings. "Why are we listening to anything this crook has to say?"

I glanced at my mother. Her lips made a tight line.

"Just wait," I said, breathless. My mom turned to me, her eyes questioning. The seven of us watched Robert Dawkins stride to a podium next to the fountain. Reporters surrounded him with their microphones aimed in his direction. A competing news station's van was positioned next to the podium.

Gel slicked Robert's dark hair. He looked pissed, like he didn't want to be there. He leaned forward and spoke into the microphone.

"I'm here today to issue a public apology, and to report new findings in the death of Francis McCarthy."

My mother's face went white. Lindsay and her mom both covered their mouths with their hands.

"I'd like to take this moment to apologize to Marian McCarthy, Audrey McCarthy, and the late Francis McCarthy, for the statements I made following McCarthy's untimely death. Furthermore, I'd like to report that a witness has come forward with concrete testimony proving that Francis McCarthy's death was caused by an error in my company's equipment, not an error made by McCarthy. A full settlement will be awarded to Marian McCarthy and family."

My breath caught. My legs went weak even though I was sitting. A settlement? He was giving us money? And saying it wasn't my dad's mistake?

Lindsay gasped. Mindy jumped to her feet and stared between my mom and me.

"Jesus, Mary, and Joseph," my aunt Linda said, and then made the sign of the cross.

"What did you do, Audrey?" Aidan asked in a low voice.

My mother covered her face with her hands, and started sobbing.

"Mom," I said, tears falling over my cheeks. She tucked her head into my shoulder and cried harder.

"You did this?" she asked into my sweatshirt. "For your father and us?" She pulled away and looked at me. "I'm so proud of you, sweetie, but how did you . . ." Her voice trailed off. She lifted the gold-framed photograph of my father from the coffee table. *"Francis,"* she said, holding him between us. His light eyes held ours, and something I didn't realize I'd lost came tumbling back.

Later, Aidan's broad frame held aside branches as we emerged onto the clearing in the secret spot behind my apartment. My breathing quickened when his hand touched my arm, and he guided me toward the water. I looked up at him. His face was still, open. Some part of me knew I was going to need him to help me figure out everything that had happened—I didn't want to keep stuff from him anymore. But that could come later.

Now was just for us.

Wind gusted through the birch trees, across the water, over the rocks stacked at the water's edge. The sliver of air between us felt thick with electricity. It was our first time together—by ourselves—in this new way, and we both knew it.

Aidan's hands reached for mine. The energy of his touch fired through me—I felt heat everywhere as he pulled me against him. His grip on my body was strong, and I wanted him to take me even closer. His gaze traveled from my collarbone to my eyes.

"I've wanted to hold you like this for so long," he said.

I took in his full scarlet lips. "What stopped you?" I asked, my voice barely a whisper. I couldn't help myself. I needed to know.

He gestured to the trees around us. "I *did* try to kiss you when we were back here before," he said with an uneasy laugh. "But you turned away." His broad shoulders lifted, then relaxed. He looked unsure, like maybe I'd pull away again. If he only knew.

"And you make me nervous," he said, his blue eyes shining. "Every time I imagined this, or being your boyfriend . . . no matter how much I wanted it, I worried I'd freak you out if you didn't. And then I wouldn't be able to be near you." He was so close I was sure he could feel the heat rising from my skin. "The best is being near you, Audrey."

I put my hands against his chest and felt his heart racing. "I'm not going anywhere," I said softly. The words felt so good. I'd spent so long wanting to escape, and suddenly, I wanted to be exactly where I was.

Leaves rustled beneath our feet as we moved closer. For

one wild second I sensed what had been between us, and how it would change into something bigger.

His hands cupped my chin and he tenderly kissed me. Warmth spread through me, and my body came alive as his lips parted. My mouth curved into a smile against his. Adrenaline, oxytocin, dopamine . . .

Whatever it was, it was *good*.

acknowledgments

I am deeply grateful to Brenda Bowen, Dan Mandel, and Alessandra Balzer.

Thank you, Brenda, for trusting me to write this book. I've learned from your great wisdom, and I've felt cared for by your kindness and encouragement.

Dan Mandel, you made my dream to write fiction a reality. Your belief in me is so strong and true—I can feel it every time we talk. I cannot thank you enough for everything you have done.

Thank you, *thank you* to Alessandra Balzer. Beyond your skills as an editor and publisher are your warmth, your unbeatable sense of humor, and your steadfast support. To work with someone so intelligent and capable—and also fair and generous—is a huge gift.

Thank you to Susan Katz, Kate Jackson, Donna Bray, Sara Sargent, Diane Naughton, Sandee Roston, Caroline Sun, Emilie Polster, Stefanie Hoffman, Patty Rosati, Molly Thomas, Andrea Pappenheimer, Kerry Moynagh, Kathy Faber, Liz Frew, Jessica Abel, Deborah Murphy, Fran Olson, Heather Doss, Jenny Sheridan, Susan Yeager, Jenna Lisanti, Brenna Franzitta, Alison Klapthor, Alison Donalty, Ruiko Tokunaga, and everyone at Balzer + Bray and HarperCollins who has helped this book. I can't imagine a more supportive group of people. I feel very lucky to be one of your authors.

Thank you to every reader. I am so grateful you spent your time in these pages. My fingers are crossed that you'll come back for the next chapter!

Thank you to Sarah Mlynowski for generous words of support.

Thank you to all of the librarians and booksellers who let me wander the aisles over the years, and to the ones who now smile even when my son throws picture books off the shelves.

Thank you to every teacher, especially Linda Harrison from Shaker High School and Siiri Scott and Mark Pilkinton from the University of Notre Dame. You taught me to dream big while being incredibly strict with me when I needed it. (Which was often.)

Thank you to the University of Notre Dame, especially the Film, Television, and Theater department, for encouraging me every step of the way.

Thank you to Mediabistro and my writing teachers: Kristin Harmel, Christa Bourg, and Ryan Harbage. Thank you especially to Micol Ostow, who taught my first class on young-adult fiction four years ago and has cheered me on ever since. Thank you to authors Anna Carey, Melissa Walker, Alecia Whitaker, Kimberly Rae Miller, and Noelle Hancock for advice and friendship.

Thank you to everyone at Alloy Entertainment for teaching me so much about writing fiction, especially Sara Shandler and Lanie Davis. Thank you to Jennifer Kasius and Perseus/Running Press for giving me my first chance at book writing.

Thank you to Tracy Weiss, Samantha Paladini, and Mark Turner for being great television agents and friends.

Thank you to Dr. Meghan Sise and Dr. Roby

Bhattacharyya for answering all of my questions about brain science and Dr. Gurung's experiment. Thank you especially to Roby for always indulging my *what-if* science questions. Thank you to Michael Smith, Brian Morrison, and Noah Harlan for answering my questions about apps, and for having patience when I had no idea what you were talking about. Thank you to Justin Rancourt and Coalesce Creative for making a perfect website.

My greatest debt of tech gratitude goes to Jason Scalia, who spent hours and hours explaining the intricacies of hacking and computer philosophy, and who made me feel like I'd gained entry into this secret world. To quote Audrey: You didn't just teach me how to do it, you taught me why. Thank you to Jason's sister, Kristen Scalia, my very first reader of *The Boyfriend App*, for the many afternoons spent in Kanibal Home discussing the plot and characters like they were real, and for letting Luke play with your boutique's register tape, greeting cards, and taxidermy.

Thank you to close friends and early readers Jamie Greenberg, Wendy Levey, Anna Carey, Debra Devi, and Morgan Oaks. Thank you to endlessly supportive friends: Megan Mazza, Tricia DeFosse, Kim Hoggatt, Jessica Bailey, Erin Murphy, J. J. Area, Brinn Hamilton, Kate Brochu, Maria Manger, Jen Singer, Molly Cesarz, Jen O'Toole, Liz Auerbach, Stacy Craft, Carol Look, Maureen Sullivan, Cara Compani, Allison Yarrow, Corey Binns, Kerrilynn Pamer, Stacia Canon, Jenna Yankun, Dani Super, Kate Gregory, Tori Watts, Victoria Hunter, Talya Cousins, Nancy Conescu, and Poppy King.

Thank you especially to Erika Grevelding, Claire Noble, and Caroline Moore, who have become like family. Thank you, Erika, for all of your insight into the job of a school social worker. I'm very proud of the work you do.

Thank you to my sister-in-law, Christine Hawes, who I'm lucky to call one of my closest friends and my family, for your support during our daily phone calls as we rehashed our babies' sleep schedules (or lack thereof) and cheered each other on during the most important year of our lives. Thank you to my mother- and father-in-law, Carole and Ray Sweeney, who read everything I write and offer unwavering support. Thank you to Robert and Theresa Sise, Linda and Bob Harrison, Tait and Walker Hawes, and all of my extended family. Thank you to my brother, Jack, and my sister-in-law, Ali, for your encouragement, and for being such wonderful people to call family. Thank you to the most amazing sister of all time, Meghan Sise, for supporting and loving me since you arrived in the world.

Thank you to my mom and dad. I am forever grateful for the way you raised and loved me. Dad, it was easy to write Audrey's relationship with her father because of what we have. Your support of this book has meant the world to me.

The Boyfriend App was written while my son, Luke, napped. Thank you, Luke, for being such an awesome napper. Thank you even more for waking up with the smile that makes my heart swell every time. There's nothing better than being your mom.

Words cannot express my gratitude to my husband, Brian. No app necessary—I'll love you for the rest of my life.